D0880535

TEMPTED TO TOUCH

Trent didn't plan the next move. It just happened. He leaned forward and brushed his lips against hers, very gently and slowly. Renee didn't reciprocate, but she also didn't pull back. That electric charge he had felt the first time they touched was back with a vengeance, flowing down his back with sharp intensity. Trent kissed her again, this time tugging on her lower lip and teasing it lightly with his tongue. He wanted to pull her closer and delve deeper to taste her sweet wetness, but he had enough sense to put on the brakes.

When he pulled away to look down at her again, Renee had her eyes closed. Sensing his gaze, she looked up at him and Trent saw a mix of surprise and confusion on her face. He stepped back a little and finally released his hold on her hand. She let out a long breath, and Trent fully anticipated she would have some scathing words for him.

"Good night," she said simply before brushing past him to walk quickly into the lobby of her building.

Also by Sophia Shaw

What Lies Between Lovers
A Rare Groove
Moment of Truth
Depths of Desire
Shades and Shadows

Published by Dafina Books

Tempted
to Touch

Sophia Shaw

Kensington Publishing Corp.

http://www.kensingtonbooks.com

DAFINA BOOKS are published by

Kensington Publishing Corp.
119 West 40th Street
New York, NY 10018

Copyright © 2010 by Sophia Shaw

All rights reserved. No part of this book may be reproduced in any form or by any means without the prior written consent of the Publisher, excepting brief quotes used in reviews.

If you purchased this book without a cover, you should be aware that this book is stolen property. It was reported as "unsold and destroyed" to the Publisher and neither the Author nor the Publisher has received any payment for this "stripped book."

All Kensington Titles, Imprints, and Distributed Lines are available at special quantity discounts for bulk purchases for sales promotions, premiums, fund-raising, and educational or institutional use. Special book excerpts or customized printings can also be created to fit specific needs. For details, write or phone the office of the Kensington special sales manager: Kensington Publishing Corp., 119 West 40th Street, New York, NY 10018, attn: Special Sales Department, Phone: 1-800-221-2647.

Dafina and the Dafina logo Reg. U.S. Pat. & TM Off.

ISBN-13: 978-0-7582-3477-3
ISBN-10: 0-7582-3477-5

First mass market printing: July 2010

10 9 8 7 6 5 4 3 2 1

Printed in the United States of America

To my mother
Iris Deloris Thomas
I am so grateful for all the ways
in which I am exactly like you!

Acknowledgments

Book #6 has been a very interesting journey! As always, I couldn't have done it without the love and support of the amazing friends and family around me.

To Maya and Jasmine Johnson—my awesome babysitters! Thank you both for always being there and being so good to your cousins. I really appreciate it. And to Fay Johnson, their mother and my very good friend. You are an inspiration to me, and I hope I can be the kind mother you are.

To Sandra Skinner and Karen Goodchild—you guys have gone above and beyond to support my writing, and I am so very grateful. I named Renee and Trent after you both, and I hope you enjoy their story.

To Scott Henderson—you were right there for every idea and every word. Thank you for being in my life and providing your unwavering support. I now understand how easy love should be, and I am holding to it tightly with both arms.

Love always,
Sophia

Chapter 1

Renee Goodchild was pissed off.

It wasn't the yelling and swearing kind of pissed off either. This was the kind that left her too angry to speak and on the verge of tears. She stood frozen in the front hall of her apartment, still trying to process the evidence in front of her.

The whole situation had started out so small. Insignificant, really.

First, it was a pair of crystal earrings. They were inexpensive, but with the right outfit, they sparkled like one-carat studs. Then it was her favorite travel mug—the only memento from her college days in Pittsburgh that had miraculously survived the numerous moves in the last six years.

Now, several weeks and various other items of increasing value later, it had come to this!

Renee picked up one half of her most prized possession, pinching it with the very tips of her fingers as though she could catch a fatal communicable disease off the surface. Her face revealed a mix of disbelief and outrage as she examined the still-wet, salt-stained leather of her perfectly sculpted, cobalt-blue platform pumps.

No! her mind screamed.

How many times had she walked by that boutique on 52nd Avenue, admiring the pair on display like art and wishing she had the impulsiveness to spend four hundred sixty dollars on shoes just because they were beautiful? And even when the price was reduced to under two hundred dollars in a post-Christmas sale, Renee still had to talk herself into buying them. In the weeks that followed, she had worn them exactly twice, but only inside the office, and only for very special client meetings.

Now they looked as though they had trudged through the dirty slush still lingering on the Manhattan sidewalks: beat up, worn out, and ruined!

Renee finally focused her eyes on the closed door of her guest room. She imagined her childhood friend, Angela Simpson, inside sleeping off another night of reckless drinking, oblivious to the turmoil that her thoughtless actions had caused.

How dare Angela wear her suede shoes without asking, and out in the February weather!

Though it had been well over three years since the women had been in regular contact, Renee had tried to be a good friend by agreeing to let Angela crash at her apartment for a few weeks until she found a job. But it was a bad situation from the beginning. Angela seemed to lack any consideration, discipline, or basic common sense. At twenty-eight years old, she was older than Renee by about six months, yet she still behaved like she was in high school.

Renee threw down the shoe in frustration, then rubbed at her forehead, trying to calm down. She squeezed her eyes tight to ward off frustrated tears and to stifle the need to scream. Things had just gone too far now, and something had to be done. Angela was going from bad to worse, and Renee was not going to put up with it anymore. It was time for her to get the hell out of the apartment.

But, of course, Renee had no time to address it now. She had a client presentation at nine-thirty, and that gave her about fifteen minutes to pull everything together and another twenty minutes or so for the cab ride into midtown Manhattan. As an interior designer for the small design firm the Hoffman Group, Renee always had to be at the top of her game in the competitive, high-end New York market.

Her newest client, Cree Armstrong, was a middle-aged B-movie actress who could be described as eccentric at best. She had a penthouse condo off 5th Avenue and wanted to revamp the décor in celebration of the recent revival of her career. After a couple of meetings to discuss the design theme, Cree had settled on a new interpretation of 1950s Hollywood glam. The meeting this morning was to finalize the design and decide on fabrics and some of the new furniture pieces.

Despite her sour mood, Renee made it to her client's appointment on time and with a cheerful smile on her face. Cree Armstrong's mood was also sunny, but it was soon obvious it was probably drug-induced. But

Cree was agreeable, and Renee left the apartment with a clear feeling of accomplishment. The project was big, including a redesign of all eight rooms in the two-thousand-square-foot space, but did not require any major construction. Cree's new television role would start filming in two weeks in Burbank, California, and was expected to go into late spring. The apartment would be relatively empty for at least three months, and Renee committed to have the full redesign completed in that time frame.

With their meeting over by late morning, Renee decided to run a couple of errands before the office staff meeting at two o'clock. Almost four years ago, she had joined the Hoffman Group as the assistant to the owner, Amanda Hoffman. By the end of the first year, Renee was leading client meetings and contributing design ideas for large projects. Then she started bringing in her own clients and projects and was promoted to associate designer before her second anniversary.

Renee loved her job, but Amanda was not the easiest woman to work for. She was temperamental and demanding, and not easily impressed. From what Renee understood, the Hoffmans were a wealthy family with old money, and Amanda and her brother had been raised as part of New York's upper-class elite. But sometime during the early 1990s, much of their money disappeared into bad investments and extravagant spending. The worst of it wasn't realized until her playboy father died suddenly. At around thirty years old, Amanda found herself practically broke and with no means or skills to support her lifestyle. She

TEMPTED TO TOUCH

started Hoffman Designs in 1996 after doing several successful renovations and design projects for family friends. It eventually grew to the Hoffman Group with the addition of four associate designers.

By the time Renee was hired, Amanda was mainly doing magazine features and was a regular contributor to several local talk shows. Now there were four full-time designers, including Renee, who did regular client projects. Two years later, Renee was still the most junior designer on the team, but she had a good, well-established reputation and a growing client list. She also had the freedom of managing her own time and doing the bulk of her planning work at home. Her trips into the office were mostly for weekly Monday-afternoon status meetings, large team projects, or the occasional one-on-one meeting with Amanda.

The Hoffman Group was located on the second floor of a restored 1940s building on Lexington Avenue near 41st Street, right in the heart of midtown Manhattan. Renee made it there by 1:30 P.M. with a large spinach salad in one hand and a selection of new upholstery fabric samples in the other. She had just enough time to eat and return a few phone calls before the meeting.

"Hey, Renee," announced the receptionist, Marsha Adams. She had been with the firm almost from the beginning and was the source of almost all of the details Renee knew about Amanda Hoffman.

"Hi, Marsha," Renee replied with a warm smile as she walked by the front desk.

"Wow, is that a new hairstyle?" Marsha asked, clearly taken aback.

Renee stopped walking long enough to touch the top of her head, lightly exploring the unusual texture of her short and spiky hair. She smiled shyly. "Yeah, I just got it done on Saturday. I'm still getting used to it."

"It makes you look so much younger! And the color is perfect. I love it!" declared Marsha.

"Thanks. I was worried that it was too light. My stylist wanted to go blond, but thank God I talked him into light brown highlights instead."

"It looks a bit like a Mohawk, doesn't it?"

Marsha had already stepped out from behind her desk and was up close inspecting the hairstyle with fascination. Renee was not offended by the reaction. Though Marsha had worked in the interior design industry for about ten years, she was still a very conservative middle-aged woman from New Jersey, and all things African American remained new and intriguing to her.

"It's called a 'faux-hawk,' actually," Renee told her with a light giggle. "It's just styled like a small Mohawk with a bit of gel, but it's really just a short cut."

"Well, you just look stunning, my dear. It really brings out those big, beautiful cat eyes."

"Thanks, Marsha," she replied bashfully before continuing the walk to her desk.

Apparently, the change of her hair from a boring, shoulder-length cut to a funky, spiky crop was more of a statement than Renee had anticipated. Everyone she passed in the office stopped to comment and compliment her, though a couple of her coworkers were actually speechless for a few seconds. By the time she started eating her lunch, there was less than ten minutes before the staff meeting. When her desk phone rang, she picked it up quickly without thinking, her mouth half full of salad.

"Good afternoon, this is Renee Goodchild," she stated.

"Good afternoon, Miss Goodchild," the female caller replied in a cool, professional voice. "I'm calling on behalf of Mr. Trent Skinner. He was referred to you by a colleague and would like to book a meeting with you for Wednesday afternoon if you are available."

"All right. Is this for an interior design project?" Renee asked. The name didn't sound familiar, but she was excited to meet any new clients. She quickly opened the calendar on her computer to check her schedule.

"Yes, I believe he is looking to redecorate a room in his home."

"This Wednesday, right?" she asked.

"Yes, ma'am. Mr. Skinner is free at two-thirty P.M. and would like you to meet him at his residence in Greenwich."

"I'm sorry, did you say Greenwich? Greenwich, Connecticut?"

"Yes, ma'am. If two-thirty works, I will send a car for you at one-thirty."

Renee paused with surprise and was about to ask more questions until she realized that her meeting was in less than five minutes. She scanned her schedule and saw that there were a couple of meetings booked in the morning, but they should be done by at least one o'clock.

"Okay, I think that will work. And it was Trent Skinner, right?"

"Yes, ma'am," the woman confirmed.

"Did he mention who had referred him to me?"

"I'm sorry, no, he didn't. Now, I'll get your address for the car and we'll be all set."

They spent a few more seconds on the phone; then Renee had to run to the boardroom, leaving half her lunch on her desk.

The staff meeting went smoothly. Amanda seemed a little distracted, listening to each designer give a status update of his or her project without adding any questions or comments. Once the team had finished its review, Amanda had an announcement of her own. She was going to Aruba for a month for some relaxation and to work on a client's vacation home. The news was a little surprising, since Amanda rarely took time off, but she assured everyone that she would stay in touch daily and would be easily reachable by e-mail or phone if needed.

Renee was just as startled as everyone else but had struggled to stay focused for most of the meeting. She kept replaying the mysterious phone call regarding the new client meeting and pondering how odd the whole thing seemed. The idea of a new project was exciting, but the call had been so strange and formal. Who was Mr. Trent Skinner, and why couldn't he call her himself to set up a meeting? Why would someone she didn't know want her to do a design all the way in

Greenwich, much less send a car for her just for the first meeting?

The minute she got back to her computer, Renee did a Google search on her new prospect. According to a professional networking site, Trent Skinner was a senior funds manager with Goldwell Group, a private equities firm in Greenwich. There wasn't much else. She went through several pages of search results but could not find anything else that seemed relevant.

Eventually, Renee put the mystery in the back of her mind and got back to work. Rather than pack up early and restart at home, she decided to stay in the office to complete a long list of calls to suppliers and stores to check on orders or works in progress.

She had three major projects under way, including the job for Cree Armstrong, all at various stages of completion. One was a small redecoration for a long-standing client, Margaret Applebaum, who just wanted to redecorate her guest room. Renee was only waiting for the upholstery and fabric work to be completed; then she would paint and finish the room. It was scheduled to be finished in about four weeks.

The other was a large renovation of a classic New York brownstone. It was for new clients, Wayne and Rachel Gibson, a couple with a young son, and they were redoing the second-floor bedrooms and bathroom. The structural changes were currently in progress, and Renee was still working with the clients to decide on furniture and finishes. She spent about two days a week working on the design and managing the contractors. Cree's project would take an additional two days a week until completed, so Renee felt comfortable that she could take on another small commitment. This Connecticut client might be ideal if the project wasn't too complicated.

Finally, at about six-thirty, she packed up and left the office. The subway ride uptown took only a few minutes, but it was enough time for her to remember the situation that was waiting for her at home. Since it was almost dinnertime, it was pretty likely that Angela would be in the apartment, watching television and waiting to see what Renee brought home to eat or volunteered to cook. But Renee vowed to herself that it wasn't going to be like that anymore. She wasn't as angry about the shoes anymore, but the situation was still unacceptable. She and Angela were going to have a long talk, and it wasn't going to be pleasant.

Chapter 2

At 1:45 P.M., Wednesday afternoon, Trent Skinner was standing in his office staring out the window with his back to the closed door. The view wasn't very impressive. It faced the side of another building in the crowded business district of downtown Greenwich, Connecticut. But Trent wasn't really looking at anything in particular. He was deep in thought, his mind shifting through several issues at the same time but not focusing on any one thing. He was very aware that he needed to head home in the next fifteen to twenty minutes. Renee Goodchild was scheduled to meet with him there at 2:30.

"Trent, did you call Colin McDougall back?" asked his assistant, Nancy Cavanaugh, as she cracked open the office door and stuck her head in.

Trent swung around to face her. She was a very attractive girl, somewhere in her early twenties, with rich brown hair and bright blue eyes. Most men would not be able to get past her pretty face and firm, athletic body, but Trent had seen the determination in her eyes the minute they met. When he hired her over eighteen months ago, it was for her sharp mind and natural ability to handle difficult people and situations.

"Yeah, I just got off the phone with him a few minutes ago. He seems fine now, but do me a favor and set up another call with him on Monday? I want to make sure we stay on top of the situation. We're too far into negotiations now for this leveraged buyout to go sideways. And have the team look at the books again to make sure there aren't any red flags we missed," he explained.

"Sounds good," replied Nancy. "Did your cousin get in touch with you?"

"He left me a message. I'll call him in a few minutes."

"Okay. Bob Smiley is still confirmed for your four-thirty call. Are you coming back here for the meeting, or will you join from home?"

"I should be back, but I'll let you know if I won't be."

Nancy nodded before walking away, closing the door behind her. Trent checked his watch again. It was just after two o'clock. He let out a long breath, then picked up his cell phone and checked for his wallet inside his suit jacket. He grabbed his overcoat from the hook behind the door and headed out of the office.

Trent's town house was located on a lakefront development overlooking Greenwich Harbor. It was several blocks south from the office. Once he got his car out of the underground parking lot, it was about a ten-minute drive on a slushy, winter afternoon. Trent used those few minutes to call his cousin back.

Nathan answered after the first ring. Anxiety made

his cousin's voice high and sharp. "Trent? I've been waiting for your call for over two hours!"

"Sorry, man, I've been in back-to-back meetings."

"Well, it's almost time. Are you at the house yet? Is she there?" Nathan demanded, barely waiting to hear Trent's excuse.

"I'm heading there now," replied Trent in an even, cool voice. "I'll be there shortly."

"Okay. So, what are you going to do? What if she doesn't take the bait?"

"Nathan, calm down, all right?"

"How can I calm down? Trent, if this plan doesn't work, I'm screwed, man!"

"Nate, just relax," Trent said sharply. "Everything is going to work out the way we planned. Once this chick thinks I can offer her the good life, she'll forget all about you and the promise of a measly ten thousand dollars. Let me meet with her, turn up the charm, and take it from there. But freaking out isn't going to solve anything."

Nathan let out a long breath. They were both silent for a few seconds.

"Sorry, Trent. I know you're just trying to help," he finally replied.

"No problem. I have to go. I'm pulling up to the house, and there is a Town Car behind me. I think it's her. I'll call you back after the meeting."

Trent hung up the phone just as he parked the car in his driveway. He was standing at the front door of the house about to unlock it when the Town Car door opened and the passenger stepped out.

Nathan had described Renee Goodchild to him a

couple times over the last week or so, yet the woman who now walked toward Trent with strong, determined strides looked nothing like he had pictured. For one, she was far more beautiful than he anticipated. According to Nate, he first met Renee when she had caught his eye in the middle of a crowded party. So Trent knew she would be attractive. He had not expected mind-blowing gorgeous, and he was completely unprepared for her stylish, professional appearance.

"Hi, Mr. Skinner? I'm Renee Goodchild," she stated in a soft voice with one hand extended. Her dark, serious eyes looked straight into his without guile.

Trent found himself momentarily speechless. The tightening at the base of his stomach told him this seduction was not going to be as easy as he had planned.

"Nice to meet you, Renee," he finally replied, shaking her hand, ignoring the electric charge that ran from her fingers to his upon contact.

They stood like that for several seconds until she finally looked away from his face to the door behind him.

"Should we go inside?" she asked. "It's pretty cold out here."

When Trent looked away from her eyes, he saw that her teeth were clenched tight as she tried to prevent them from chattering. Her rich, almond-colored skin was getting a little red in the cheeks.

"Of course," he replied before turning away to unlock the front door.

Once inside, they both removed their winter coats. Trent put them in the hall closet.

"Come, let me show you around," he said as he led her into the only living space on the first floor. It was a generous room that was empty except for a large desk with a stack of files on top of it.

"This is supposed to be a den or office I think," Trent explained. "I haven't decided what to use it for yet."

Renee nodded as she walked into the space and did a full three-hundred-sixty-degree walk around. Her face was quite expressive, and Trent could tell she was already seeing the potential.

"Is this the space you would like to redecorate?" she finally asked when she walked back to him.

"No, I'm going to leave this for now. I was thinking I would start with my bedroom."

She nodded and gave him a polite smile. Trent found himself staring down at her again. It wasn't until she blinked a few times that he realized she was politely waiting for him to continue the tour.

He cleared his throat, then turned toward the stairs at the other side of the hall.

"The kitchen and main rooms are on the second floor," he explained on the way up.

"How long have you lived here, Mr. Skinner?" Renee asked politely.

"I moved in last spring, so almost a year. And, please, call me Trent."

They were now standing near the living room, which faced large patio doors leading out to a wide balcony and revealing a breathtaking view of the harbor.

"Wow, that is quite a view," she stated. "I knew we were near the waterfront, but I hadn't realized you were right on it."

"I know. It's the reason that I bought the place. It's so quiet and peaceful, yet just a few minutes from downtown."

Trent watched as she did another circular walk to take in the generous open space of the second floor. The large U-shaped kitchen was on the right with white wood cabinets, high-end stainless-steel appliances, and polished black granite countertops. It was spotless, and the counter was virtually empty except for a toaster oven. There was a breakfast area in front, but it was empty, as was the more formal dining room at the far end of the space. The only furniture sat in the living room and included a chocolate-brown leather sectional with an attached chaise, two dark wood end tables, and a matching coffee table. They faced the gas fireplace with a large flat-screen television mounted over it. There was nothing else on the walls and very few personal items.

"I'll work on the dining areas after the bedroom," Trent felt compelled to explain as he was forced to see the barrenness of the rooms through her eyes.

Renee flashed that brief, polite smile up at him again, her face devoid of any real reaction. It took Trent aback for a second. His simple plan of seduction hinged on her greedy character being highly impressed not only by his looks and charm, but also by his house and obvious success. But, other than her appreciation for his view off his balcony, Renee Goodchild appeared pretty underwhelmed by what she had seen so far, and maybe even a little disappointed. Trent was starting to see that he was going to have to revisit his game plan.

The third floor had the very spacious master bedroom and bathroom under a lofty ceiling, plus two spare rooms and second full bath. Trent had very little furniture up there also. His bedroom had a California king–size mattress set, covered by a sky-blue sheet set and a blue and white striped duvet. There was also a chest of drawers and a heavy wingback chair covered in dark hunter green leather. Again, the main feature was the large double French doors in front of the bed, leading out to another balcony with a spectacular view of the marina and the Long Island Sound behind it.

Trent let Renee walk around to inspect the room unimpeded for a few minutes. It gave him the opportunity to watch her freely. She wore a close-fitting black pantsuit made from fine wool. The jacket was short, ending at midhip, and was cinched at the waist with a wide belt. It accentuated her trim waist and displayed the shape of her lower half. Her pants clung around her hips and thighs before flaring out slightly at the bottoms. They discreetly revealed the high, round swells of the most perfect bottom Trent had seen in a long time. His eyes were immediately captured by the way the curves bounced lightly with each step she made. It was hard for him to stay focused on the task at hand.

Renee eventually made her way into the adjacent bathroom. Trent waited for about a minute before he followed her in. He needed the time to decide his first move.

"So, tell me what you are thinking for your bedroom and bath?" she asked when she saw him. "The space looks great, and all the fixtures are beautiful. Are you just looking to finish it off?"

Trent nodded as they looked around the bathroom together. Next to the view, the master bathroom was his second favorite feature of the town house. It had been done with beautiful, creamy oversized marble tiles and elegant pewter hardware. It was also laid out very well, giving him plenty of room to move around. Trent was a pretty big guy at six foot two and two hundred thirty pounds. It was important for him not to feel cramped in his space.

"I think that a basic update is what I want. The walls could do with some fresh paint, and I will need a headboard and new furniture. Other than that, I am completely open to your suggestions," he told her.

"Okay, let's go back into the bedroom."

Trent followed her as requested.

"Do you have any thoughts on style or colors?" she continued.

He sat on the edge of the bed, but she stayed standing.

"I'm not sure. I don't think I would like anything too traditional or country. I bought that dresser several years ago, because I liked the height and the number of drawers, but it's a bit too ornate for me now. Maybe something simpler but still practical?"

"What about the chair? It's beautiful but quite traditional."

"Yeah, I guess. It belonged to my father," Trent explained simply.

Renee looked at him steadily for a few seconds with those cat-shaped, intense eyes, as though reading more into his brief statement. But she looked away without probing further.

"And colors?" she asked instead.

"I'm open. They should fit in with the view, I think. And I'm partial to blue, but that's about it."

"Is there anything else you want in here?"

"No, I don't think so. The closet can use some rework maybe, with some additional shelving."

"Okay, I'll take a look at it before I leave. What about your budget? Do you have a target that includes the furniture?"

"Again, I'm open. Let me know what you think is needed and I'm sure it will be fine," replied Trent with a slight note of arrogance.

She only nodded, then continued with the business at hand.

"Timeline? When are you expecting it to be completed?"

"Sooner rather than later. How long do you think you will need?" he asked.

"Well, that depends on what direction we go with the furniture and fabrics we choose. If they are in stock, then maybe four weeks. But if you prefer something that is custom made or requires a special order, it could take a few more weeks."

Trent checked his watch. It was almost three-thirty. He stood up and stepped closer to her. He watched her eyes open slightly with surprise at his sudden closeness. She was only about five foot six, so his close proximity forced her to look up at him. It was as though she noticed his size for the first time.

"What are you doing Friday?" he asked in a smooth voice.

Her eyes widened again.

"I'm sorry, what do you mean?"

"I am looking forward to seeing your suggestions. Can we meet on Friday?"

"Oh. I'll have to check my schedule, but I'm pretty sure I have a couple of other commitments. How about next Wednesday?"

"Friday evening, then?" he persisted, as though he missed her suggestion. "I will be meeting a client in Manhattan, anyway, so we can talk over dinner."

"That's quite soon. I'm not sure I can have anything ready for you by then."

"That's okay; we can just review your ideas," Trent concluded before he turned away from her and headed out of the room and back downstairs. "Nancy arranged for the car to come back for you at three-thirty, so it should be outside now."

"Wait. I was hoping to take some measurements."

"No worries. We'll have you come back whenever you need to," he replied over his shoulder.

There was a brief pause before he heard her following behind him.

Neither of them spoke again until they were on the first floor near the front door. Trent removed their coats from the closet.

"I'll pick you up from your office at about six

o'clock Friday, but I'll give you a call tomorrow to confirm," he told her.

She nodded and had that polite smile on her face again. But it barely hid her confusion and surprise. They both went outside into the cold air. As planned, her ride back to New York was waiting in the driveway.

"It was nice meeting you, Trent," she said. "I appreciate the opportunity to work on this project for you."

They shook hands again.

"My pleasure," he replied. "I'll call you tomorrow."

Chapter 3

Renee spent at least half of the drive back to Manhattan thinking about the meeting with Trent. She pulled out her notebook and wrote down a few key ideas, finishing the comments with his expectation to meet for dinner on Friday.

What's that all about? she asked herself, now doodling on the paper as her mind wandered. Why was he so insistent that they meet again so soon? Judging from how sparsely furnished the rest of the house was, he could not be in a rush to decorate his bedroom. And a meeting over dinner? It was a little inappropriate.

Renee's fingers went still as she remembered the moment he stepped up to her, so close she could smell his light, fresh cologne. Renee had noticed his height and considerable size from the moment they had met, but those details were just part of her inventory of his space along with the spectacular views and sterile kitchen. Yet, when he was right in front of her in his bedroom and looking into her eyes from a height that forced her head to fall back, she had stopped breathing.

Now she was scheduled to see him again in two days, and whatever she thought she felt in those few seconds was irrelevant. The most important fact was that Trent Skinner was way out of her league with his million-dollar waterfront town house and top-of-the-line sport sedan. More importantly, he was now a client. And judging by the amount of work that was needed in his town house, he could become a pretty lucrative one.

Once Renee drew the line in the sand regarding Trent, she spent the last leg of the drive on her phone doing work. If she was going to have a few design options ready for Trent by Friday evening, she could not afford to waste the hour staring out the window. If she worked late tonight on sourcing furniture for the Gibson project and spent tomorrow on the Armstrong condo design, she could then focus on pulling together two or three themes for Trent's bedroom.

Keeping busy on the ride back to the city also prevented Renee from thinking about the situation back at her apartment. Though Angela had been home on Monday evening, she had been unusually quiet and preoccupied. Renee had used the opportunity to bring up the ruined shoes. Though she had been braced for one of Angela's arrogant, belligerent responses, Renee was surprised at how smoothly the brief talk had gone.

Angela had been sitting on the couch watching *Judge Mathis* when Renee entered the apartment.

They exchanged brief hellos while Renee put away her briefcase and the mail she had picked up in the lobby. As usual, the living room was littered with every item that Angela had used during the day, from plates and cups to nail polish and beauty supplies. Renee took a deep breath, deliberately ignoring the mess in order to focus on the bigger issue. She walked back to the front closet where her shoes were still tossed in the corner, looking no better than they had that morning.

"Angela," Renee stated in a soft but firm voice. She was now standing near the couch with a shoe in each hand.

The expression on Angela's face went from distracted to guilty in about two seconds. Her mouth formed an oval shape and her eyes were wide and unblinking.

"What happened to my shoes?" Renee finally asked.

Angela looked back at the television. A stretch of silence hung between them while Renee waited for a response. In the past, she might have bit her tongue and let the matter drop. But this time, Renee was going to stand her ground regardless of how Angela responded.

"Angela!" she demanded, this time louder and sharper.

"What?" she demanded. "What about your shoes?"

"Angela, you ruined them! And you wore them without even asking me."

"Okay, I borrowed them, Renee. What's the big deal?"

Renee clenched her teeth so hard she could hear

them squeak. "The big deal is that they were very expensive, and you have no respect for my things."

"All right, all right!" Angela interrupted while rolling her eyes. "I'm sorry I borrowed them, okay? I'll take them to the shoemaker tomorrow and get them cleaned up. And I borrowed your laptop today, by the way, just in case that's a problem too."

She turned her head back to the television as though her petulant apology was enough and the matter should be dropped. Renee had been standing on the wrong side of Angela's turned back on many occasions in the past, and it had always meant the same thing: Angela was done talking, and any attempt to continue discussing the topic was just going to get ugly. Renee had thought she was prepared for that moment and had built up the resolve to push forward and say everything she needed to express about their deteriorating friendship. But now that she was in the situation, the fight seeped out of her. She definitely did not have time for a long, fruitless debate. And until she determined exactly when and how she was going to ask Angela to move out of the apartment, there wasn't much else to say on the subject.

Renee put her shoes back in the front hall and then went into the kitchen to make something for dinner.

Angela had hung around on the couch for a few more minutes before heading into the spare bedroom where she spent the next hour between there and the bathroom. She then left the apartment at around nine o'clock, dressed to the nines in all her own clothes.

Renee was left wondering where on earth she could be going to party on a Monday night.

The two women briefly crossed paths again mid-morning Tuesday, and now, as Renee directed the driver to her apartment, she wondered what mess and drama would be waiting for her. She also silently vowed that when the next incident happened—and there was no doubt that there would be another one— she would tell Angela to find somewhere else to live.

When Renee got to the apartment, she could hear Angela in the shower. Renee took the opportunity to quickly change out of her suit and into jeans and a sweater. She threw her notebook into an oversize purse along with her wallet, pen, and a few other essential items before heading back outside. The bathroom door was still closed when she left.

Renee jumped on the subway and headed to her favorite furniture outlet in the Bronx. Henry Interiors was a small wholesale operation run by two brothers who started out as reupholsterers. They featured designer samples and unique pieces from all over the world. They also did custom pieces based on their own designs right there in their shop. Renee had met the youngest brother, Frederic, at a decorating convention a couple of years ago, and the two of them quickly became friendly. She met his brother, Albert, at her first visit to their store.

Frederic was the first to see her when she walked in. "Hey, gorgeous!" he stated while walking toward her. His voice still held a hint of a childhood Scottish accent. "Don't you look hot! When did you change your hair?"

Renee laughed, still not used to the reactions to her new look. "Hey, Freddie."

They hugged tightly with genuine affection. He playfully tried to mess up her hair with the tips of his fingers. Renee ducked away and slapped his hands, laughing.

"Well, look who has blown in from the Upper East Side."

Renee turned around and watched Albert saunter toward her. The brothers were about eighteen months apart in age but looked like identical twins. They were tall, thick, and way too good-looking for their own good. Both were in their early thirties and had a full head of thick reddish brown hair, though Albert wore his in a low buzz and Frederic had longer locks, which he pulled into a small ponytail at the base of his skull.

"Hey, Albert," she replied before he, too, pulled her into a hug.

His squeeze was so tight she could hardly breathe. He then looked her up and down but didn't comment on her new look.

"To what do we owe the pleasure?" he asked instead.

Renee was used to Albert's sardonic nature, so she was unfazed by his sarcasm. She wrinkled her nose at him teasingly. "What? Can't I just be visiting my favorite furniture designers?" she asked with feigned innocence.

Both men rolled their sky-blue eyes, smirking at

the idea that she would travel all the way to the Bronx just to visit.

"Please, darling," quipped Albert. "If that were true, you should have called. I would have sent Freddie here out on a long errand so we could have had plenty of time to ourselves."

Renee gasped at his naughty flirting, then slapped him playfully on the shoulder. He responded with a rare, devilish grin that revealed matching dimples.

"You wish, brother." Freddie snickered.

"Okay, I need your help," Renee finally admitted. "I need some fresh, new furniture pieces for a couple of projects. I'm pretty sure that Pottery Barn just isn't going to cut it for these clients."

"Okay," Albert stated, all business again. "What rooms are you working on?"

Both men started walking toward the main showroom. Renee walked quickly to keep up with their long strides and started explaining her ideas about the furniture she had in mind. The three of them spent the next couple of hours looking at stock items, catalogs, and Henry Interiors' custom designs. By the time Renee caught a cab back to Manhattan, she felt pretty satisfied with the options for the Gibson brownstone and the Connecticut town house.

After being dropped off, Renee stopped into a restaurant near her building and bought a chicken dinner from the takeout counter. When she got home, the apartment was empty. Renee was relieved. It had been a long day, and she was looking forward to watching a little television while she ate.

She dropped her things on the dining room table and went into her bedroom to change into her pajamas. Once dressed, she washed her face in the bathroom to remove her makeup, then headed back into the living room. Finally, Renee could sit back and eat her meal with a sitcom playing in the background.

The phone rang about twenty minutes later. Renee recognized the phone number of her friend Jennifer Smith.

"Hi, Jen, what's up?"

"Hey, Renee. Nothing much. How are you doing?"

"I'm okay. Just got home not too long ago."

"Wow, that's a long day. It's almost nine-thirty," Jennifer commented.

"I know." Renee sighed. "I went up to the Bronx to look at some furniture. I met a new client today, and I needed to get some fresh ideas."

"Oh, okay. Well, I won't keep you. I'm calling to invite you to a fashion show on Friday night. It's for a local designer, and it's supposed to be a pretty hot event. Do you want to go with me?"

Renee remembered her meeting with Trent Skinner.

"Oh, I'm sorry, Jennifer. I wish I could, but I have a client meeting on Friday evening."

"That's too bad. What time will be it over? Maybe you can come to the after-party," Jennifer suggested.

"Maybe. I'll have to see. He's picking me up at six-thirty, so I'm guessing we'll be done by nine o'clock?"

"Hmm, that sounds like an interesting business meeting," Jennifer said mischievously. "He's picking you up for dinner on a Friday night? Who's this mysterious client?"

Renee let out a deep breath and smiled at the teasing. "Well, it's the same guy I met today. And *mysterious* is definitely the right word. I got a call out of the blue from his assistant to arrange to meet him in Greenwich."

"Greenwich? Connecticut? Are you serious?"

"I know. That's what I thought. Aren't there plenty of qualified designers up there? Then he sends a car service for me."

"Wow, that sounds pretty nice," Jennifer replied. "So how did you guys end up with a dinner date?"

"It's not a date," denied Renee.

"It sounds like a date to me. Unless, of course, he's short and ugly."

Both women laughed.

"Is he?" Jennifer insisted.

"No, he's the exact opposite of short and ugly," Renee admitted.

"I knew it!"

"Well, it doesn't matter. Regardless of how sexy he is, he's still just a client."

"All right, if you say so. But let me know if you want to meet after your dinner and go to the after-party."

"I will. And thanks for the invitation."

They hung up soon after.

Renee spent a few guilty moments remembering just how attractive Trent Skinner was, with his tall, firm body and creamy brown skin. Then there was the look in his eyes as he stepped close to her in the bedroom, as though he wanted to touch her. . . .

She shook her head sharply, pulling herself out of the daydream. Thoughts like that were only going to get her in trouble. Renee quickly cleaned up the garbage from her dinner, then went back to watching mindless television.

Chapter 4

After the meeting with Renee, Trent drove back to the office for his 4:30 meeting and to finish off a few things. He called Nathan from the car on the way.

"Well?" his cousin asked without any small talk. "What happened? How did it go?"

"We're having dinner on Friday evening," Trent told him bluntly.

There was a small silence.

"Wow, Trent. You really work fast."

Nathan's voice held an awkward mix of admiration, relief, and bitterness. Trent ignored it, as usual. Even though he was twenty-nine years old, Nathan still had the emotional maturity of a teenager.

"We need to move fast, don't we? Didn't she give you a deadline of this Saturday to come up with the money?" he replied.

"Yeah," confirmed Nathan with a big sigh.

"Okay. So, you need to call her tonight and tell her you will give her the money, but you need two weeks."

"I don't know, Trent. The last time we talked, it got pretty nasty. Renee made it crystal clear that either she got the money on Saturday or she would tell Ophelia all about our relationship. And you know that can't happen. Ophelia would put me out on the street in a heartbeat."

Trent rolled his eyes. "Nate, think about it. Renee just wants the money. Telling your wife will get her nothing. She'll wait a couple of weeks for it."

"Let's say you're right," Nathan replied quickly. "Then what? I won't have the money in two weeks either. I don't have that kind of cash available, not without Ophelia finding out about it."

"You don't have to. We're just buying time, remember? By then, Renee Goodchild will be too busy trying to hook what looks like a much bigger fish: me. Or, at the very least, it will give me enough time to find any evidence she might have."

"She suggested there were pictures," Nathan threw in.

"Have you seen them?" asked Trent.

"No."

"Then how do you know they exist? Didn't you demand to see them? She could be playing you, man!"

"I—"

Trent cut him off impatiently as he pulled his car into the parking lot beneath his office. "I'm back at work, so I have to go," he told Nathan. "Call her tonight and tell her you will need at least two more weeks, and you need to see the evidence."

"Okay," agreed Nathan before they hung up.

Trent banged his fist on the steering wheel to vent his annoyance. He loved his cousin to death, but Nathan could really test his patience at times. It was inconceivable that Nathan had put himself in such a ridiculous situation and seemed so helpless to get himself out of it.

Nathan Frost was Trent's first cousin on his mother's side. They had been quite close as kids in Chicago, where they were both raised. While Trent was the only child of a single mother, Nathan lived with both his parents and had two older sisters. Trent's father, whom he didn't meet until he was fifteen years old, was a high-ranking officer in the Jamaican army, while Nathan's was a manager at a local insurance company. Their upbringing could not have been any more different, but for some reason, they still grew up like brothers. Though Nathan was only three years younger, he had looked up to Trent his whole life, always turning to his cousin for advice and support.

Trent was not surprised that Nathan made a habit of cheating on his wife during the course of the six years of their relationship and their three-year marriage. The two men had never discussed it outright, but Nathan wasn't very discreet. He had made enough innuendoes and suggestive comments to give Trent a good idea of what he was up to. But Trent had just assumed his cousin had the good sense to be smart about it. Apparently not.

At the same time, now that Trent had met Renee Goodchild, he could not find fault with his cousin's taste. She was just as beautiful as Nathan had described, but in a totally different way. Trent had expected to find her obvious and artificial, both in her appearance and personality. Instead, he found the complete opposite. She had been professional and credible as a designer, subtle and feminine as a woman. Not at all the image of a money-hungry slut.

Back in his office, Trent dove back into work, hoping to put the whole sordid mess out of his mind. He stayed occupied well into the evening, and he didn't shut down his computer until almost eight-thirty. As he headed out the door, he paused to check his cell phone, still in his coat pocket. There was a missed call and a voice mail message. The caller history indicated the number was an overseas extension.

Trent checked the message as he made his way down to his car.

"Hi, Trent," said the caller in a flirty, bubbly voice. "It's me, Brianna. It's almost midnight here, and I was hoping to catch you before bed. Paris is beautiful, and the shopping has been just fabulous. My feet are killing me from walking all day, but wait until you see the dresses I bought at this tiny boutique downtown. Anyway, give me a call back if it's not too late. Otherwise, I'll call you tomorrow morning your time. Good night."

Trent deleted the message.

Brianna Chamberlin was the daughter of one of his clients. At twenty-three years old, she was very sweet and beautiful, but way too young and pampered. Trent met her at a charity event about five weeks earlier and found her fun and lighthearted at first. He asked her out a few days later, and they had been dating pretty steadily ever since. She had flown to France on Monday with her mother to spend a few weeks shopping in Paris and relaxing at a spa in Nice.

Though Brianna was a nice girl, and they had had a lot of fun over the last few weeks, she could be a little too chatty at times. Trent now tried to avoid conversations with her during work hours as much as possible. She worked occasionally for her father's company and didn't seem to understand the concept of limited time during work hours.

It was definitely too late for him to call her that evening, since Paris was six hours ahead. Trent made a mental note to try and call her the next day when he had some time.

On Thursday, he had a full day of meetings and client calls booked. Yet every hour or so, a reminder popped up in his calendar prompting him to call Renee to confirm their dinner plans. The more he thought about the whole situation, the more his involvement made him uncomfortable. Something wasn't right, and he had spent a good part of the previous night trying to put his finger on it, but with no luck.

Ironically, Trent was the one who came up with the whole plan to seduce his cousin's lover-turned-extortionist. Nathan had called him about the situation within hours after Renee's first demand for money. At that point, Trent had been pretty dismissive of the whole situation. His advice to Nathan had been to buy her some jewelry and firmly end it. But Nathan did not have the assertiveness to do the job right. Apparently, Renee happily took the gift and increased her demand to ten thousand dollars. At that point, Trent knew that she smelled blood and would not stop squeezing Nathan unless she found a more lucrative victim. Nathan was skeptical of Trent's plan from the beginning, but he was also too desperate to object.

By three o'clock Thursday afternoon, Trent knew he could not put off making the call any longer. He pulled Renee's business card out of his wallet and dialed her cell phone number. She answered after the second ring with a professional greeting.

"Hi, Renee. This is Trent Skinner," he stated simply.

There was a small pause before she replied.

"Mr. Skinner. How are you doing today?" she asked politely.

"Trent, please," he insisted again. "I'm doing well. How about you?"

"I'm good, thanks . . . Trent."

"Good to hear. I'm calling to confirm dinner tomorrow. I will be downtown until about five-thirty. Why don't I pick you up at six o'clock?" he suggested.

There was another pause before she answered.

"All right."

"Good. I have your card, so I'll pick you up at your office on Third Avenue," confirmed Trent.

"Wait!" she interrupted. "I'll be working from home tomorrow, so . . ."

"Oh, okay. Then I'll pick you up at your home address. Where are you?"

"No, really, that's not necessary. Why don't I just meet you somewhere?"

"Renee, I'll pick you up," he insisted in a voice that did not invite further debate. "Do you live in Manhattan?"

He could sense that Renee was frustrated with his heavy-handed approach. She let out a loud sigh, and he grinned to himself.

"I'm on the Upper East Side," she finally told him.

"Great. Why don't we make it six-thirty, then? What's the address?"

She finally gave him the details. They confirmed the time again before hanging up.

Trent still had a satisfied smile on his face. He was suddenly looking forward to the evening. Renee Goodchild was turning out to be a complicated puzzle, and he was looking forward to solving it. Though, if Trent thought more deeply about it, he would have to wonder if his interest was purely to fix Nathan's problem, or something much more selfish.

He would also wonder why he completely forgot to return Brianna's call.

Chapter 5

It was the last few days of February, and winter had New York City in a tight, icy grip. The sky was a brilliant, cloudless blue, but the air was so cold and still that it hurt to breathe. New Yorkers scuttled around the city, bundled in fashionable layers and enveloped in the clouds of white, billowy exhaust from the constant traffic.

Renee spent all day Friday in her apartment wearing her flannel pajamas and with the thermostat set at least two degrees higher than was necessary. She had her work spread out on the couch and coffee table, and the television played softly in the background. Occasionally, she would take a break to look out the window at the drama on the street below and wish she didn't have to go outside that evening. Renee kept her fingers crossed that Trent Skinner would cancel their meeting due to the extremely cold weather.

By four-thirty in the afternoon, there was no call from Trent, and Renee resigned herself to the inevitable. On her laptop, she put the final touches to her designs for him and saved the file. Renee then sent the five-page presentation to her printer in the spare bedroom before cleaning up her work into a neat stack on the coffee table. All she had left to do was arrange the printed presentation in a nice folder; then she would have plenty of time to get dressed for dinner.

Renee had not seen or heard anything from Angela all day, and she was pretty sure she had not come home on Thursday. But she knocked lightly on the door to the spare bedroom just in case, then pushed it open when there was no response. She walked over to her desk, which was set up along the far wall under the window, carefully stepping over discarded clothing and shoes along the way.

The pages of her presentation were waiting on the printer, but Renee sifted through them with dismay. They were all blank except for about half of the first page. The printer was out of ink. She let out a frustrated groan, mentally kicking herself for not remembering to buy more ink over the last couple of weeks. The only option now was to run over to the small printing shop down the street before Trent came to pick her up.

Renee quickly ran through the options in her head and decided to get showered and dressed for dinner first, then go to the printer. They had self-service machines that were usually available, and Renee figured she could be in and out in fifteen minutes. If she was running late, she could call Trent at the last minute and ask him to wait for her in front of the building.

Once she decided what to do, Renee sprung into action. First, she had to save Trent's presentation on a flash drive. She had bought one on sale at a business-supply store several months back but had never used it. Renee was fairly certain she had left it on top of her desk. A quick search of the surface came up empty. The flash drive was not there. She then checked the desk drawers and the floor around the area in case it had fallen but found nothing.

Renee straightened up and looked around the bedroom. Stress and panic were starting to crawl up her neck and create pressure around her temples. Where else could it be? She started looking around again with more scrutiny, starting with the bookcase beside the desk, then moving to the bedside table. Finally, she found it in one of the lower drawers. Renee let out a big sigh of relief, grabbed the device, and ran to the living room to save the file. She could not afford any time to think about why she would have stored the flash drive in such an odd place.

She got dressed and ready in record time and managed to reach the printing store before six o'clock. However, both the self-serve machines were being used, and judging from the stack of papers each customer had, Renee knew they were not going to be free any time soon. She quickly went to the service desk to have the document printed for her. Thankfully, the young man behind the counter was available and took the flash drive and instructions right away.

Renee was checking her e-mail on her phone when he came back to her.

"'Xcuse me, ma'am, but which file did you want printed?" he asked.

"Sorry, what do mean?" Renee replied, distracted and confused by his question. "There is only one file there."

"Ahh, I don't know. There looks like a couple."

He turned away from her to check out the computer screen.

"There's one document called 'Skinner Greenwich' and a folder," he told her while pointing to the screen so she could see.

"A folder?" she repeated dumbly.

Renee stared at him blankly for several seconds, trying to remember when she had used the drive and what she had put on it. Nothing came to mind. The store employee stared at her with raised eyebrows, clearly waiting for her to give him some instructions.

"Oh, um . . . it's the document, the Skinner Greenwich file. Thanks."

She spent another few seconds worrying about her forgetfulness, but then the beeping of her phone pulled her back to the e-mails until the document was ready.

Renee got back upstairs to her apartment with the presentation completed and ten minutes to spare. She double-checked her makeup and hair, straightened her pantsuit under her coat, then switched from thick-soled snow boots to a high-heel pair. Once satisfied with her appearance, she headed back downstairs to the lobby a couple of minutes early.

While she waited, Renee called Jennifer to let her know that she wouldn't be going to the fashion-show party. It turned out that Jennifer found it too cold to venture out also and was already wearing her pajamas and wrapped in a warm blanket.

Trent Skinner pulled up in front of her building exactly on time. Renee recognized his sleek sedan right away, and she stepped out into the frigid night air before he had come to a full stop. By the time she got to the vehicle, he was walking around the car to open the passenger door for her. She gave him a small, polite smile before lowering herself into the luxurious black leather bucket seats. Within seconds, the seat warmer was penetrating through the layers of her clothing.

Trent slid in beside her and pulled away from the curb.

"It's a pretty cold night, isn't it?" he asked as they joined the flow of traffic heading west toward Central Park.

"I know. I was kind of expecting you to call and cancel," she replied, trying to sound humorous, though she was being honest. "The drive from Greenwich must have been difficult."

"Not at all," replied Trent. "The roads were dry, so it was nothing. And there is no way I would cancel. I've been looking forward to seeing you again."

He gave her a sidelong glance full of intensity. Renee looked away quickly, focusing on the view out the window as she tried to process what his words might be implying. The seconds stretched awkwardly.

"I can't wait to see your ideas for my bedroom," he finally added.

Renee looked back at him and nodded. She wasn't sure what to say.

"Do you like Italian food?" he asked a few moments later. "I always have Italian when I come into the city. But we can have whatever you like."

"Italian is fine."

"Good. I've made reservations at my favorite place."

She smiled at him, nodding slowly.

There was silence between them again. A few minutes later, Trent turned on the stereo and soul music started playing at a low volume. Renee didn't immediately recognize the artist, but the first couple of songs sounded familiar. She found herself relaxing back into her cozy seat.

The ride to the restaurant lasted only about ten minutes, but with the lack of conversation, it felt much longer. She did sneak in a few quick glances toward Trent. His posture was relaxed, but his face was firm, almost pensive. Every minute or so, from the corner of her eye, she could see him rub at his temple with his thumb. She could not help but wonder what was on his mind.

They pulled up to a small restaurant on 44th Street, about half a block from Fifth Avenue. The parking valet quickly opened the door for Renee. She ran inside the building with Trent close behind her. They were immediately approached by the hostess, a tall, stunning blonde with a slender body and overly generous breasts.

"Mr. Skinner," she stated with a big smile. "So nice to see you again."

"Hi, Maria," he replied easily. "It has been too long. I've been craving Angelo's lasagna for months."

"He'll be glad to hear it. It's on the menu tonight," Maria replied as she led them toward a table at the back of the room.

While Trent and Maria chatted, Renee took in the décor. She had never been to Italy, but she imagined that there was a restaurant somewhere in Naples that looked exactly like this one. It was dripping with ornate, old-world design charm. Heavy iron chandeliers provided low, ambient lighting, and tall pillar candles flickered from stands mounted on the walls. The tables were solid mahogany and surrounded by large leather armchairs with a brass stud trim. Renee could not help but run her hands along their smooth curved arms as she took her seat.

Maria handed her a menu and asked if she would like something to drink. She requested water, while Trent ordered a bottle of red wine for them to share.

"Do you like wine?" he asked once they were alone.

Renee was tempted to suggest sarcastically that perhaps he should have asked the question before ordering a full bottle. But he was her client, so she smiled nicely instead.

"I do like wine, red in particular," she told him truthfully.

"Good," he replied with a pleased smile. "You'll really like the one I ordered."

"I'm sure it will be fine," Renee said. "But I'm not a connoisseur or anything. I probably couldn't tell the difference between an expensive import and something cheap."

Trent laughed and seemed genuinely amused. His face completely transformed from masculine austerity to boyish charm. Renee found herself smiling also, a little captivated by the sparkle in his eyes. She wanted to ask him what was so funny.

"I don't think there is a real difference. Stick to what you like and that's all that matters," he replied, still chuckling. "Last year, I found this California cabernet somewhere on sale. I think I needed it to cook something, but I can't remember. Anyway, I tasted it and it was really good. Better in my mind than some of the trendy labels you buy for gifts or dinner parties. I went back and bought about ten bottles, and I put it out in a decanter the next time I had people over. There's this one guy I work with whose wife was going on and on about their expensive wine collection, and the last two-hundred-dollar bottle she ordered from somewhere overseas. So, while she was blabbing away, she drank glass after glass of my cheap stuff."

Renee was smiling more broadly now, listening to him tell his story. Her chin rested in the palm of her hand, propped up on her elbow.

"Finally, near the end of the night, she started bugging me for details about the wine. But when I told her exactly what it was and where I bought it— for about six dollars—she was so drunk that she didn't believe me and kept insisting it was some South African vintage that she also had at home. Eventually, I just gave up and agreed with her."

They both laughed for several seconds. It wasn't

until their waitress arrived with their drinks that Renee realized how much she and Trent had naturally leaned into each other in the dim light. She quickly sat back into her chair, and he followed at a slower pace. Her heart was racing.

Renee quickly skimmed the menu and picked out a simple chicken pasta dish, but she kept the menu open for several minutes longer. The air at the table suddenly felt less like a business meeting and more like a date. It wasn't so much that Trent was being amusing and flirtatious; many of her male clients were like that. Several were downright suggestive, and she was quite capable of politely ignoring inappropriate overtures. So, even though she sensed that Trent Skinner might be making a move on her, it was irrelevant if she was not interested. It was her own attraction to his smooth smile, strong lips, and kind eyes that was changing her impression of the evening.

Kind eyes? Where the hell did that some from? she thought. One funny story and her body heat had gone from zero to one hundred in sixty seconds!

Eventually, she had to close the menu and face him again.

Chapter 6

Trent ordered what he always did from Al Pesto—a Caesar salad and Angelo's four-layer lasagna with ground veal, spinach, and a mix of white cheeses. He was sure most things on the menu were excellent, and if he lived in Manhattan and was able to eat there regularly, Trent would sample more of them. But like most things in his life, once he discovered something he liked, Trent was pretty loyal to it.

He watched Renee mull over the thick menu, though he suspected she was just avoiding looking at him. He had sensed the minute her attention to their conversation had turned from polite interest to real enjoyment. Her stunning eyes had looked deep into his, and she even ran her tongue over her top lip while brushing her fingers over the buzzed hair at the nape of her neck. These were all signs of attraction that Trent knew very well. His plan was working, and he should have been satisfied with the results. But Trent was more confused than ever.

Renee Goodchild, a supposed shameless, manipulative whore, was not at all impressed with his waterfront town house, expensive car, or the high-end restaurant he chose. She didn't even try to order an overpriced drink or pretend to have upper-class taste. But she came alive the minute he told a funny story about pretentious people.

And why had he even told her that story? That was the type of thing he would laugh about with his friends. Yet, the minute Renee mentioned her lack of knowledge about wine, with that sweet smile and direct gaze, the scenario popped into his head and the words poured out of his mouth without his usual filters.

Trent rubbed his finger along his temple, then brought it to rest against his lips. He watched her put down the menu as their waitress approached to take their orders. She requested one of the least expensive dishes, no appetizers or salad. His brows lowered, creating parallel grooves deep in his forehead. He was so taken aback that it took him several seconds to realize the two women were looking at him expectantly, waiting for him to place his order.

Trent quickly asked for his usual, and the waitress walked away. Before he could say anything further about her meal, Renee reached into the oversized handbag hanging off her chair and pulled out a presentation portfolio.

"I've put together a few ideas for your bedroom so that we can get a little closer to understanding exactly what you want," she stated, all business and focused.

"All right," Trent replied as he accepted the folder. He opened it up and found five printed pages.

The first three were computer-generated images re-creating the dimensions of his bedroom, each with a different theme of style and colors. The fourth page was a furniture list, including several options for bed frames, dressers, and chairs. The last page had three price points with some summary comments for each. Trent flipped back to the first design and went through them each more slowly. They were all really nice. Simple and masculine, but they also looked very comfortable and inviting. The last one was by far his favorite.

The walls were a rich gray with a hint of blue. Trent was surprised that it didn't look dark or dingy, though it might have if there wasn't a ton of light flooding in through the French doors. Renee's illustration showed them with his white plantation shutters open, but with dark gray curtain panels hanging along the sides.

She had moved his bed from the back of the room to the side wall so it sat beside the patio doors. There was only a simple, tall headboard made of dark wood with decorative trim creating six raised panels. Renee used his preference of light blue in sheets, covered by a dark gray duvet with a textured square pattern that mimicked the headboard panels. Two slightly different oval side tables flanked the bed. She added a tall chest of drawers against the wall across from the bed, and his dad's wingback chair was placed beside it, still in its original dark green leather.

Trent wasn't sure how long he spent looking through the pictures and reviewing all the details. Renee sat quiet, patiently waiting for his reaction. When he

finally looked up, she was leaning back in her chair
with her legs crossed and her face expressionless.

"The third one," he stated simply.

She smiled broadly, showing two rows of even
white teeth, including slightly pointed incisors. Trent
thought they made her look a little mischievous, and
he smiled back.

"Okay," she replied, laughing lightly. "That was
easy."

"Well, it's exactly what I'm looking for, though
I'm pretty sure I didn't know that before," he replied,
chuckling also.

At that point, the discussion turned to the details
of the design. Renee asked him to flip to the last two
pages of the presentation and walked him through
the different furniture options, price points, and
finishes.

In those few minutes, Trent became so engrossed in
the idea of his new bedroom that he lost sight of the
end game. The dinner arrived, but they continued
talking as they ate. He was surprised, almost thirty
minutes later, to find them still discussing her designs
with their empty plates in front of them. They paused
for a few seconds as their dishes were removed, and
their waitress asked if they would like any dessert of
coffee. Trent ordered an espresso and talked Renee
into having one also.

"I don't think you've told me who referred you to
me?" asked Renee once they were alone again.

"Oh, yeah. There was a woman at an event I went
to a couple of months ago. I don't remember her name,
but she had been talking about some decorating she

had done and how much she loved it. She gave me your card," Trent replied smoothly.

"Really?" she replied, sounding surprised and a little skeptical.

"And now that I've seen your suggestions, I can see why she was so happy with your work," he added.

She beamed, but lowered her head shyly.

"How long have you been an interior designer?" he asked, seizing the opportunity to get the conversation back on track.

"About four years now."

He nodded.

"Well, you've clearly done really well so far. Are you from New York originally?" he asked.

"No, Pittsburgh, actually. I moved here right after college."

"Steele town," he added. "Why Manhattan?"

Renee shrugged. "It seemed the best place to have a good career in design."

"True, but it's a big move for a young woman alone. Or did you move with someone?" he asked. "Like a boyfriend or husband?"

She smiled pleasantly, then shook her head. "Nope, no boyfriend or otherwise," she finally replied.

Trent sat back in the chair, looking at her speculatively.

"What?" she finally asked when his stare become uncomfortable.

Trent shrugged. "Nothing, really. It just seems odd to me that a beautiful, young, single woman would move to big, bad New York all by herself."

"Why?" she asked defensively. "People do it all

the time. I'm sure the city is filled with women just like me, just pursuing their careers."

"No," stated Trent definitively. "There are none quite like you, Renee."

Their eyes met and held as she tried to read the meaning behind his words. He knew the second she got the message. She smiled politely, but straightened in her chair.

"Well, I'm glad you like the designs," Renee finally stated. "If you're ready to move forward, I will need to take some measurements before we can start the work."

Trent smiled slowly until it became a grin. She was backing away from what his eyes were telling her, and he wanted her to know he knew it. A charged silence settled between them.

"Look, Trent," she started in a low, direct voice. "I really appreciate the opportunity to work on your town house. I'm excited about the project, and I think it will be beautiful in the end. But I need to be clear that it will strictly be a professional relationship. I hope you are okay with that."

Trent didn't know exactly what he had expected Renee to say, but it wasn't that. He was completely caught off guard by her direct but gentle rejection, and his smile faded a little. Renee was clearly waiting for his reaction, and he scrambled to find an appropriate response.

"All right," he stated in a light tone. "I can respect that."

"Great, I'm glad. I will have to double-check my

calendar for next week, but I would like to stop in to get started."

"Sounds good."

The conversation on the drive back to her apartment was a little stilted but polite. Renee talked a bit more about the process needed to complete his bedroom, and Trent responded as needed. But he was very preoccupied, trying to decide what to do next to salvage his plan. He was also fighting a feeling of disappointment that he knew had nothing to do with Nathan's situation.

When they reached her building, he stopped in front with the engine running and quickly walked around to the passenger side to let her out.

"Thanks again for dinner, Trent. It was very nice," she told him as they stood facing each other in the frigid night air. Her gloved hand was extended to shake his.

"My pleasure."

He took her hand, shook it slightly, but then pulled her into a platonic hug. Their cheeks met, and Trent brushed his lips against a spot near her ear. Renee pulled back to look up at him. Her bright, beautiful eyes showed surprise and a little confusion. Trent didn't plan the next move. It just happened.

He leaned forward and brushed his lips against hers, very gently and slowly. Renee didn't reciprocate, but she also didn't pull back. That electric charge he had felt the first time they touched was back with a vengeance, flowing down his back with sharp intensity. Trent kissed her again, this time tugging on her lower lip and teasing it lightly with his tongue. He wanted to pull her closer and delve deeper to taste her sweet wetness, but he had enough sense to put on the brakes.

When he pulled away to look down at her again, Renee had her eyes closed. Sensing his gaze, she looked up at him, and Trent saw a mix of surprise and confusion on her face. He stepped back a little and finally released his hold on her hand. She let out a long breath, and Trent fully anticipated she would have some scathing words for him.

"Good night," she said simply before brushing past him to walk quickly into the lobby of her building.

Trent turned to watch her leave, making sure she entered the security doors safely. He then got into his car and drove away.

Nothing about this whole messy situation was working out right. His plan for an easy seduction to distract Renee was obviously not going to work. In fact, it was a disaster, and his irrational behavior just now could have ruined everything. She had made it very clear that she was not at all interested in his romantic attention, and Trent was lucky that she hadn't slapped his face.

He now realized he and Nathan may have to move on to plan B. If things didn't change drastically soon, Nathan would have to call Renee's bluff to tell his wife about the affair by threatening her with legal action if she did not produce her evidence and disappear forever.

Chapter 7

Renee didn't remember the walk up to her apartment. Somehow, she found herself leaning against the inside of her apartment door. Her mind was reeling, and her lips felt tingly and tender. Slowly, she walked into her bedroom and began to remove her clothes.

Why had he kissed her? And, worse, why had she let him?

She ran over all the details of the evening, and nothing in it could have prepared her for that kiss, including his harmless flirting. It was the most bizarre thing that had ever happened to her. One minute she was shaking his hand and doing an excellent job of keeping her promise to herself to enjoy being single for a while. The next minute, his gorgeous mouth was brushing her skin and then her lips.

Even now, as she pulled on loose flannel pajamas, Renee wondered if she had imagined the whole thing. Men like Trent Skinner just did not seriously pursue women like her. They might test the waters in the search for an easy lay, and Renee was smart enough to see that coming a mile away. Her statement to Trent about maintaining a strictly professional relationship was specifically to put that idea out of his mind. But there was nothing about his kiss that felt casual or trifling.

In her bathroom, with her face scrubbed clean of makeup, Renee stared hard at her reflection. Yes, he was a gorgeous example of a man: tall with smooth, milk-chocolate skin. He seemed strong and unyielding, with a firm jawline and a beautiful smile. But he was her client and way, way out of her league. She did okay, making a modest income that was steadily growing, but she was nowhere near the tax bracket Trent fell into. Taking his advances seriously would be a big mistake for her career and her heart.

With new resolve, Renee headed to bed.

Her weekend went by quickly. The city was still in a deep freeze, so she stayed close to home, catching up on work and venturing outside only to do some basic shopping. As usual, Angela was hardly there, only stopping in on Saturday afternoon to take a shower and change her clothes.

Despite her lingering discomfort, Renee called Trent's office on Monday morning to arrange a return visit to the town house, ideally that Thursday. His assistant answered the call and introduced herself as Nancy. She took the details and promised to call Renee back quickly with confirmation.

When the phone call came later that afternoon, Renee was unprepared to hear Trent's voice on the other end of the line.

"How was your weekend?" he asked her after they exchanged greetings.

"Relaxing, thank you," she replied politely. "How was yours?"

"Cold," he stated simply with a deep chuckle. "But, hopefully, spring's just around the corner, right?"

"Let's hope so," she said. "I let your assistant know that I'm available on Thursday to come up to Greenwich and take some measurements. Will that work for you?"

"Yeah, Nancy gave me your message. That could work, but I will need to be in the office most of the day. I'll send a car for you, and you can pick up the keys from my office before you head to the house. I might be in meetings, but Nancy will have everything you need."

"That sounds good. But there is no need to send a car. . . ."

"I insist, Renee," he dismissed. "What time would be good?"

"The earlier the better, I think."

"Okay, I'll have the driver pick you up at nine o'clock. That way you can avoid some of the traffic."

"All right. Thursday at nine o'clock it is," she confirmed.

"Now, I was thinking about the furniture choices, and I wouldn't mind looking at a few more before I make a decision. I'll be in the city tomorrow. I'm sure you're quite busy, but I have some time in the afternoon available. It would be a good opportunity for us to look at some other options."

Renee had a strong suspicion that the shopping

trip was an excuse for them to see each other. She could not imagine that he was that anxious to buy new furniture.

There was a brief pause as she tried to decide how to respond. "I think I can free up a few hours if I move a couple of things around. Is after three o'clock okay?"

"That's perfect," he replied.

"Okay, then I'll line up two or three stores that we can go to."

"Great, Renee. I appreciate it."

Renee sat back after hanging up the phone. She ran a finger over her lips, remembering those last few seconds with Trent the previous Friday. She probably would have spent a lot longer thinking over the whole situation, but her phone rang again a couple of minutes later.

"Hi, Renee, this Maya Johnson from the *Daybreak Show*."

"Hi," Renee replied, somewhat confused as to why they were calling her.

The *Daybreak Show* was a daily morning TV show based in Manhattan. They had a weekly segment on home decorating, and Renee's boss, Amanda Hoffman, was one of their regular contributors. Amanda's work on the show had started just before Renee began working as her assistant, so Renee had also been on set several times, helping out behind the scenes. But that was a couple of years ago.

"I am producing the interior design and renovation show this Friday," Maya continued. "Apparently, the designer we had lined up broke her leg over the weekend and had to cancel. I called Amanda

Hoffman's office, but she is going to be on vacation. Her assistant suggested you might be available to step in?"

"Oh, I see," stammered Renee.

"I understand you have some experience with live television broadcasting?"

"Yes, but not on camera."

Renee went on to describe what she had done for the shows that Amanda had appeared on.

"Excellent. This week's show will focus on what's new for spring. So, we would need to do a fifteen-minute segment highlighting some of the newest trends," explained Maya. "We will have two other designers on also—Kevin Adams and Sonya Sheridan. Kevin is going to showcase the before-and-after of a large renovation, and Sonya is going to talk about what's new for indoor and outdoor paints."

"Okay," Renee stated as she quickly made notes in her notebook.

"So, I'm thinking you can focus on new furniture design, accent pieces, what's new in color and fabrics. Stuff like that."

"That sounds great."

"Good. So, will you be able to do it, Renee?"

"Absolutely, I would love to be on the show," stated Renee. "What time does it start?"

"We go on air at ten o'clock, so you'll want to be at the studio at about eight-thirty."

Maya went on to discuss the logistics, including a list of stores that would provide her with whatever items she needed. By the time Renee got off the phone again, she was feeling very excited but also a little overwhelmed. The first thing she did was call Amanda's assistant, Claire, and thank her whole-heartedly for the referral. She then opened her calendar again to figure out how she could make time for all her commitments. It soon became apparent that the shopping trip with Trent was really a blessing in disguise. She would just take him to the stores on the *Daybreak Show* sponsorship list and kill both birds with one stone.

Renee spent the rest of the day on the phone moving around appointments and project commitments. By Tuesday afternoon, she felt more organized. The only thing left to do was get the right outfit for her television debut. As she was getting ready to meet Trent, Renee flipped through her closet to see if there was anything suitable. Her work wardrobe consisted of slacks, button-down shirts, and several pantsuits, all in some shade of brown, blue, gray, or black. None of them were going to work.

As she got dressed in black pants and a gray turtle-neck, she tried to think of when she might have time to go shopping. Wednesday night after work looked like the only available opportunity. Once she finished her hair and makeup, Renee left a message for Jennifer, who was a merchandise manager at Bergdorf Goodman. Jennifer had an excellent sense of style and could help her pick out the right outfit, fast.

Trent called her cell phone at about quarter after three and indicated he would be there in ten minutes. Renee checked her appearance again before pulling on a thick, black leather jacket, comfortable black boots, and the rest of her winter gear. She waited in the building lobby for a few minutes before his car pulled up.

He welcomed her with a smile as he opened the passenger door for her.

"Okay, where are we heading?" he asked once they were both seated and buckled in.

"Let's head down to Thirty-second and Park. There are a few stores in the area that we can start with."

Trent pulled the car away from the curb and into traffic. "Thanks again for making time for this. I hope it didn't mess up your schedule too much," he stated.

"Not at all," Renee replied politely. "I just had to move a few things around, but it worked out fine."

"That's good."

"Actually, it turned out to be a very good thing," she added, then went into a brief explanation of her role on the Friday morning talk show.

Trent looked at her hard, his eyes shifting back and forth between her and the road. His face showed a mix of admiration and real surprise that seemed out of place to Renee.

"Wow," he said eventually. "That's pretty impressive, Renee. Your work must be really good."

"Well, I think it was more about being at the right place at the right time," Renee replied humbly.

"You're just being modest. It's a live show, so I'm pretty sure they did their research before asking you to participate."

Renee shrugged, unable to think of anything to add.

"Very impressive," he repeated. "It sounds as though you're doing very well for someone so young."

"I'm not that young," Renee rebutted, letting out a sharp laugh.

Trent gave her that big, charming smile. "Yeah, you are," he stated.

"Well, look at you," she returned. "You're obviously successful yourself. And I'm sure you're not much older than I am."

"I'm thirty-two," replied Trent. "And I would say you are no more than twenty-five."

Renee let out another sharp laugh. "Very flattering, thank you. But I'm twenty-eight."

He rolled his eyes and they both laughed.

"Either way, you should be very proud of your career. A lot of women move to Manhattan and get distracted by all the partying and illusion of glamour. Clearly, you've been able to avoid that."

Renee immediately thought of Angela and her destructive lifestyle.

"I'm not really the partying type," she told him.

"No? Well, a little fun is okay. What do you like to do for fun?"

They approached the intersection of their destination, and Trent pulled into a nearby underground parking lot.

"My work is fun. I know that sounds really cheesy, but it's true. What can be better than shopping and decorating beautiful spaces?"

"Come on, there must be something you like to do besides work. Do you like movies, traveling, reading? You live in New York City! Haven't you gone to the theater or the museums?"

"I like to walk in the park when it's warm," Renee admitted finally.

Trent pulled into a parking spot, then turned to face her as he turned off the engine. "Okay, that's something. But life can't be all work or it will stop being fun really fast. You need some balance."

Renee held his gaze and read sincerity and honest interest in his eyes. She nodded but could not ignore his logic, so she smiled instead. He smiled back. There was self-conscious silence before she finally looked away.

"Now, let's go shopping," he added in a light tone.

As they made their way onto the street and toward the first store, Renee was preoccupied with the tension between them. The feel and taste of that kiss was still pretty fresh in her mind. She was becoming more torn between the need to maintain a professional distance and a growing desire to explore the attraction she felt for him.

Chapter 8

"Hey, babe! Do you miss me?"

Trent rubbed the skin over his eyes with his thumb and index fingers, trying to reduce his increased stress level. It was Wednesday morning, and he had not bothered to check the caller ID before picking up the phone in his office. Brianna's voice sounded bright and bubbly as usual. However, Trent was in the middle of negotiating several high-priced deals and didn't really have the time to talk. He also didn't have an appropriate response to her teasing question.

"Hi, Bri. How is your vacation so far?" he asked, choosing not to answer her.

"It's just beautiful. We flew in to Nice yesterday, and the spa Mummy found is right on the promenade overlooking the French Riviera. Oh, Trent! You should see this place. It's just beautiful. The hotel is fabulous, with a private beach and everything."

Brianna continued with her gushing description of everything about the south of France for a few more minutes. Trent listened with half an ear but continued working on his computer. He managed to make the right sounds of interest at the appropriate moments. Eventually, when he heard a few seconds of silence, he realized her chattering had ended.

"Trent, are you there?"

"Yeah, I'm here," he stated quickly.

"Well?" asked Brianna impatiently.

"Well, what?"

"Trent! Weren't you listening to me? I asked if you got the tickets to the spring gala yet. I think I've found the most perfect dress to wear. It's yellow, but really more of a butter color. And Mummy bought me this brilliant necklace with yellow sapphires. Wait until you see it. You'll have to get a yellow bow tie and handkerchief so that you complement me. I'm sure I can find something at Hermes while I'm here, or we'll go shopping when I get back."

Her remarks continued for a few more minutes, and she never gave Trent the opportunity to tell her about the tickets. Thankfully, Nancy stuck her head inside his office at that moment to drop off several reports and documents for his next meeting at eleven-thirty that morning. Trent didn't bother waiting for an appropriate break to interrupt Brianna.

"Hey, sorry," he butted in while she was in the middle of a sentence. "But I have to run."

"Oh. Right now? I was going to tell you—"

"Brianna, I really have to go," he repeated a bit more forcefully.

"Okay, but call me in a little bit. I saw this—"

"Yeah, I'll call you later. Bye, Brianna."

Trent hung up. It was only 11:15, so he had a few

minutes to spare. But his stress level had increased by several degrees as he listened to Brianna's endless rambling. He needed those extra minutes to refocus on his work.

Though the rest of his day went by smoothly, Trent remained distracted. He had expected a call from Brianna this morning. They had exchanged only a couple of phone messages since she left for France over a week ago, but she had tried to speak with him on several occasions. Trent had been avoiding talking to her, mostly because he had nothing to say, but also because he had made a decision. It was now clear to him that things were not going anywhere between them, and it was time to cut her loose.

It wasn't his style to break up with a woman over the phone, but he also could not pretend that everything was just fine while talking with her. The only alternative now was to keep the communication to a minimum while she was overseas, then have a proper discussion in person when she returned. The delay required to address the situation with Brianna made him uncomfortable, but there was no way to avoid it.

Trent had known pretty much from the beginning of their relationship that it had a fairly short shelf life. She was beautiful and fun, and they had a good time together. There wasn't anything wrong with her in particular, but she just wasn't what he wanted or needed long-term. Trent might not have a clear picture or description of what the right woman for him looked like, but he always knew that she was out there. It was just a matter of time and patience until he found her. Until she arrived, it only made sense to enjoy life and the multitude of women in the world.

That was one of the many lessons Trent learned from his father, Lawrence Skinner, a superintendent in the Operations arm of the Jamaican Defense Forces. His dad had been a bachelor for many years before he met his wife, Nadine. He told Trent on several occasions that when the right woman entered his life, Trent would recognize her. But it would take courage to pursue that woman's love while walking away from all the others.

Though Trent was born and raised in Chicago with his mother, Andrea Pinnock, his father was Jamaican. Lawrence Skinner was a smart, disciplined man with a long, envied military career, but he had lived on the Caribbean island all his life until he died four years ago of a brain aneurysm. Lawrence and Andrea had met while she was working on the island for a summer contract, and thus had a brief love affair. By the time she realized she was pregnant, Andrea was back in Chicago, faced with having to raise her child alone.

Trent had always known who his father was, and they spoke over the phone a few times per year. But while he had considered himself practically fatherless, he was unaware of how involved Lawrence was in his life and well-being.

When Trent was around fifteen years old, he fell prey to street life and changed from a sweet kid to a thug. He identified with the large number of unsupervised young men from low-income, single-mother homes, and he became defiant, rebellious, and angry.

Soon he was spending days away from home, returning anytime he felt like with stacks of cash earned from illegal activities. His mom was at her wit's end and eventually agreed to send him to live with his father in Montego Bay, Jamaica.

Trent met his father for the first time that summer, and his life changed forever. He also learned very quickly that though his dad was not present for his upbringing, he had kept a close eye on his son and was very unhappy about the direction Trent's life had taken. Within a week of arriving in Jamaica, Trent was enrolled at Silvercreek Military Academy, a very strict boarding school for boys in the countryside about forty-five miles from Montego Bay. Silver-creek offered a regimented academic and demanding physical curriculum designed to instill discipline in teenagers. The students were from all over the world. A large number of them were from military homes or, like Trent, were troubled youth heading down the wrong path.

He spent the four years at Silvercreek, living on campus during the week, then spending the week-ends and holidays with his father and his stepmother, Nadine. The first few months were the hardest; Trent missed his mom and found it difficult to be cut off from his friends and the life he knew. But eventually, he made new friends at school and began to enjoy the structured environment.

The hardest part was not being with his mom. Once he matured enough to realize how bad his behavior had become in Chicago, and how disrespectfully he had treated her, he felt incredibly guilty. But they stayed in close contact through regular phone calls. Whenever he told her about an outstanding accomplishment in his academics or with sports, he could hear the pride in her voice. By the time he graduated high school—at the top of his class—Trent felt he was close to redeeming himself.

Most of the guys from the neighborhood that he used to hang out with on the streets didn't fare as well. Of the seven boys in his juvenile crew, three ended up in jail, one was crippled and in a wheelchair, and two were shot to death. Only one of them made it to age eighteen, living as a relatively successful drug dealer with enough street credibility to stay protected. Trent still kept in touch with two of the guys who had been incarcerated and released a few years later. Now they were productive, hardworking men with families. Whenever Trent visited Chicago, they would get together and look back on how stupid they had been as teenagers, how far they had come, and how some guys hadn't made the journey out.

It was no surprise that Trent was recruited into the Jamaican Constabulary Forces during his senior year at Silvercreek. It was a great achievement and made both his parents incredibly proud, particularly his father. Though Trent enjoyed some aspects of being a police officer, like protecting the citizens of Jamaica and upholding the idea of justice, there were other parts of the job that did not feel natural to him. He spent most of his time looking at the greedy and ugly side of humanity, the same attitude that once lured him into petty crime as a youth, and it challenged his faith in people.

Eventually, Trent left patrol and joined the crime intelligence unit. He spent the last eighteen months of his career as an officer there before being shot in the back during an organized-crime investigation. His recovery had been long and painful. Trent used the time to focus on what he really wanted to do with the rest of his life. He reached out to his classmates from Silvercreek who were doing well in various private-sector jobs. Out of all his options, finance and banking were the most interesting and seemed to offer the best opportunities. It was one of the hardest decisions he had to make, but Trent chose to leave the constabulary forces and go into investment banking. To his surprise, his father was completely supportive of his decision.

As much as Trent had come to love Jamaica, once his father passed away suddenly, he had no desire to live there on his own. He considered moving back to Chicago so he could be close to his mom again. He and Nathan had always stayed in touch, and by then his cousin was married and living in Connecticut. Trent applied for jobs in both areas. The position at Goldwell Group as a junior funds manager was the most promising, and Trent moved back to the United States after being away for fourteen years.

It took a while for him to get used to the aggressive corporate culture in Greenwich, but once he settled in, Trent's career took off. His co-workers were some of the brightest financial minds in the country, and he set out to learn everything they knew. Within two years, he made it to senior funds manager after closing several large, complex mergers. Trent's life had become a success story that he could not have imagined while running the streets of Chicago.

Chapter 9

The rest of the week flew by with lightning speed for Renee. She looked around at ten thirty-nine Friday morning, and it was all over. The last three days had been so packed with activity that she could barely remember everything she had accomplished. Her TV segment on spring and summer decorating trends went off just as she had planned, and all the pieces had fallen into place in the end. Jennifer had helped her pick out a really sweet designer silk dress from last season's line in the sale section at Bergdorf Goodman. It was light blue, and the minute Renee saw it, she knew her blue suede platforms would work with it perfectly.

Angela had not done anything to repair the damage she had done to the shoes, but thankfully, the cobbler down the street from her apartment was able to clean them by removing the salt stains. He then sprayed them with a dye very similar to the original color, and they looked brand-new again.

The shopping trip with Trent was the one event

that week that remained vivid in Renee's mind.
They had spent almost three hours on Tuesday
evening visiting Gillian Interiors and the Top Shelf,
two of the stores on the *Daybreak Show* sponsor
list. Afterward, they went to a nearby sushi restaurant for dinner. Renee was quite surprised when
Trent suggested it, but she was more than happy
with the choice. She had tried sushi for the first
time over the summer, and though she wasn't too
adventurous with the different choices, she now
had a regular craving for tempura and a variety of
maki rolls.

Renee was still surprised at how much she and
Trent had accomplished that evening. With some
trial and error, she discovered that Trent preferred
simple, traditional furniture design with classic
lines but no fussy detail. He also confirmed that her
color choices for the bedding were perfect and
wasn't willing to consider any other options she
pointed out. Her custom-made headboard and bed
frame from Henry Interiors was still in the plan,
since Trent did not like anything in the stores nearly
as much.

In the end, choosing furniture for Trent took up
less than half their time. Once Renee explained to
him all the items she needed for the show on Friday,
he became very engrossed in the process and was
more than willing to help her pick out many options.
With his help, she procured a variety of small decorative furniture pieces and accessories in the latest
colors and styles. Both stores were more than happy
to provide the items on consignment and delivered

them to the television studio Thursday afternoon at no cost. The free endorsement on the show appeared to be payment enough.

Not only was the shopping trip successful, but it was also fun. Renee was surprised to acknowledge that Trent Skinner was good company. He didn't really understand what she was looking for, so he didn't pretend to have a serious opinion about her choices. He was just very helpful, focused on the task, and appeared to have an endless amount of patience.

And he was funny! Trent had a sarcastic, critical comment about everything, and it was based solely on his complete ignorance of design basics. Renee already knew that he had good taste and a natural sense of style. It was obvious in his simple, well-cut, and expensive clothes. Even the furniture in his town house, little that there was, was excellent quality. But, like most men, he didn't really understand the point of decorating a room with anything other than functional necessities. He helped out any way he could, though.

Then, as they had started eating the variety of Japanese appetizers they ordered, Trent surprised her with a suggestion.

"Do you have any plans this weekend?" he had asked.

"Not really," replied Renee honestly, thinking it was just idle chitchat.

"Would you like to go to a dinner party with me on Saturday evening?"

"I'm sorry, what do you mean?" she asked, befuddled

and surprised. Her brain could not quite grasp what he was suggesting.

"I mean," Trent stated slowly with a teasing smile spreading wider on his face, "I would like you to come with me to a party on Saturday."

"Why?" Renee blurted.

Trent laughed out loud, like she had said the funniest thing he had heard in a long time. Her blank stare just made him laugh harder.

"Come on, Renee Goodchild, this can't be the first time you've been asked out on a date."

She looked down, embarrassed by her clueless reaction. Eventually, Trent stopped chuckling even though Renee knew he was still teasing her. She felt his hand fall on hers, gently, as though to give her comfort. His touch felt good. Even though Renee knew she should pull away and discourage even the slightest intimacy, she didn't.

"It's nothing formal," he explained. "One of my clients owns a large transportation company, and he has an annual dinner at a restaurant in SoHo. I won't really know anyone other than Conrad, the owner, so I would rather not go alone."

It was Renee's turn to laugh at him.

"You can't find a date for Saturday night? Is that what you're trying to tell me?"

"No." He brushed his thumb across the top of her hand. "I'm saying I think it would be fun if you went with me."

Renee remembered making some sort of rebuttal, something really sharp and witty, of course. Then the discussion went back and forth until she could not stall any longer, and finally she found the courage to accept his invitation. It was a spontaneous decision made just because it felt good. Her reservations about the date came hours later.

The conversation had returned to fairly mundane topics after that, but the air between them felt charged. The rest of the evening was a blur to her, except for the moment when Trent stopped the car in front of her place. He turned to gaze at her with a look that was serious and intense. Then he leaned in close and kissed her. This time, Renee was waiting for it, hoping for it.

Her mouth eagerly explored his as his tongue slipped between her lips. The kiss deepened with wet heat until the electricity in the air caught on fire. Renee remembered the moment they finally pulled away from each other, as though surfacing from a trance. She didn't know how long they had been kissing, but the car windows had steamed up. Trent looked just as dazed and surprised as she felt.

As Renee stood backstage at the *Daybreak Show* studio, her mind still lingering on the nebulous thing that was developing between her and Trent, it took a few seconds to register that her name was being called. She turned to find Maya Johnson walking toward her.

"Thank you so much again, Renee, for stepping in so quickly," Maya stated warmly. "You did a great job."

"Thanks for having me. I had a lot of fun," Renee replied with sincerity.

"I would definitely love to have you join us again in the future."

"That sounds great."

"Good," Maya said with a big smile. "The show is going to reair Sunday morning at ten o'clock. And don't worry, Gillian Interiors and the Top Shelf will send a truck to pick up their things."

The two women chatted a bit before Renee packed up and left the studio. She felt completely energized and elated, and it was only eleven o'clock in the morning. What if she became a regular on the show? It would open up all sorts of opportunities. Renee's brain was full of the possibilities, like doing design show appearances, writing a book, maybe even getting her own show on a network. Not right away, of course, but once her name was recognized and her design skills respected, there was so much she could do in her career. The possibilities for the future seemed unlimited.

The last few years in New York seemed to have flown by, and though Renee could not have predicted how her life would change, she felt proud of all she had accomplished. Occasionally, she wondered where she would be if she had stayed in Pittsburgh, still clinging to a dysfunctional relationship with her high school sweetheart, Devlin Sheppard.

She and Devlin had started dating their junior year and were practically tied at the hip for the next six years. But, while she went to college, Devlin never developed adult ambition. He was a starter on the basketball team in high school, then after graduation became a street ball player with a string of minimum-wage jobs.

Renee never saw it as a problem. He was her heart and soul, and she accepted all his life decisions without question. Then, somewhere during her second year of college, Devlin started to complain about her attention to school and lack of time for him. His resentment slowly evolved to verbal abuse, to the point where Renee felt as though everything that went wrong in his life was her fault. It took her another three years and several huge fights for her to figure out that he was going nowhere in life and resented her ambition.

Breaking up with Devlin had been the scariest and hardest thing that Renee ever had to do. It meant accepting that she had given her unconditional love to someone who didn't deserve it, and it meant being alone for the first time since she was sixteen years old. Moving to Manhattan paled in comparison.

Renee had dated over the years since then, and a few of the men had been quite nice and eligible. They just hadn't inspired anything more than friendship and a little bit of fun. So, work had been her primary focus and it had really paid off. She loved her career, and it was exciting to see the growth in her client base and the increase in the scale of her projects over the last couple of years. Getting into television would just put her on another level, where the sky was the limit.

And then there was Trent Skinner.

Trent was completely different from any guy she had ever been interested in or dated. He was mature and successful, which, up until now, had also meant boring and unapproachable. But Renee had discovered that he was pretty laid-back and easygoing, with a great sense of humor. Of course, the visceral, electric attraction between them was pretty hard to ignore. It lingered in the air between them, sparking heat whenever they touched.

Renee was finding it difficult to justify her initial commitment to keep things on a professional level. Trent made his interest obvious, and she had spent the last few days asking herself why not pursue this thing between them and see where it goes. Her biggest concern was the long-term potential. He clearly lived in a different world and at a different level than she did, so what was the likelihood that his interest would last past the physical attraction? She didn't have the answer to that question. And at this point, Renee knew she just had to wait and see, but also to stay grounded in reality as things played out.

After leaving the studio, Renee stopped at home to do a couple hours' work; then she headed to two of her project sites to check on their progress. She worked late into Friday evening to get as much done as possible before the weekend. On Saturday, after giving her apartment a quick clean-up, Renee spent the rest of the day pampering herself, getting ready for the evening with Trent. She went to see her hair-stylist in Harlem, then got a luxurious manicure and pedicure at a nearby day spa.

It wasn't until she was back at home late Saturday afternoon that Renee realized it had been a couple of days since she had seen Angela.

As she walked by her spare bedroom, Renee knocked on the door. There was no answer, so she opened it to look inside. The space was a mess, with clothes and other items strewn around. Angela was typically pretty disorganized and untidy, but this was different. It looked at though everything she owned had been dumped on the floor and rifled through, as if she had been desperately looking for something. She then noticed that most of the items on Renee's desk had also been shuffled around, and one of the drawers hung open.

Renee stood there for a few seconds, biting her lip, unsure what to do. She was about to close the door when Angela came into the apartment. She appeared distracted and did not notice Renee's presence until she was halfway into the hallway.

Angela stopped suddenly, clearly surprised. "Hey," she stated as she resumed walking into the apartment.

"Hey," replied Renee casually.

"What's going on?" Angela asked.

She was now standing beside Renee on the threshold of the spare bedroom. They both looked inside, then back at each other.

"Nothing," Renee told her. "I was just a little worried. Is everything okay?"

"Why? What do you mean?" asked Angela dismissively.

"Angela, your room looks like it was ransacked. What happened?"

"Oh, it's nothing," she replied, stepping into the room and starting to pick up some of the clothes strewn all over. "I was just looking for something, that's all."

Renee nodded, but something about Angela's flippant response made her uneasy. Her gut told her that something more was going on, but she could not think of a way to ask additional questions.

"Is that nail polish?" Angela asked, reaching out and taking hold of Renee's hand to examine her fingers.

Renee looked down also, admitting that her pale pink manicure looked really good.

"Yeah," she replied shyly. "I know. Weird, huh? I never wear nail polish."

"And a pedicure too?" Angela added with exaggerated shock. "Wow, Renee. You've gone all out! It must be a pretty special occasion."

Renee could not help but laugh, because Angela's words were completely accurate. Other than religious visits to the hair salon, it had been many months since Renee had done any frivolous, girly things like applying nail polish or getting other expensive spa treatments. She just didn't have the time and could not see the point. Angela, on the other hand, seemed to spend hours grooming every week, including her perfect false nails and various other pampering rituals.

"Well, it's nothing important. I'm going to a dinner party, that's all."

"Really?" probed Angela, clearly a little surprised. "You? Going to a party? This is a first."

"I might not go out every night like you, Angela, but I do have a life, you know."

"Hey, I'm just saying that you spend every weekend working or watching TV. I'm glad to see you get out and enjoy yourself. Where is this party?"

"I'm not sure. Somewhere in SoHo I think. I'm going with someone," Renee replied evasively.

"Like a date? Renee Goodchild, you sly bitch! Why didn't you tell me you were seeing someone?"

Angela stepped forward and punched Renee on the shoulder lightly with feigned insult.

"It's nothing, honestly," she protested. "It's really more a work thing. . . ."

"Please! That doesn't matter. Is he cute?"

Renee couldn't help but smile.

Angela laughed loudly, punching her again. "Okay, so you have the hair and nails done. What are you wearing?"

"I'm not sure. It's going to be pretty casual, so I was thinking a pair of dark jeans."

"All right, that could work. I think I have the perfect top that you could wear with it," Angela told her, and immediately started riffling through the clothes still scattered about.

When she found a silky blouse a few moments later, she held it up for inspection and Renee had to admit it was absolutely perfect.

"Good, right?" asked Angela as she took Renee's hand and started leading her toward Renee's bedroom. "Now, let's go try it on with the jeans. What shoes are you wearing?"

Chapter 10

"I still think it's a bad idea, Trent," Nathan stated.

His face had a petulant frown and his eyes were red and bloodshot.

The cousins were sitting in Trent's living room on Saturday afternoon with a basketball game playing on the television in the background.

"Look, we've gone over this, Nate," replied Trent. "The plan is obviously working. You just said that Renee hasn't returned your call since Tuesday, right? If she was still hell-bent on getting the money from you, I'm sure you would have heard from her by now. She's distracted and that's what we wanted. And after tonight, I guarantee that you won't hear from her again. I will make sure she thinks that I'm a bigger payoff than a few thousand dollars from you. Then I'll have lots of time to find whatever evidence she has."

Trent was pretty good at reading his cousin. When Nathan started biting his nails, Trent knew he was searching for more reasons why Trent should not take Renee out tonight.

"This is what you wanted, right?" Trent finally asked. "You wanted me to take her off your hands and make the whole thing disappear, right?"

"Yeah, of course," his cousin replied, but his voice did not hold any conviction, and his eyes remained focused on the TV.

"Well, then everything is going as planned," added Trent.

"I guess."

Nathan crossed his arms, and there was silence for a few minutes. Trent hoped that was the end of the discussion, but his instincts told him different. Something was bugging Nathan, and had been for the last few days. Trent knew if he waited long enough, whatever was eating at him would come out.

"It's just that something isn't right," Nathan finally stated.

Trent could not help rolling his eyes.

"I know you think she's merely a gold digger, but Renee's just desperate for help. She was so distraught and upset the last time I spoke to her. Her mom's getting sicker, and the medical bills are piling up. She was almost in tears. I just don't understand why she hasn't called me back."

"Nathan, I just saw her on Thursday. She was right here, in this house, working away. There is no sick mother, all right? It's a scam," Trent replied, frustration clear in his voice.

But even as he said the words, Trent felt a needle of doubt. The same uncertainty had been bugging him from the minute he had met Renee Goodchild, and it had gotten worse over the last two weeks.

Something wasn't right about the whole situation, but he could not put his finger on it. The picture that Nathan portrayed of the distraught, greedy slut who was threatening his marriage was the absolute opposite of the woman Trent had gotten to know. *His* Renee was smart, classy, and funny and focused on her successful career. She also had an effortless sexiness that stirred up a primal desire right at the pit of Trent's stomach; because he knew what Nathan said she was, Trent tried hard to deny the feelings.

Nathan stayed for another hour, then left to go to his in-laws' house. While he and his wife lived in a downtown Stamford condo, about seven miles from Trent's house, her parents lived in North Stamford in a sprawling mansion, situated on over two acres of forested property. Ophelia spent almost every weekend at her childhood home, and Nathan was expected to be there also, a requirement that he resented but complied with nonetheless.

Soon after Nathan left, Trent headed up to his bedroom to shave and shower. He then got dressed in dark blue jeans and a white cotton twill button-down shirt that he left hanging over his pants. By six o'clock, he was heading out the door and on his way to Manhattan. He was picking Renee up at seven o'clock but stopped along the way at the drugstore to pick up some gum and other supplies that may be needed for the evening.

About fifty minutes later, as he turned off the Robert Kennedy Bridge and headed south on the FDR, Trent called Renee to let her know he would be there in a few minutes. She was waiting just inside the front doors when he arrived.

As Trent walked around the back of the car to open the passenger door for Renee, he admitted that she looked incredibly hot. March had arrived a few days earlier and brought with it a break from the frigid winter cold. She wore a short, fitted, white leather biker jacket over tight narrow black jeans, and black high-heeled stiletto pumps. Her cropped hair was styled into a tousled crown of soft waves. The serious professional had been replaced by an edgy, sexy Manhattanite ready for a night out. Trent found himself fascinated again by another side of her personality.

As he drove them into the center of the city through the thick traffic, they made small talk about the mild weather. They arrived at the restaurant just after seven-thirty and were immediately taken to a private dining area in the back. There were already about thirty-five people there, and their host, Conrad, greeted them enthusiastically at the entrance to the room. He was a big, burly black guy, at least six foot four, with a shiny bald head and a full beard and mustache. His dark complexion had a reddish tone that suggested a Native American heritage.

"Trent! I'm glad you could make it, man!"

"Glad I could make it, Conrad," he replied as they shook hands, and Conrad pounded Trent's back with his bear-paw hand. "This is Renee Goodchild."

"Hi, Renee, welcome," Conrad said in his deep, booming voice, and gave her a big smile.

"Nice to meet you," Renee replied with a polite smile.

"Well, come on in and take off your coats. There's

plenty of food and drink, so help yourselves to whatever you'd like."

He urged them farther into the room and pointed to a row of coatracks along the wall. Trent quickly shook off his wool overcoat, then helped Renee out of her jacket. She had on a sheer white top with soft cap sleeves and a low, draping front. Trent let his gaze sweep over the curves of her breasts, which swelled deliciously above her blouse's neckline. His eyes met hers and lingered there long enough to let her know what he was thinking.

A waitress walked by at that moment with a tray of drinks. Trent took one filled with red wine for Renee, and requested a bottle of beer for himself.

"Are you hungry?" he asked her.

"I'm getting there," she admitted.

"Okay, let's see what we can find."

They spent the next hour or so trying out the food from the different buffet tables that were placed around the room. Occasionally, they were introduced to other guests and pulled into a group discussion. During one of these conversations, the topic turned to investments and the economy. Renee listened politely for a short while, then excused herself to go to the bathroom. Trent pretended he was paying attention to the guy next to him babbling on, but his focus was on Renee as he watched her walk away. Her backside looked very tempting in her tight jeans. By the way her hips swept graciously from side to side, he had the feeling she knew he was watching. Trent smiled to himself before refocusing on the conversation around him.

Ten minutes later, when she still had not returned, Trent casually started walking around to see where she was and make sure everything was okay. He found Renee on the opposite side of the room surrounded by four women who all looked very excited. As he got closer, he heard them talking about her television appearance from the day before. Renee looked surprised and a little uncomfortable with all the attention, but she politely listened to their comments and responded to their questions. When she discovered Trent standing beside her, she introduced him to the other women.

Trent learned very quickly that only one of the women, Sheila, had seen the show live on Friday morning, and the other three wanted to hear all about it.

"Now I feel like I've met a television star," Sheila stated excitedly.

"Oh, no," Renee replied, shaking her head. "I was just a fill-in. I'm not sure if I will be back on anytime soon."

"Oh, I'm sure you will be. You were a natural, dear."

"When will it be on again?" asked one of the other women. "I watch the *Daybreak Show* almost every day, but I had a doctor's appointment yesterday."

"I'm sure it will be on again tomorrow," stated Sheila. "They always reair the shows on the weekend on channel thirty-one."

"Friday's show will be on tomorrow morning at ten o'clock," confirmed Renee.

"Great," stated two of the other women at the same time.

"So, do you do any consultations?" asked Sheila. "I've been thinking about redoing our kitchen, but I don't know where to start. And my husband, Bob, is just useless! Our dishwasher broke over a year ago, and he still hasn't gotten around to fixing it."

The women went on for a while, discussing various decorating challenges in their homes, peppering Renee with questions and asking for advice.

When Trent suggested he was ready to leave the party, it was a few minutes before ten o'clock. They were back in her neighborhood about thirty minutes later, and he parked his car in an available parking spot across the street from her apartment, then turned to face her.

"I'll walk you upstairs," he said, but his tone let her know he wasn't asking a question.

Renee's gaze did not quite meet his eyes, and Trent sensed she was trying to decide how to respond.

"All right," she finally stated in a soft voice.

He immediately turned off the car, and they walked into the building side by side.

"Thanks again for coming out tonight," he told her smoothly as they rode up in the elevator. "I don't usually go to these things for clients, but I really like Conrad."

"He seems very nice," she replied.

"Yeah, he's a pretty humble guy. I met him about three years ago just after his divorce. His business had been in rough shape financially, but he listened to my advice and made some great decisions. Now he's pretty much set for life."

"That's great. It must feel really good to help your clients achieve goals like that."

"Yeah, it does. It's the best part of my job, particularly for hardworking people like Conrad."

The elevator door opened, and they walked to her apartment, which was a couple of doors down the hall.

Renee smiled up at him. "Would you like to come in for coffee or something?" she asked shyly.

"Sure. It's still pretty early," he replied casually, smiling back.

She started to unlock the door, then stopped and turned back to him.

"What?" he asked, puzzled by her hesitation, but also afraid that she may have changed her mind.

"Nothing . . . It's just that I have a friend staying with me. It's Saturday night, so I don't think she's home. She has a pretty active social life. But I thought I should warn you just in case."

"No problem," replied Trent with a chuckle.

"Okay," she stated, then let him into her place.

They walked into a long front foyer with a framed mirror running along its length, then into the open living room and dining room. She stopped at the front closet to hang up her jacket and kick off her shoes. Trent followed her example.

The apartment was modest but even nicer than Trent expected it to be. Renee had kept a lot of the building's historical architectural details but had decorated the space with dark hardwood floor and warm taupe-colored walls. The furniture looked comfortable and inviting, with accents of blue and yellow scattered around in pieces of art, pillows, and other beautiful objects.

Renee walked ahead of him and turned into the kitchen. "Have a seat. The coffee will only take a minute," she told him.

Trent took the opportunity to look around her space more closely. His attention was caught by a group of pictures mounted on the wall next to the window. He found himself smiling as he looked through them, particularly the ones that looked like family events. Several of them had Renee at various ages with a woman who looked like an older version of herself. Trent assumed this was her mother. Then there was a wedding picture of her mom and a tall, handsome man, and two other pictures of the new family of three in Renee's teenage years.

Her other pictures were mostly of her high school and college years, where she managed to look beautiful and adorable through various questionable fashion trends. Trent was looking at one photo in particular, of Renee and another girl, arm in arm. They were wearing matching high school cheerleader outfits and smiling broadly. He was caught by the striking similarity between them, as though they were twins.

"Okay, here we go," Renee stated as she walked into the living room carrying a French press and two coffee mugs. She placed them on the coffee table. "How do you take your coffee?" she asked, heading back to the kitchen.

Trent followed her to help. "A little cream and lots of sugar. I have a bit of a sweet tooth," he confessed with a lopsided smile.

She reached into the fridge to get the cream while

Trent grabbed the sugar bowl off the counter, then headed back to the living room.

"I know," he stated a minute later while scooping the fourth teaspoon of brown sugar into his cup. "I know. It's really bad, isn't it?"

"What?" she said, laughing lightly. "I didn't say anything."

"You didn't have to. I can feel your eyes on me," he replied sheepishly. "It's horrible, I know. I have an intimate, destructive relationship with anything sweet. It's my one weakness."

Renee laughed out loud. "Only one weakness?" she asked. "That's not too bad."

"Well, it's the only one that I will admit to."

She smiled at him and took a sip of her coffee.

"What about you, Renee? What's your weakness?"

"I'm sure I have more than one."

"Really? That's pretty intriguing. What's your biggest?"

She didn't answer right away. Instead, she drank more coffee while glancing at him with a secret smile.

"How bad can it be?" Trent finally asked.

"Okay. I would say . . . French fries."

"French fries."

"Yup. My biggest weakness is hot, salty fries."

"Wow, that's just . . . horrible."

"I know, isn't it? And I don't even try to resist them," Renee added.

"No. I mean it's horrible, and just sad, that your biggest weakness is fries! It should be something bad for you, maybe even dangerous."

"Really?" she demanded with a twinkle in her eyes. "Something dangerous like sugar?"

"That's right!"

They both burst out laughing at their silliness.

"I've just remembered another weakness," he stated after a few minutes.

Renee looked at him expectantly, still smiling.

"I definitely have a thing for beautiful women," he told her seriously as he put down his drink on the coffee table and turned to face her fully. He then took her cup out of her hand and put it beside his.

Her eyes widened in surprise.

"Do you want to hear another confession?" Trent added. "I didn't come up here for coffee."

Chapter 11

Renee sat frozen at the edge of the couch. Her mind stopped working while her heart started beating fast and hard. His hand ran up her back until it cupped the base of her head. As though in slow motion, she watched as Trent leaned toward her and pressed his mouth on hers. The kiss started out gently, exploring the feel of hers, as though introducing intimacy and asking her permission to go further. She parted her lips in response, silently inviting him in.

Trent groaned softly and pulled her into a close embrace. His tongue swept over the contours of her mouth before delving into its heat. Renee shuddered and a liquid pool collected at the base of her stomach. Her tongue met his to mimic his explorations until the kiss became intense and their breath labored.

"Wow," whispered Trent as he ran his lips along the line of her jaw.

He then began to explore delicate swirls of her ears with the slick tip of his tongue. Renee could barely breathe from the intense shivers of pleasure that ran down her back. Trent moved to that sensitive area just below her ear. He lightly bit the tendon at the side of her neck and she moaned deeply. He bit it harder, then soothed it with his soft lips before nipping it again and again.

"Oh, God," Renee whimpered while clutching at his shoulders.

She couldn't think and she couldn't seem to get enough air. All she could do was disappear into the desire that was mounting in her body. Renee started pressing kisses along his neck and running hands over the thick slabs of his chest. Her fingers worked at the buttons of his shirt until it was open down to his navel. She then continued her exploration, paying special attention to the hard nubs of his nipples, pausing only when Trent's lips hit a spot near her throat that left her immobilized with intense pleasure.

When they finally came up for air, they sat with their foreheads pressed together for several seconds. Renee had her eyes closed tight, feeling their hearts beat at the same racing pace. Trent was the first to move, sliding his hands over her shoulders and down her arms. He swept them up again, then along her collarbone. With one index finger, he traced a line down the center of her chest until it disappeared into the valley between her breasts. Then both his hands slid over the swelling mounds and squeezed their fullness.

Renee's breath came out in a loud rush. She opened her eyes to find him watching her face with an intense gaze. His palm found the hard tips of her nipples and massaged them in slow circles. She could not resist throwing her shoulders back, making her ample curves completely available to his touch.

Their eyes locked again, and Trent pulled her across his lap until her thighs straddled his, and he relaxed back into the sofa. He pulled her toward him and kissed her deep and hard while his hands roamed her back. Renee wasn't sure who instigated the action, but soon they were both working together to remove her top. It was tossed aside and she sat upright in only her lacy bra.

"Wow," he mumbled while brushing his fingers along the delicate edge of the fabric. "Just beautiful."

Renee felt so aroused with his powerful thighs between her legs and his hot gaze running over her exposed flesh. She was overwhelmed by the need to feel his hands on her again, but thankfully she didn't need to wait long. Trent resumed his exploration of her breasts, now heavy and taut with desire. He added his lips and tongue to savor the taste and feel of her soft skin. Extra attention was put on her thick, erect nipples as they pressed through her bra, begging for his touch. Finally, he pulled the lace down to reveal the sensitive nubs. He quickly sucked one deep into his mouth, and Renee let out a deep, uncontrollable groan. Trent sucked harder, then scraped it with his tongue.

"Yes!" she whimpered.

"Do you like that?" he asked breathlessly.

"Yes . . . yes . . . ," she stammered.

Trent patiently gave the same attention to her other

breast, and Renee now had her head thrown back, completely lost in sensation. His hands slid down her back to cup her bottom. He squeezed her round curves and pulled her hips closer to him until the apex of her thighs brushed the bulge of his arousal. They both let out deep sighs.

Renee flexed her hips against his, savoring the feel of his hard shaft against the center of her passion. She stroked him over and over, losing herself in the mounting excitement.

"Stand up," he whispered.

She followed his direction and allowed him to undo her jeans and work them down the length of her legs. Trent brushed his hands up her legs while his eyes swept over the contours of her body, now naked except for her underwear. When his fingers reached the top of her thighs, he turned her around to look at the rest of her. With her eyes closed, Renee could feel the heat of his searing gaze on her skin. When his fingers slid along the outside of her hips, she shivered with anticipation. She glanced over her shoulder, down at Trent looking sexy and flustered, and she knew instantly that he was just as caught up as she was.

Renee reached out her hand. He took it and stood up. They didn't need words as she led him into her bedroom. The room was dark, but the curtains were pulled back from the windows, and the city lights provided subtle illumination. She stopped in front of her bed and turned to face him. Trent immediately pulled her into a tight embrace, his lips entwined with hers while his hands flowed up and down her back.

They could have been standing like that for an hour, kissing hungrily between panting moans, or it may have only been ten minutes. When Trent finally pulled back, it was only so that he could grasp Renee firmly by the underside of her bottom and lift her up until her hips met his. She gasped with surprise, then wrapped her legs around his body. They kissed as he carried her forward and smoothly placed her on the edge of the bed.

Trent proceeded to slowly remove the skimpy strings of her underwear. Renee could only watch with heavy, hooded eyes and lift her hips as needed. He then kissed down her stomach, starting from just under her breast and ending just below her navel. She held her breath with greedy anticipation as he knelt on the floor in front of her, still fully dressed, and gently urged her thighs apart. His fingers gently stroked her inner thighs while his lips brushed the area around her knees. When his fingers finally brushed the flesh between her legs, Renee shuddered with excitement.

He stroked her quivering, dewy mound again, sweetly exploring her secrets until he found the magic button.

"Yes!" moaned Renee.

Trent gave her what she wanted, caressing the center of her desire slowly, deeply. His lips played around near the top of her thigh, gently nipping her hot skin with tiny bites, then tracing circles with his tongue. Renee was overwhelmed with passion, her body taut with pleasure. She tried to stay calm, relaxed, and just enjoy his incredible touch, but the sensations he created were too overwhelming. The room became filled with her heavy breathing and stifled moans.

Then Trent grabbed her hips to pull her closer to him, and his lips replaced his fingers, his tongue stroking deep and hard over her throbbing clitoris. Renee could not slow down her mounting climax. It was building fast, creeping up her thighs and tightening in the base of her stomach. And Trent did not stop. She tried to pull him back by grabbing his head, but she lost focus and stroked his hair. Then he placed a thick finger to the wet core, and her breaths started coming in short, urgent pants. Trent slid his finger in again and again, deep and long while his lips worshipped her now-swollen, quivering flesh.

Her climax finally came with such intensity that Renee became lost in every tremor and spasm. Her eyes were clenched tight, and her fists grasped at the blanket beneath her as she moaned loudly. When she finally came to an exhausted and depleted rest, Renee opened her eyes to find Trent standing in front of her, gloriously naked and fully aroused. His stiff, hard penis stood straight and strong, already covered in protection.

"Wow," she whispered.

Trent grinned devilishly before leaning forward to place one knee on the bed beside her. "Wow," he echoed before kissing her sweetly, gently.

With one sure stroke, he penetrated her moist, ready body. He paused with his thick length filling her completely, allowing her to adjust to his size.

"Oh my God," she moaned weakly, stunned by the power of his presence.

"Beautiful," he whispered roughly with his face pressed into her neck. "So beautiful . . ."

He withdrew completely, then slid deep again and again. Renee wrapped her legs across his back and used her hips to match his pace. Trent's strokes became faster, more urgent, and his breath became labored. She ran her hands feverishly over his body, savoring the feel of his strength and hardness.

His orgasm matched the intensity of hers, shuddering through his body in a violent wave that left them both breathless.

Renee wasn't sure what woke her up. It could have been the sunlight shining through the windows, or the cool air on her bare bum. She blinked a few times, trying to put this in focus and take stock of her surroundings. Very quickly, she remembered the cause of her nakedness.

She glanced over at the spot on the bed beside her but it was empty. Trent had left.

Renee fell back onto the bed with her eyes squeezed closed. Very vivid images of the night before started flashing through her mind, and she covered her face with her hands in embarrassment.

What had she been thinking?

After a few minutes, she sat up and rolled out of bed. The clock beside her bed said it was 9:13 A.M. In her bathroom, she washed the faded makeup off her face and brushed her teeth. At some point, when back in her bedroom, she caught a whiff of something that smelled like bacon. Renee sniffed the air with her brows knit, but then ignored it, assuming it was her imagination or that it was coming from a neighboring apartment.

She was pulling on an oversized T-shirt when she heard sounds that were definitely coming from inside her apartment. It sounded like banging cupboard doors and the clang of pots.

Renee's first thought was that Angela had finally returned and was making some breakfast. But that seemed unlikely since Angela was rarely if ever up before noon, and Renee had never seen her use the stove or a pot. Once outside of her room, the delicious aroma of coffee and sizzling butter surrounded Renee and she continued walking toward the kitchen. The door to the spare bedroom was closed as usual, and it was not Angela she found cooking up a storm.

Trent Skinner was bent over her stove wearing only black boxer briefs that left little to the imagination. There were two plates on the counter with buttered toast on each, and a fresh pot of hot coffee was brewed in her French press with two mugs beside it. He must have sensed her presence and turned quickly to face her. Renee could only look around the small kitchen, then back to him, her mouth hanging slightly open with surprise.

"Good morning," he finally stated with a bright smile. "I hope you're hungry."

"Wow," she replied. "Good morning. I'm starving, actually."

"Good. Your timing is perfect. I was looking around

for a tray so I could bring it all into the bedroom for you, but no luck," Trent confessed.

"I don't have one," she told him as she walked forward and started to pour the coffee.

Trent took her by the shoulders and tried to steer her away from the counter and back out of the kitchen.

"No, no . . . You go have a seat at the table and I'll bring everything out," he insisted while urging her out of the space. "I made your eggs over hard; I hope that's okay."

"That's perfect."

Renee reluctantly followed his directions but reached back to take the coffee and cups with her. She sat at her small dining table, and Trent soon arrived with two plates loaded with eggs, bacon, and toast. He went back to get cream and sugar before sitting beside her.

"This looks amazing, Trent. Thank you."

"My pleasure," he replied with a charming smile and a wiggle of his eyebrows.

Something about the look in his eyes and the twitch in his grin brought back sharp memories of the night before. Renee cleared her throat awkwardly and looked down at her plate to hide her embarrassment. Trent laughed and they ate the entire breakfast in silence.

Chapter 12

After waking up starving, Trent polished off his food quickly. He then spent the next few minutes watching Renee eat her breakfast at a much slower pace as he sipped his coffee. He could tell that she was uncomfortable under his inspection, but eventually she stopped dodging his gaze and stared back defiantly and unabashed. It became a game to see who would say something first, and the topic would likely be about last night.

"Soooo," he finally stated, dragging out the word and grinning as her eyes widened. "Did you sleep well?"

Renee blinked a few times. "I did, actually. How about you?"

"I slept like a baby," he told her.

"Good."

There was another pause in the conversation.

"What time does your show air this morning?"

She quickly checked the clock on the wall in the living room.

"It will be on in about ten minutes," she told him. "Can you stay to watch it?"

"Of course," Trent confirmed without pause. "Let me wash up a bit. You wouldn't happen to have a spare toothbrush, would you?"

Renee confirmed that she did.

They cleaned up the table together; then Trent followed Renee into her bathroom, where she provided him with a towel and the toothbrush. After a quick shower and a toothbrushing, he quickly got dressed in his clothes from last night. His cell phone was in the back pocket of his pants, and Trent noticed that he had missed a call from Nathan about fifteen minutes earlier.

Trent cracked open the bedroom door and could hear Renee in the kitchen running the water. The television was also playing. He decided it would be safe to call his cousin back and give him a quick update.

Nathan answered after the first ring. "Well, how did it go? What happened?" asked Nate right away.

"I'm still at her apartment," Trent told him in a hushed tone.

"What? Since last night?" demanded Nathan.

"Look, I can't really talk. She's waiting for me in the living room. But I did a quick look around this morning while she was still sleeping, and I couldn't find any pictures or anything else really obvious. Did you tell her that you want to see the evidence she claimed to have?"

"I haven't been able to reach her, Trent," Nathan replied weakly.

"So, is it a picture she has? Or did you send her e-mails, text messages?"

"No, it's not e-mails for sure. Maybe text messages, but I don't think I ever sent anything really bad. . . . I don't know, Trent."

"Well, you're going to have to find out for sure the next time you talk to her about the money," stated Trent in a hard tone. "I might have a chance to look around again, but unless I know what I'm looking for, it's pretty impossible."

"All right. But she still hasn't called me back, Trent. I'm getting a little worried that—"

"Good," interrupted Trent impatiently. "It means she's distracted, and that's what we wanted, right? We're about to watch her appearance on that morning show, so there's lots of reasons why she might be rethinking about hitting you hard for that money. You might just get lucky and dodge this thing faster than we thought."

Nathan started to reply, sounding skeptical and much less enthusiastic, but Trent heard the water turn off in the kitchen.

"Listen, I have to go," Trent stated in a hushed voice. "I'll call you on my way back home."

He hung up the phone without waiting for a response from Nathan, then tucked his phone into his pants pocket. When he got back into the living room, Renee was still cleaning up the kitchen, watching the start of the television show from there. They smiled at each other, and he casually sat on her sofa. She joined him a couple of minutes later, just as her image appeared on the television as she was being introduced to the audience.

Trent had to admit that she looked great on camera. He quickly became fully engrossed in the show, watching her talk and interact naturally with the host. She spoke in a way that was very knowledgeable but also down-to-earth. He thought it showed credibility but without pretense.

They were halfway through her segment when Trent's cell phone beeped, indicating a text message. He ignored it, not wanting Renee to think he was distracted or not completely focused on her television appearance.

When her section was over and the show went to commercial, he turned to her with a big smile on his face. "That was really good," he stated simply.

"Thanks," she replied proudly. "I was more nervous watching it than I was when I did it. I was afraid that it wouldn't be as good as I thought it was. But it was all right."

"It was better than all right. You're a natural."

She shrugged a little, but didn't say anything more, and they went back to watching the show.

Trent's phone beeped again, and this time he took it out of his pocket. There were two messages, both from Nathan. The first said Call me now! The second said It's not her!! Call me!

He stood there for a few seconds with his brow furrowed tightly.

"Is everything okay?" Renee asked.

"I'm not sure," he told her vaguely. "I just have to make a phone call. Excuse me."

He stood up and walked toward her front hallway so that he could get a little privacy. Once he was out of her eyesight, he hit the REDIAL button.

"What are you talking about?" demanded Trent as soon as Nathan answered.

"That's not her, Trent," he stated frantically.

"Who's not? What the hell are you talking about?"

"I just watched her on that television show, and *that* Renee Goodchild is not *my* Renee."

Trent was speechless as he looked toward the living room. "That's not possible, Nate. She's the person you told me you met, right? Everything about her is what you told me."

"I know! And she looks a lot like Renee, but I'm telling you, it's not her, man!"

"No, no, it's just the lighting and stuff, Nate. The makeup," Trent insisted. "Television makes people look a little different, right?"

"Trent, I'm telling you. The woman who was on TV just now is not the Renee Goodchild that I . . . that I got to know. There is no question in my mind."

Trent let his head fall back and ran a hand down his face. His mind was racing but nothing was clear. He was absolutely speechless.

"Trent, are you still there?"

"Yeah, yeah, I'm here," he finally replied.

"Could there be two of them?" Nathan suggested.

"What? Two women with the same name who look alike and work at the same interior design firm in Manhattan? Come on! Obviously, one of them is a fraud, Nathan. I'm pretty damn sure it's not the one I just slept with!"

His voice had started to rise in frustration, but Trent caught himself in the end, finishing the last sentence in a harsh whisper.

"You slept with her?"

Trent didn't respond. He just hung his head, shaking it from side to side. The full weight of what he had done landed square on his shoulders, and it was crushing.

"I'll call you later," he eventually replied.

"Wait! What are you going to do?"

"I have no damn idea."

Trent stood in the front hallway with his back against the wall and his head hung low. If only he could walk away from the whole situation. Just walk out the door of that apartment without looking back and pretend the events of the last two weeks had never happened. Unfortunately, walking away from a problem wasn't in his nature. He was going to have to face what he had done.

The messy, sordid problem that his cousin was caught up in had just become messier and even more distasteful. Except now Trent was an ugly participant.

"Is everything okay?"

Trent turned quickly toward Renee when he heard her voice and found her peeking around the wall. He straightened up and walked toward her, trying hard to remove all traces of stress from his face.

"Yeah . . . yeah. Everything's fine," he stated.

"Are you sure? You look like you just heard some bad news," she insisted.

"No, it's nothing major. My cousin was just telling me about a situation he's dealing with."

"Oh. Nothing too serious I hope."

They were both now standing just outside of the kitchen.

"He's going through some stuff with his wife, that's all."

Renee nodded with sympathy.

"So, your show's over?" he asked.

"No, it's still on, but my part's done. Did you want to see the rest?"

"I would like to, but I have to get going. My cousin is pretty down, so I promised to meet him a little later. And I'll have to stop at home first."

"All right," she replied. "I'll get your coat."

Neither of them said much as he got ready to leave. Within a few short minutes, they were standing near her front door facing each other awkwardly. It was hard to ignore all the intimate details from the last twelve hours, but the memory was in their eyes.

"Sorry I have to leave so quickly," Trent finally stated.

"It's no problem. Staying here last night wasn't really planned, right?" she replied easily.

"No, not really."

They both laughed a little.

"Okay. I'll give you a call later today?" he suggested.

"Sure."

Trent leaned forward and gave her a tender, soft kiss on her lips, followed by a peck on her forehead.

"Bye," they said at the same time.

The drive back to Greenwich was smooth and uneventful. Trent spent the time doing a lot of thinking.

He usually had a sharp ability to measure someone up very quickly, and he should have trusted his instincts from the beginning. Looking back, it was so obvious to him that the Renee Goodchild he had met and spent time with could not be the same woman who was extorting thousands of dollars from his cousin. The doubts had been there from the beginning, but he chose the easy way out and stuck with his ridiculous, arrogant, half-baked plan to dig Nathan out of his mess.

That realization took about ten minutes for him to formulate in his mind. Trent spent the rest of the ride home coming to terms with why.

His Renee Goodchild, the real Renee, just seemed too good to be true. She was smart, independent, and absolutely gorgeous. Sure, there were lots of women with that combination, but from Trent's experience, they usually also had a viper personality that went along with it. Renee did not seem to have an ounce of negative, greedy energy in her perfect, petite frame.

Then there was the physical reaction Trent had in his lower stomach whenever he was near her. It was so strong that it disarmed him and kept thoughts of her floating around in his mind long after he left her. In the face of what Nathan had claimed Renee to be over the last couple of weeks, having those kinds of feelings for her was completely absurd, and it scared Trent to death. That was the real reason that he ignored his judgment and instincts. He had quite successfully warded off the persistent claws of dozens of social-climbing women in recent years and was not about to fall for the worst example.

Trent waited until he got home before he called Nathan again. By then, he was starting to see that this morning's turn of events was very good news for their end game. Trent felt pretty confident that once his cousin confronted his former lover with his knowledge of her fraud and identity theft, the woman would back off and most likely disappear altogether. Hopefully, it would also scare her enough to stop using the false identity and leave the real Renee relatively unharmed by the scam. And maybe Trent would never have to explain his part in the business.

Chapter 13

"So what do you feel like eating?" asked Jennifer.

It was Monday evening, and the women had arranged to meet after work to grab some dinner. Renee was waiting for her near the front entrance of Bergdorf Goodman.

"Anything's fine," Renee stated.

"Well, I've been craving a steak," Jennifer told her. "There's a pretty good place about a block away."

They started walking down 5th Avenue toward 56th Street.

"I'm glad you could make it tonight. But how come you're not working?"

Renee glanced at Jennifer, surprised by her question.

"What do you mean?" she asked.

"Nothing really. It's just you're not usually available during the week, that's all," Jennifer told her.

"Am I that bad?"

Jennifer laughed lightly. "Yes, you are. But it's no

big deal. You're busy. I get it and that's cool. But I'm glad we can hang out for a bit, get caught up."

Renee smiled in response, but she was a little troubled by Jennifer's comments.

She and Jennifer had met over three years ago, when Renee was still Amanda Hoffman's assistant, and Jennifer managed a furniture store prior to her current position. They became friendly over several months as Jennifer helped her with several projects and special orders. Jennifer then invited Renee to a get-together at her house with a few other women. Since then, they'd gotten closer, touching base regularly by e-mail and hanging out on the weekends once or twice a month.

It was true that Renee was often unavailable, particularly during the week, always because of work. It had not occurred to her that Jennifer might feel put off by the limited amount of time they spent together. It wasn't because she didn't enjoy Jennifer's company. They always had a great time together. But Renee had always been a bit of a loner, perfectly content with her own company and busy with her studies and now her work. That's one of the reasons why it wasn't that difficult to move to a big city alone.

Renee had spent the last few years building a life for herself in New York and felt pretty fulfilled and satisfied with what she had accomplished. She knew she spent too much time working and probably needed more of a social life, but she loved her job and found it fun. There were only a few people she considered good friends in the city, with Jennifer being at the top of the list. Frederic and Albert were great to work with and were always good at industry events. At the office, there were also a few women who Renee sometimes had lunch with or had drinks with after work.

Was she missing out on something by not being more open and available to new friendships?

"Well, I'm going to try and spend a little less time working after hours," Renee told Jennifer. "Spring is almost here and I plan to enjoy it. Who knows, after the show appearance, my career could end up going in a whole new direction."

"That's right," replied Jennifer with excitement. "I told everyone at work to watch it, and, of course, they all commented on how fabulous you looked in that dress. You did so good! Are you going to do another one?"

They had just arrived at the popular steak house Jennifer suggested. Inside, it was still busy for a Tuesday, and the hostess suggested they wait at the bar until the table was ready, which would be about thirty minutes. They each ordered a glass of wine.

Jennifer repeated her question about Renee appearing on the *Daybreak Show* again in the future.

"I hope so," Renee replied. "Maya, the producer, seemed pretty happy with how things went. But they only called me because their scheduled designer got injured and Amanda is on vacation. What's the likelihood that will happen again?"

"Hey, if they like you, then you're the first on the list for the call, right?" Jennifer suggested.

"Maybe. I'm not sure how Amanda's going to feel about that. You know how she is. Doing these talk shows is her thing, and I'm not sure she would appreciate me stealing opportunities from her."

"You think she'd be upset? You would still represent Hoffman Designs, so it's free advertising, right?"

"True," Renee admitted. "Maybe I am being a little paranoid."

"Either way, it's your career and you can't turn down opportunities like this even it does piss off your boss."

"Oh, no, I have no intention of turning anything down regardless of how Amanda feels about it."

"Good," stated Jennifer. "'Cause I'm kind of liking the idea of having a famous designer as a friend."

Both women laughed.

"Speaking of that, do you still want to do some work on your apartment?" Renee asked.

"Absolutely, but the reality is that my budget is pretty tight right now. I'm still really glad that I moved to the East Village, but my bank account hasn't really recuperated yet."

"Hey, I know what you mean. But we don't have to do anything expensive. I'm telling you, there is plenty we can get just at Target," Renee told her with a grin.

The women continued talking about ideas for Jennifer's apartment until the hostess let them know their table was ready.

"Hey, what happened with that job in Greenwich? Did you ever figure out who referred you for it?" Jennifer asked after they had ordered their meals.

Renee tried not to blush. When she and Jennifer had gone shopping last week for the show, Renee had told her a little about Trent and his bedroom project.

At the time, Renee had left out the parts where Trent asked her out on a real date and kissed her.

"It's going okay. I was in Connecticut again on Thursday doing the measurements," she replied briefly.

"Did he have his driver pick you up again?" Jennifer asked with a mischievous grin. "It's like a scene out of *Pretty Woman*!"

"Oh, please! Thanks for the reference, but I'm not exactly a prostitute. And it wasn't his driver, just a car service," she rebutted. "A really nice car service with fully stocked luxury sedans and chilled designer bottled water."

They both laughed.

"What a life, huh?" added Jennifer. "I still can't believe the kind of bank accounts some people have. I mean, I'm not broke, not like when I was growing up in Brooklyn, but every paycheck still counts. Then, there are people who can spend a few grand on a purse at Bergdorf without blinking. It's like they don't know the value of money, you know?"

Renee nodded.

"I know. I'm being hypocritical, right?" continued Jennifer. "I make my money off of them spending absurd amounts of theirs. That's kind of the point of high-end fashion, isn't it?"

"Yeah, it is," Renee replied with a sardonic smile.

"All right, all right. I'll shut up about it."

"But you're right. Interior design is pretty much like the clothing industry. It's all driven by fashion. I love it as much as you do, but there are some things that are just ridiculous. I've seen beautifully hand-carved wooden furniture priced cheaper than trendy fiberboard designer stuff. I try to explain the difference to my clients sometimes, but they don't really care."

"I know! The label is now more important than the quality. That's the power of marketing dollars. It makes it so much harder for new designers to start their own line."

"Are you still thinking about launching yours?" Renee asked.

Jennifer sat back in her chair with her eyes focused on the last ounce of wine sitting in the bottom of her glass.

"I'm thinking about it," she finally admitted.

"What's stopping you?"

"Time, mostly," replied Jennifer with a shrug.

"Oh, come on! Give me a break," dismissed Renee.

"What? It's true! I've taken on a few new lines for the store, and it's been crazy lately."

"All right, if you say so. I haven't seen your designs yet, since you won't show them to me, but I know your style. I'm absolutely certain that if you had your own line, it would be a huge success. But if you don't have time . . ."

Jennifer looked back at Renee with an innocent, blank stare.

"Weren't we talking about your client in Connecticut?" she replied.

Renee was unprepared for the change in topic, and she could not hide her surprise or conceal her emotions.

"What else is there to say?"

"Oh, Renee! What are you not telling me?"

Their food arrived while Renee pretended she didn't know what Jennifer was talking about.

"Well?" Jennifer probed once they were alone.

Renee started eating her chicken salad.

"Come on, Renee. You're not a very good liar. What's going on?"

"Okay!" she finally acknowledged. "Really, it's not a big deal, but Trent and I went out on a date last Saturday night."

"No way! Just like in *Pretty Woman*!"

Renee rolled her eyes. "Jen, get off the *Pretty Woman* bit. I'm not a prostitute, remember?"

"Sorry," Jennifer replied, giggling. "It was on TV last Sunday. But you must admit there are some similarities. He's your wealthy client, and now he's falling for you."

Renee rolled her eyes again and went back to eating her meal.

"Fine, I'll stop. Tell me about your date."

Finally, Renee put down her fork and told her friend all the details of her night with Trent.

"What happens now?" Jennifer asked.

"To be honest, I'm not sure. He's been calling me every day, and we're going to dinner after work tomorrow."

"Wow, it sounds like you have a boyfriend."

"Well, I wouldn't say that exactly."

"Why not? He took you out to meet people he works with, then spent the night with you on the weekend. Now he's asking to spend time with you on a regular basis."

"Yeah, but I'm sure I'm not the kind of woman he

usually dates, Jennifer. I can't stop wondering why he's slumming."

"Okay, now you're just being silly, Renee. Why wouldn't he be attracted to you? I know you don't date much, but it's not because you don't get any offers," Jennifer stated. "So what if he has money? That doesn't automatically mean he only wants a Barbie on his arm."

"I know, you're right." Renee sighed. "I guess it's more about my own insecurities. Like you said, I haven't dated much in the city, and I never figured out what kind of man I fit in with here. I went out with that teacher, Kevin, last summer. He seemed like my type. Serious and smart, very responsible. But I just couldn't find anything we really had in common. Before that, there were a couple of guys from Brooklyn that I talked to for a bit. They were your typical, hardworking guys, doing pretty good for themselves."

"So why didn't anything happen with one of them?" asked Jennifer.

Renee shook her head. "I have no idea. I don't remember anything wrong with them. I just didn't have any interest beyond the first couple of dates. My mind was completely focused on work, and I knew these guys wanted a woman who was more available than I was willing to be."

"So, what's different now?"

"I don't know. I'm still very focused on my career, so I'm not even sure if I want a relationship right now. But something about Trent makes me anxious and excited at the same time."

"Maybe you feel a little intimated by his lifestyle," Jennifer suggested.

"Maybe. I know I did at first, but he is so down-to-earth and easygoing. I'm not sure if it's still an issue."

"Renee, if you're not ready for a relationship, then just forget about what he wants and why he wants to go out with you. It doesn't matter. Just have a good time for as long as it lasts."

Renee thought about those words of advice for the next few days and decided that Jennifer was right. There was no reason to worry about what Trent wanted from her until she understood her interest in a relationship.

Chapter 14

Goldwell Group was one of the most successful private equity firms in the United States, with several impressive equity funds and a lengthy list of investments in various industries. Though Trent worked out of their Greenwich office, Goldwell's head office was in downtown Manhattan, and the company had locations in every major city on the East Coast.

Trent usually only went into New York occasionally for client meetings, but his trips into the city had increased to two or three times a week over the last few weeks. At first, it was to facilitate his plan to get closer to Renee; then it became purely about spending time with her. In the week since he discovered Renee's innocence, Trent drove down to see her twice, and they had plans to see a movie on Saturday evening.

It was now Friday evening, and he was on his way to pick up Nathan at home; then they were to meet Nathan's friend, Richie, to watch a Stamford basketball game. Trent arrived at his cousin's condo just after six o'clock. His wife, Ophelia, answered the door. She was a tall woman, almost five foot ten, and as thin and straight as a rod. But, as the owner of a high-end boutique clothing store, she had an excellent sense of style and only wore clothes that flattered her body.

"Hey, Trent," she said, greeting him with a warm hug.

"Hi, Ophelia."

"Nate just got out of the shower."

Trent followed her into their apartment. It was a spacious penthouse unit with twelve-foot ceilings and all the high-end finishes that money could buy, compliments of Ophelia's parents.

"Well, he better hurry up. The ball game starts in about forty-five minutes."

"You know Nate, Trent. Time has no meaning for him," she replied lightly. "Do you want something to drink?"

"I guess a beer couldn't hurt," Trent told her.

She handed him a chilled bottle a few moments later.

"So, what are you up to tonight?" he asked her after taking his first sip.

Ophelia shrugged. She had on a polite smile, like she always did, but Trent sensed she was wearing a mask tonight.

"Nothing really. I'll probably just order some food and curl up on the couch. I have a week of television shows I TiVoed that I need to catch up on."

"Why don't you come with us?"

Before she could answer, Nathan entered the room dressed in jeans and an expensive designer shirt.

"Come where?" he asked while buckling his belt. "Hey, Nate."

The two cousins shook hands and patted each other on the shoulder. "I was just telling Ophelia that she should come out with us tonight," explained Trent.

"Nah. Phelie doesn't want to hang out with guys all night watching basketball and trash talking," he replied with a dismissive snort.

Trent looked over at Ophelia as Nathan was talking, and there was a look of pure sadness in her eyes. Or was it loneliness?

"We don't have an extra ticket anyway," Nate continued.

"I'm sure we could figure something out," insisted Trent quietly.

"Come on, it's a guys' night out. Trust me, she doesn't want to be around us. Right, Phelie?"

The thin smile was back on his wife's face. "You guys go out and have fun. I'm looking forward to a night to myself," she replied.

Trent looked at her for a few seconds longer, but Ophelia just nodded with gratitude. She then walked back to the kitchen and started to flip through a small stack of restaurant takeout menus.

"Come on," urged Nathan as he brushed by Trent. "Let's get going. I don't want to miss the tip off."

"See you later, Ophelia," Trent stated.

"Why did you have to do that?" Nathan asked as soon as they were in the elevator.

"What?"

"Go on and on about Ophelia coming out with us."

"I didn't go on and on, Nate. I just made a suggestion. What's the big deal?"

"If I wanted her to come out with us, I would have suggested it, Trent. I'm entitled to go out with the guys sometimes."

Trent glanced over at his cousin with a look of confusion. "What are you talking about? You act like you're tied to her hip or something. You go out with the guys plenty, Nathan."

"Oh, no. Here we go again. Are you going to give me another one of your preacher-man lectures? 'Cause I'm a grown man, Trent. I don't need your input about my marriage."

Trent didn't reply. He knew his cousin was referring to the conversation they had last weekend after he left Renee's apartment and returned to Connecticut. During the drive, Trent had done a lot of thinking about Nathan's situation and what they had just learned about his lover. Trent felt pretty confident that Nathan's troubles were over. He asked Nathan to meet him at the town house to talk about it.

"The way I see it, she has way more to lose at this point," Trent stated as they stood in his kitchen discussing how to handle future contact with Nathan's ex-lover.

He handed Nathan a glass of juice.

"I don't know, Trent. If we threaten her with fraud charges, she may get pissed off and contact Ophelia anyway. And we still don't know who she is, so how are the police going to be able to help?" Nathan asked.

"Nathan, she was never going to tell your wife

about the affair. The only way this situation works out for her is if you still think she is Renee and you still want to keep your affair a secret from your wife. In that scenario, you're scared enough to give her the money and she remains anonymous. She has nothing to lose," explained Trent. "She has nothing to gain by telling your wife, except out of sheer spite or if she felt betrayed by you in some way. Now, from what you've told me, you guys only knew each other for a few weeks, and you were honest with her from the beginning, right? So she doesn't have any reason to want to hurt you personally, right?"

Nathan nodded. "No, I don't think so. I mean, it's not like we were in love or anything. We both understood that it was just for fun while I was in the city," explained Nathan.

"Exactly. And if her intentions were innocent, she would not have pretended to be someone else from the moment you met. That woman was looking for a mark from the beginning, and you walked into her net, that's all."

Nathan had the good sense to look embarrassed.

"So, if she doesn't realize we know she's a fraud, the only risk she has is that you will call her bluff and refuse to give her the money," Trent continued. "In that case, she'll just try her game with another victim. Even then, I guarantee she will keep threatening you for a good amount of time before walking way. But the minute you tell her that you know her game, she'll disappear before you blink."

"You think?" Nathan asked, clearly not convinced that it would be so easy.

"Trust me. Now she has everything to lose. We might not know exactly who she is, but we do know she looks a lot like Renee, and she obviously knows Renee in some way. Or at least knows enough about her life and social habits to pretend to be her without running into people who know the real Renee. It would not take too much police investigation to pick up her trail. So, her only option will be to walk away now and forget she ever met you."

Nathan let out a deep breath. He still looked worried but not quite as anxious. "So, what now?" he asked Trent. "She hasn't returned any of my calls."

"Now we wait. If you're lucky, she may know that Renee was on that television show on Friday and decided the game is too risky. Either way, I think your troubles with this girl are over."

"I sure hope you're right."

Trent looked at him for a few seconds, trying to decide if there was any remorse in his voice to go along with his relief.

"I hope that means that you're not going to put yourself in this situation again, Nate," he finally stated.

"What are you talking about, Trent? It's not like I planned any of this."

"No, but if you continue to play with fire, it's only a matter of time before your ass gets singed."

"Come on, man. It ain't like that. I don't go out of my way to play around, but you know how it is," Nathan replied dismissively.

"No, I don't know how it is. You chose to get married, Nate. So be married or get out. Do whatever you need to do to be happy. But the cheating is just wrong and you know that."

"Man, don't be a hypocrite," he replied bitterly. "How many women have you cheated on, Trent? Don't act like your behavior is better than mine."

"That's where you're wrong. You think you know me, but you don't. I have never cheated on a woman who I was committed to, Nathan, and I never will."

"That's right. You just never commit, right?" Nathan asked sarcastically. "You spend just enough time with a woman until she wants something more; then you lose interest and walk away. Or you just start dating someone else. And you think that makes you better than me?"

"Look, I never said that," Trent replied sharply. "I never compared myself to anyone. You did that. But looking at my life doesn't make your choices any better."

"Whatever, man," Nathan replied sullenly.

Trent was used to his cousin's childish ways and had let the matter drop at that point. But as much as he hated to admit it, Nathan's words had struck a chord somewhere in his conscience. He thought of his decision to break things off with Brianna. More importantly, why had he chosen to go out with her in the first place? Why did he always choose to pursue women who he knew from the beginning were not what he wanted long-term?

His dad had always told him to be ready for the right woman when she appeared and to have faith that she would. Trent always thought that meant that he should enjoy himself until the right one arrived. But he now wondered if he should have been spending more time looking for her and less time with the ones he knew were wrong.

Now, as he and Nathan got into his car and drove toward the Stamford University campus, Trent realized that nothing he said to his cousin was going to divert Nathan from the path he had decided to take in his marriage. Though Trent had very little patience and sympathy for people who cheated in their marriage, he was honest enough to admit he was now in a situation of his own that was blurring the line of faithfulness. He had allowed himself to become enamored with Renee, spending as much time with her as possible, yet Brianna would return from France in a couple of weeks expecting them to pick up where they left off.

Nathan's treatment of Ophelia was unacceptable, but until Trent cleaned up his own mess, he could hardly criticize.

Chapter 15

"If you didn't have to work for money, what would you do with your time?" Trent asked Renee.

It was Saturday afternoon, and they were walking through Central Park. The weather had been unseasonably warm for the last few days, melting most of the ice and snow. They had just finished seeing a movie at an uptown theater, and were walking back to Renee's apartment. The afternoon sun was warm and bright.

"That's a really good question. I don't know," replied Renee after a long pause. "Honestly, I would have to say exactly what I'm doing now."

"Come on, you can do better than that. The possibilities are limitless. There has to be something else you would do with your time. What about traveling to exotic locations? Or wine tasting around the world?" Trent insisted.

"Well, you know my amateur knowledge of wine, so that's definitely not on the list," she replied with a short laugh.

"But that's how you could learn, right? You would be a world-class connoisseur within a few months."

"Is that what you would do?" Renee asked, looking up at him.

"Nah. Well, maybe for a few weeks." They both laughed, then he continued. "If I didn't have to work and money wasn't an issue, I would buy a small resort on the beach in Jamaica. Something I could run with one or two employees."

"Really? I would never have guessed that."

"Why not?"

"I don't know. You just don't strike me as the beachcomber type, living the lazy life by the seaside."

Trent let out a humorous snort. "You're right, that doesn't sound like me. But I could be very happy with a simpler life. Perfect weather year-round and a nice plot of land overlooking the ocean where I can grow all the fruits and vegetables I need. What could be better than that?"

Renee looked around the barren landscape of the Manhattan park, and Trent's vision of tropical paradise sounded like a great idea. She glanced back at his face, and something there made her believe his description of an ideal life was more than just a random or spontaneous thought.

"Why Jamaica?" she finally asked.

"My dad was Jamaican," he replied simply.

"Really? That's very interesting. Do you get to go there often?"

"Yes and no," Trent told her with a wry smile. "I actually lived there for about half my life. I lived with my mom in Chicago's south side until I was fourteen;

then she sent me to live with my dad in Jamaica. Let's just say I was headed down a pretty destructive path, running the streets with other stupid kids in the hood. So, my dad put me in a military boarding school there."

Renee was speechless. It never occurred to her that Trent could have come from anything other than a privileged and secure background. He displayed such natural grace and class, as though he was born with innate power and influence. It really surprised her that he came from the same humble upbringing that she did.

"I didn't move back to the States until three years ago, after he died."

"I'm so sorry to hear that. Were you close to him?"

Trent looked up at the sky, but his face held a mix of amusement and nostalgia.

"My dad was a superintendent in the Jamaican army. He was a pretty hard guy to get close to, particularly when I was an angry teenager meeting him for the first time. Things were pretty simple for him. Do what he told me to do and we would get along fine. He wasn't interested in being friends. But eventually, sometime in my twenties, we started to understand each other."

They walked in silence for a few minutes.

"Did you think of anything yet?" Trent asked her.

"What do you mean?"

"What would you do with yourself if you were independently wealthy?"

"Oh, yeah. Okay . . . Wow, this is tough," she

admitted, biting her lip in concentration. "I know! I would restore and renovate old homes."

Just saying it made her feel excited and energized. But Trent looked completely unimpressed.

"Come on. That's only one step away from being an interior designer."

"Fine. Then I would restore and renovate old homes around the world."

They both burst out laughing. It was very clear that she had a one-track mind, and that was the extent of her imagination.

"It's pretty sad, huh?" she added.

"Yeah, it is."

They chuckled some more.

"I guess there was something else I wanted to do at some point as a kid. But for as long as I can remember, interior design has been my thing," explained Renee. "My mom and I lived in a pretty dodgy part of Pittsburgh. It wasn't Section 8 or anything, but our building was pretty run-down. Anyway, we spent many weekends shopping for the most inexpensive way to decorate our apartment."

"So that's where you got the bug. From your mom."

"I think so, but she doesn't agree. The way she tells it, I was the one who forced her to apply gold leaf to every surface that fateful winter of 1992."

"It was just the two of you?" Trent asked. "Was your dad around?"

Renee shook her head. "No, I never knew my real father. He left town before I was born, apparently. But my mom remarried when I was about thirteen, and now Kenneth is Dad to me."

At that point, she and Trent exited the park a few blocks from her building. There were a number of restaurants along the way, and they discussed the options before finally choosing a place that offered an eclectic menu of dishes from various Mediterranean countries.

As they ate, Trent continued to tease her about her inability to dream big. He insisted that with the right coaching, she could find other ways to live a fantasy life. Renee played along but could not help but be distracted. Her life was moving in an unusual direction, complete with a growing career, new friends, and maybe even a boyfriend. It was pretty exciting but also quite daunting.

While growing up in Pittsburgh, she had always been a bit of a loner with only a couple of close friends around her. For many years, since they met in fourth grade, it was just her and Angela as a team. They told each other everything and were practically inseparable. Their moms became friends as single parents living in the same neighborhood, and the four of them did lots of stuff together. Then, when Renee was thirteen, her mom, Anna, met Kenneth Blake, and within a year they were married. It was a little awkward at first having a man in the house and seeing her mom in a real relationship for the first time. But Kenneth was a good man, hardworking and reliable. They all soon adapted and became a family unit.

While Renee's family life had positive changes, Angela's headed in the opposite direction. Her mom, Janette, was diagnosed with lupus, and her health slowly declined. The friendship between Anna and

Janette did not survive the changes. Renee and Angela tried to stay close, but eventually it became harder and harder for them to relate to each other.

In high school, Angela became a big social butterfly. At first, Renee went along for the ride. They joined the cheerleading team together and became part of the popular crowd. While Angela loved being a member of an elite, envied group, Renee found it tedious and superficial. Then Renee met Devlin her junior year, and he became her new best friend. The once-close relationship with Angela faded further to the point where it was almost nonexistent.

In her heart, Renee still considered Angela to be her best friend, the one person in the world who knew all her childhood and teenage secrets. She had believed they could reconnect at any point and continue the relationship they shared as girls. But after sharing an apartment with Angela over the last few weeks, that possibility no longer seemed realistic. It was very sad.

It was about six-thirty when they finished dinner and continued the walk to Renee's place.

"Would you like to come upstairs?" she asked once they reached the lobby.

"For coffee?" suggested Trent with a devilish smirk.

"Hey, you better watch yourself, or you'll be lucky to get a glass of water," Renee replied sharply, but her eyes were dancing.

"Yes, ma'am."

They spent the rest of the evening watching television and a couple of movies from Renee's slim collection. She did make them some coffee at some point.

Then they both fell asleep on the couch with his arm wrapped around her shoulder and her head resting on his chest. At some point in the night, Trent woke her up and they made the move into her room, stripping off their clothes to sleep in their underwear.

Renee woke up to find him pressed against the length of her back. She lay there for several minutes, listening to his deep breathing and trying to keep hers smooth and steady. Sunshine was peeking in through the window curtains, and it was toasty under the covers. She could tell that it was midmorning, but Renee closed her eyes again and snuggled closer to the warmth of Trent's body.

He groaned softly and ran a hand over her hip. She froze and held her breath, not wanting to wake him up. After a few seconds, Trent's breathing deepened again and his arm went slack.

It felt really good to wake up on a Sunday morning wrapped in the arms of a strong man. Being with Trent like this, at a level deeper than dating or just sleeping together, was surprising and unexpected. Renee spent a few minutes thinking back on the last couple weeks. She tried to put her finger on what made this connection with Trent different than with any of the men she had dated over the last few years. What about him captured her attention enough to put aside work to see him whenever they were both available? Where did this evolving feeling of long-term potential come from?

"Good morning, gorgeous," Trent whispered into her ear before she knew that he was awake.

"Morning," she whispered back. "Did you have a good sleep?"

"Hmm. I don't even remember what time we went to bed," he replied.

Renee smiled to herself. "I don't know either."

"How about you? Did you sleep well?" Trent wrapped his arms around her from behind.

"I did, and I was just wondering how late it is. It looks like the whole morning is gone."

She felt him rise up onto one elbow so that he could look down at her face.

"Oh, sorry. You probably have plans for the day. . . ."

"No, it's okay. I don't have anything special booked."

He lay back down and they shifted around under the covers into more comfortable positions. It was hard to say when their embrace shifted from relaxed and cozy to sexually charged. Renee was suddenly intensely aware of how much of their bodies were in contact and how little fabric there was between them.

Trent's hand found her hip again and slid upward over the soft surface until it came to rest high on her rib cage. Her breathing became slower and deeper, and her skin tingled with anticipation. As though reading her mind, he cupped her breast gently.

"Hmm, you feel so good," Trent told her.

He squeezed the sensitive mound, teasing her nipples with the center of his palm. Renee sucked in a deep breath, trying to relax and enjoy his touch. The firm length of his arousal now nudged at her bottom. She arched her back to encourage his touch and let out a soft moan.

They were both still drowsy from their long sleep,

and it made their lovemaking slow and languid. While they remained spooned, Trent used his position to explore every part of Renee's body that was exposed to him. He kissed her neck and shoulder while his fingers plucked, stroked, and rubbed her peaks and hidden valley. She felt pampered and indulged, completely at the mercy of his touch and her mounting pleasure. When she finally came, it was in long, drowning waves that flowed through and stole her body.

As the final tingles of orgasm exited through her toes, Trent paused to slide on a condom. He then lifted her leg over his and slid his hard shaft deep into Renee's wet sheath from behind. He held her tight and stroked deep until he shuddered in climax.

Chapter 16

The next week went by for Renee much like the last. Once she and Trent finally got out of bed on Sunday morning, they showered together; then she made him a light breakfast before he left for the drive back to Connecticut. Later that evening, they talked on the phone for several hours, about everything and nothing in particular. Trent came into the city Tuesday to take her to dinner, and Thursday to shop for fabrics and paint for his bedroom.

At some point, Renee realized that it had been several days since she had seen Angela in the apartment. Their last real conversation had been on that Saturday almost two weeks ago when Angela had helped her get ready for her date with Trent. Since then, Angela's presence had become more and more scarce.

It was now Saturday, early in the afternoon, and Renee had just gotten home from the hair salon. Once again, Angela was nowhere to be found. Renee took off her winter boots and opened the hall closet to hang up her coat. At that moment, she noticed that several of Angela's extra jackets and shoes were missing. Renee put her coat away, then stood in the hall for several seconds, her brow furrowed in confusion. She then went to her spare bedroom and looked at the door that had been closed for days. She knocked first, then opened the door when there was no answer.

Now, as she stood in the doorway of her spare bedroom, which was almost completely empty of Angela's belongings, it was very clear that the division between them may be irreparable. It had been at least a week since Renee last saw her in the apartment, and as usual, Angela had been rushing out, dressed up for a night on the town. There was still no sign of her securing a job or doing anything more productive with her time than partying.

The room was almost empty except for a few random, abandoned items scattered on the floor. A yellow Post-it note was sitting on Renee's desk, and she walked across the floor to read it. The brief message had only a few words written in Angela's handwriting, saying she would call Renee soon. She put the note down and looked around again, seeking additional information.

It really hit her at that moment just how distant she and Angela had become. She didn't have a clue what was going on with her childhood confidant, including where she was living now and why she departed so quickly without any notice or discussion.

Renee then let out a deep breath before going through the bedroom and putting Angela's remaining belongings into a neat pile in the closet. The sad reality was that if Angela had found a new place to live long-term, then it saved Renee from having to ask her to leave. They may not be close anymore, but it would have been a very uncomfortable conversation.

Renee also liked the idea of having her privacy back. Despite her initial objections and hesitation, it now appeared that she and Trent were going to be seeing each other regularly. Though Angela hadn't been around a lot in the past few weeks, and had always been gone when Trent stopped by, her presence was unpredictable. Now, Renee did not have to worry about a roommate walking in at an inappropriate time.

Once Renee finished tidying up Angela's things so it resembled her office again, she headed into the shower. Trent had gotten them matinee tickets to the Broadway production of *Chicago.* They had left the rest of the day open for them to get something to eat and do some shopping. She was secretly hoping this weekend would end the same as last—with her waking up wrapped in Trent's arms on Sunday morning.

At almost one-thirty that afternoon, Trent called to say he was parking his car nearby, and Renee got ready to meet him downstairs. Though the temperature outside wasn't as warm as last weekend, it was a few degrees above freezing, with clear skies and a mild breeze. She was shrugging on a cozy down jacket when her home phone rang. Renee answered it quickly, expecting it to be Trent again.

"Is this Renee Goodchild?"

The question was asked by a deep voice, devoid of

any emotion. Renee was certain she did not recognize it. She took a second to look at the caller ID, but the number was unlisted.

"Yes?" she replied cautiously.

"Renee Goodchild? You work at the Hoffman Design Group?"

"Yes," she stated again, this time more forcefully. "Who is this?"

There was a click and the phone went dead.

"Hello? Hello?"

It took her a few seconds to realize that the person with the unfamiliar voice had hung up the phone. She stared at the receiver, trying to understand what had just happened and why. As she was about to place the phone back on the kitchen counter, it rang again.

This time it was Angela, sounding a little uncomfortable. "Renee, I'm glad I caught you!"

"Angela? Where are you? What's going on?" Renee asked, surprised.

"Nothing, nothing. Everything is okay."

"Are you sure? I haven't seen you in days, and your stuff is all gone. When did you leave? Have you found somewhere else to stay?"

"Yeah . . . I have a friend who's invited me to stay with him for as long as I need to. I took most of my stuff yesterday."

"Okay," stated Renee, dragging the word out to reveal her surprise. "Why didn't you tell me?"

"It kind of just happened. I've been hanging out at his place most of the time anyway. It's not like I could stay with you forever, right?"

There was an awkward pause before Renee replied.

"I know," she stated simply. "But you could have said something, you know? We could have talked about it."

"I know. I didn't plan it like that, Renee. I tried to wait around for you yesterday, but it got late. . . ."

"I put the rest of your things in the bedroom closet," stated Renee.

"Okay. I'll try to come by soon."

"Are you sure you're going to be all right, Angela?"

"Come on, girl. You know me. I've got everything under control."

Renee was skeptical but kept her opinion to herself. Instead, she felt the need to try and reach out. "Angela, we should stay in touch. I know we didn't spend much time together so far, but we still can."

"That would be good," Angela agreed.

"Do you have a phone number where I can reach you?"

"No, not really. But I'll be getting a cell phone soon. I'll call you with the number when I get it."

The two women ended their call soon after, and Renee made her way downstairs to meet Trent.

After her call to Renee, Angela sat back down on the armchair to watch television. The apartment belonged to Winston Thompson, who was now asleep, stretched out on the couch. She had met Winston at a club soon after she had arrived in New York in early January. They had stayed in touch over the phone and met up a few times to hang out casually. He lent her money occasionally and even bought her clothes when she saw something she liked. Even so,

Angela had been very honest with Winston over the last couple of months, letting him know she didn't see him as anything more than a friend. But he didn't seem to care and was content to remain platonic.

Though he was a very nice guy and somewhat attractive, Winston wasn't Angela's type at all. He was just too straightlaced and tame. As a New York City transit worker, he was also only a working stiff with no real money. His apartment in Brooklyn was all right, but it was definitely not a luxury mansion. Angela had not come all the way to Manhattan to live hand to mouth like she did in Pittsburgh.

One of the reasons she had accepted the invitation to stay with Winston was because she could tell her time was running out with Renee.

Renee had been visiting her mom and stepfather over Christmas in Pittsburgh when Angela ran into her in the mall. They exchanged phone numbers and spoke vaguely about getting together. When Angela needed to leave the city for a while, she hopped on the train to Manhattan and called Renee for a place to crash until she found a job. Renee had always been the nice one in their friendship and welcomed Angela with open arms.

Now, over two months later, Angela could tell the warmth was fading fast. A job never materialized, and Angela was low on cash, so couldn't really help out with the bills. Renee also seemed to be very possessive of her stuff, a trait that Angela did not remember from their childhood.

Either way, it was time to move on, and Winston's invitation came at a perfect time. Angela had plans to improve her financial status, and it did not involve getting a nine-to-five. She was pretty sure that Renee would not appreciate the ingenuity of her plans. Staying with Winston and sleeping in his bed was just a temporary stop on her way to financial freedom.

Which brought to mind the second reason Angela had moved in with Winston.

Purely by chance, she had been watching television on Friday morning just over a week ago and was shocked to see a promo for Renee Goodchild as a guest on the *Daybreak Show*. It kind of surprised Angela that Renee had not bothered to mention her television debut, but the two women had not talked much in the last few weeks. There was lots of stuff that Angela hadn't shared either.

But, unfortunately, Renee's television appearance now made it impossible for Angela to continue pretending to be her.

When Angela decided to introduce herself at exclusive parties as Renee Goodchild and pretend Renee's life was hers, it had been just for fun. It gave her an instant identity that was glamorous and fit in with the lives of the people she was meeting. It was much better than telling everyone that her last job was as a cashier at a hardware store in Pittsburgh. Or it was until they fired her for credit-card fraud. And Renee never went out, anyway, so it seemed pretty harmless.

Nathan Frost was the first mark that Angela had set up. She met him at a hotel party when she caught him giving her the eye. He was very good-looking, with a honey-brown complexion and stunning gray-green eyes. Even better, he seemed to have some money and liked to impress her with it. Nathan had been honest from the beginning and told her about his marriage. At first, she only intended to have some fun and let him take her to expensive restaurants. Then, once they were sleeping together, he started buying her things like jewelry and shoes. It was great, and Angela decided she wanted more.

One night, after an evening of hot, kinky sex, she asked him for a few thousand dollars to pay off some bills. Angela could tell he was a little put off by the request, but he handed her the cash less than a week later. About two weeks after that, she went in for the kill and asked for ten thousand dollars. She didn't really think he would give her the whole amount, but she was getting bored with him already and there was nothing to lose. The story was that her mother was sick and needed expensive medication but didn't have health insurance.

Her excuse was based on the truth. Angela's mom had been suffering from the effects of lupus for over fourteen years. It was a painful and debilitating disease, and the cost of medication to control the multiple symptoms had put her mother on the edge of bankruptcy. Angela's use of stolen credit-card numbers started out with the need to help her mom pay their bills. Somewhere, in the back of her consciousness, she still intended to use any financial windfall to help out her mother.

At first, Nathan seemed very concerned about her situation and told her he would see what he could do to help out. Another week or so went by, but he didn't bring it up again. By then, Angela had moved up in the world of New York elite. She had just met a Broadway producer, Nigel Bloom, who liked to host wild parties in his penthouse apartment. From what she could ascertain, his friends were into anything and everything, without limits. Her options had grown exponentially almost overnight, and Nathan's contribution to her welfare seemed less essential.

The next time Angela saw Nathan, she asked him bluntly about the money. At first, he hemmed and hawed and tried to give her the impression that he was still working things out so he could give her something to help her out. When she persisted on confirming when and how much, Nathan finally admitted that there was no way he could give her any more cash. His wife kept tabs on everything and would know immediately if that kind of money disappeared. Angela saw an opportunity and took it. At first, she cried a bit, showing real stress about her mother's health and financial situation. Then she told him quite firmly that if he didn't get her the money, she would have to go to his wife. It was a bluff, of course, but Nathan clearly believed her. His anger and fear were palpable.

They spoke again a couple more times, and with each conversation, Nathan begged her to forget about the money. He was so pathetic that Angela enjoyed toying with him a bit and gave him a deadline to come up with the cash. That was the last time they spoke, though he had left her several messages over the last couple of weeks as the deadline came and went. He sounded so agitated and desperate as he begged for more time that Angela almost felt sorry for him. Eventually, she planned to put him out his misery, but not before she scared him out of a few more dollars.

In the meantime, she had a bigger fish on her hook and it was time to reel him in.

Chapter 17

Though the bright afternoon sunshine and slight breeze made walking around comfortable that Saturday, the temperature dropped as soon as the sun started to set. The weather forecast had called for snow in the evening and through the night, predicting an accumulation of several inches by Sunday morning. Earlier in the day, Trent had suggested to Renee that it would be better if he stayed the night and drove back to Connecticut on Sunday after the snow had cleared up. He had also confessed that he had brought a change of clothes, hoping that she would be fine with his plan. After the play, Renee and Trent walked to his car to grab his overnight bag, then headed back to her apartment quickly, huddled together to preserve the little body heat they still had between them. They decided to pick up some Chinese food at a small restaurant along the way and spend the rest of the evening watching television. By the time they reached the front door of her building, a light snow had started falling.

As they rode up in the elevator, they talked about their plans for Sunday. Renee thought it would be a great opportunity for them to choose some of the finishes for his bedroom, like the bedding and paint color. They were discussing the best places to go shopping as they approached her apartment. Renee had her back to the door as she searched through her purse for her keys, and something about the door frame caught Trent's eye and made him freeze. There was too much light coming through the crack, as though the trim around the frame was loose or warped. He had his overnight bag slung over his shoulder and the takeout containers in one hand. Trent used the other hand to quickly move Renee behind him.

"What are you doing?" Renee blurted out as she stumbled over her feet from his sudden manhandling.

Trent gave her an intense look and pressed an index finger over his lips, indicating she should be quiet. Her eyes were wide with surprise and confusion, but she followed his instructions. He pressed lightly on the door near the lock. The dead bolt rattled a bit as though loosened. He pushed a little harder and the lock gave way under the pressure. The door swung open freely. He heard Renee let out a sharp cry of dismay.

"Stay here," he instructed softly.

Renee grabbed at his arm, trying to stop him. Trent glanced at her quickly over his shoulder to keep her calm and to make sure she understood the seriousness of the situation.

"Stay right here," he repeated more forcefully.

She nodded, but her fear was clearly visible in her eyes.

Trent pushed open the door as quietly as possible, then leaned his head into the apartment to look down the foyer. There wasn't anyone within his immediate line of vision or anything that looked out of place. He paused for a few seconds, listening for any movement. It was completely silent. Trent then crept inside and stealthily made his way down the hall with his back pressed against the wall.

When he reached the living room and dining room area, he found the room literally torn apart. Everything that Renee owned was tossed around and pulled apart. Trent ignored the chaos and disarray, and focused on trying to detect any sound or movement indicating the perpetrator might still be in the apartment. A quick but thorough inspection of the open space and the kitchen came up empty. He did the same in the bedrooms and bathrooms before he knew for sure that the apartment was empty except for him.

It took Trent less than two minutes to clear the unit. When he got back outside, he found Renee exactly where he left her. Her keys were still clutched in one hand, and she now had her cell phone in the other. Trent wasn't sure if she planned to call for help or use it as a weapon.

"Is everything okay?" she asked frantically.

He let out a deep breath, dreading the look on her face and how she was going to feel when he told her what happened.

"Renee, your apartment has been broken into."

"What? What do you mean? I've been robbed? Oh, my God!" she exclaimed.

Before he could stop her, she rushed inside.

"Damn," he muttered under his breath.

Trent took his time before he followed her, wanting to give her a few minutes of privacy. He found her standing in the middle of her living room, immobilized by what she saw. Her shoulders were slumped, and one hand covered her mouth as though stifling a scream. She looked at Trent with eyes wide with shock. He felt her pain deep within his soul.

"Renee, it's bad, I know. But we have to get out of here and call the police," he tried to explain in a gentle tone.

His voice seemed to unfreeze her, and she took a couple more steps into the living room toward the windows. All around them were the remnants of her furniture and personal items. Her couch was turned over with all sides slashed open to reveal the stuffing. The cushions were thrown around and ripped up, leaving down filling scattered all over like snow. All the paintings were ripped off the walls with their frames and glass broken. Her flat-screen television had been knocked over and lay facedown on the floor. Everything that was loose, including papers, magazines, and knickknacks, was strewn everywhere.

It was bad. The minute he saw the mess, Trent knew that this was not a robbery or a random break-in. Someone was looking for something, and judging from the extent of the unnecessary damage, they also wanted to deliver a loud message.

"Renee, we have to get you out of here," he repeated, and stepped close to her.

"What? What do you mean? I'm not going anywhere!" she stated loudly, stepping back from him. "Look at my stuff. I . . ."

Her voice broke before she could finish her sentence. Tears welled up in her eyes, but she walked away from him before they could escape. He swallowed his emotion and reached out a firm hand to stop her. Trent knew that every second they stayed in that apartment was dangerous to her.

"Renee," he stated firmly. "Please, grab a change of clothes and anything you absolutely need. We have to get out of here, now."

"I just told you, I'm not going anywhere!" she exclaimed as she tried to pull her arm free of his grasp.

Trent tightened his grip, not enough to hurt but firm enough to get her attention. She looked up into his face, clearly startled by his display of control.

"Listen to me," he stated in a low voice. "Someone broke into your apartment looking for something. If they didn't find it, they will come back. Trust me, you don't want to be here when they do. Do you understand? We are leaving in two minutes. Grab as much as you can. Now."

Though it pained him to do it, Trent knew that unless he put the fear of God into her, she was going to continue fighting him out of anger and despair. They just did not have the time it would take for him to explain reality to her nicely.

Renee now looked up at him with eyes wide with realization.

"Now, what do you need?" he asked in a more compassionate voice.

She finally looked away from this face and around the room.

"My laptop," she stated. "And my project files. I need my project files."

"Okay. Go and get some warm clothes, and I will find your computer."

Renee nodded sharply and walked away quickly. By the time she returned with her clothes in a small knapsack, Trent was holding what was left of her computer. It was bashed in and completely destroyed. She came to a full stop once she saw it, and there was absolute terror in her eyes. Trent tossed it on the ground and pulled her into his arms.

"It's okay. Everything is going to be okay," he whispered soothingly.

"I'm all right," she told him after a few seconds, then pulled away. "I just need to collect a few files from the office."

Trent took her bag out of her hand; then she rushed off to the spare bedroom. He used those few minutes to try and find anything that could be a clue as to who had done this or why. He sifted though her belongings, eventually turning over her discarded photos. One of them caught his eye, and he picked it up to examine the image further. It displayed Renee as a teenager, wearing a high school cheerleading outfit and looking healthy and radiant. But it was the young girl standing beside her that captured his attention. He was struck again by the strong resemblance between them. Instinctively, Trent dismantled the broken frame and tucked the picture into the bag still slung over his shoulder.

"All set?" he asked when she returned with a portfolio bag.

"I think so."

"Okay, let's go."

"What about the food?" she asked as they passed the kitchen.

The forgotten takeout containers of Chinese food were on the counter. Trent now remembered that he had handed their dinner to Renee before he went into the apartment to check for an intruder. She must have brought it in afterward.

"We'll leave it in the fridge," he told her as he stopped to put it away.

When they finally left the apartment, Renee tried fruitlessly to lock the door behind them. Her key was useless and the dead bolt was too loose to hold. Trent finally told her to just leave it closed. He was then on full alert as he shuttled her out of the building, but they did not run into any residents or other people who could be a threat.

There were so many things that they needed to talk about, things that Trent needed to understand, but he decided to wait until they were somewhere safe before bringing any of it up. Renee seemed too shocked to have a meaningful conversation at that point anyway.

Once they were in his car in the parking lot near her building, Trent instructed Renee to call the police and report the break-in. He listened as she did a good job letting them know she was too scared to stay at her place but could be reached on her cell phone. At one point in her conversation, she glanced at him questioningly, and he took the cue.

"The Marriott on East Ninety-second Street," he supplied before she could ask the question.

She looked at him, completely puzzled by how he knew what she needed, but she repeated the information to the police operator. They were halfway to the hotel by the time Renee got off the phone with a promise from the operator that the police would go to her apartment soon to investigate. Police officers would also meet them at the hotel soon after.

As Renee finished up her report, Trent made a quick phone call himself to his good friend Robert Drummond. Robbie was a detective in the NYPD Homicide Division and was a former colleague in the Jamaican Constabulary Forces. He had married his American wife, Beverley, over six years ago, and then moved to the Bronx and joined the New York Police Department. The two men stayed in touch despite the distance and reconnected when Trent returned to the United States.

The conversation with Robbie was short and rather cryptic. Robbie agreed to meet Trent in the lobby of the Marriott in about an hour.

Chapter 18

"Look, I know you're just doing your job, but I've told you everything I know. I have no idea who would break into my apartment, much less why," Renee repeated in a weary voice.

She was sitting at the desk in the hotel room that Trent had booked them into at the Marriott. He had left the room soon after they arrived, telling Renee that he had to meet with a friend in the lobby. Two policemen had been sent to take her statement about the break-in and now stood in front of her. Only one officer bombarded her with repetitive questions. Detective Brown was a tall, stocky, older man with red, blotchy skin and a body that looked sweaty and out of shape. The other cop, whose name she could not remember, was a younger version of his partner and just made notes while watching her closely.

After almost an hour of interrogation, Renee was starting to lose it. She really did understand that they needed answers in order to start an investigation, but she was frustrated that she did not have anything to offer them. And she was also becoming preoccupied with what she would do with her life until this mess was sorted out.

"All right, Ms. Goodchild," stated Detective Brown. "But from what we have been told, the kind of damage done in your apartment was not random; it was personal. So if there is anything else you can remember that can help our investigation, please let us know right away." He took out a business card and handed it to her.

Renee nodded as she took it. "I will," she told him solemnly. "Do you know when I can return to my apartment?"

The two men looked at each other.

"That's hard to say," said the second detective. "We'll be finished processing the scene in another couple of hours. But we wouldn't advise you to go back right away. Do you have someone you can stay with for a few days?"

"Why? I don't understand," questioned Renee.

"Ms. Goodchild, we know it wasn't a robbery. Nothing of value was taken, including your television, laptop, or several other valuable items. Instead, they were destroyed. So, whoever did this was there for a reason. And you haven't been able to tell us anything to suggest what that reason could be or if they accomplished their goal. So, until we find some evidence or you remember something to tell us, there is the real possibility that they will return."

Renee could only stare unblinkingly. Her heart started pounding in her chest until she could hear the beat in her head.

"Do you need to go back for anything?" Detective Brown asked after a few seconds. "Our guys will be there for a little bit, or we can have someone escort you in the morning."

"Ahh . . . no. No, I think I'm okay," Renee finally replied in a whisper.

The only reason she was anxious to go home was to start cleaning up, and hopefully have her life return to normal as soon as possible. If she couldn't do that, there was no point in returning now just to review the destruction all over again. Trent had forced her to take all the essentials already.

"Do you have someone you can stay with?" he asked, echoing his partner's earlier question.

"She can stay with me," stated Trent as he walked into the middle of the room to stand beside Renee.

She was surprised by his presence and shocked at his statement. She had not heard him walk in and now wondered how much of the discussion he had heard. Until Trent spoke, she really had no idea where she would go until this mess was figured out. Her mind was blank of options, and she was about to start a mental calculation of how long her bank account would allow her to stay in the hotel.

"Gentlemen, I'm Trent Skinner," he stated, extending his hand to the officers. "Renee will be staying with me for as long as it takes to solve this case."

Both men shook his hand, but they were clearly distracted by another man who had walked into the room behind Trent. Renee noticed him for the first time. He was about an inch shorter than Trent and had a darker, smooth complexion and a more slender frame. Like Trent, he had an intangible air of importance. Renee stood up.

"Officers," the stranger said in a soft, melodic voice that suggested a Caribbean accent. He also shook hands with Detective Brown and his partner.

"Detective Drummond," replied the two cops at almost the same time. They seemed surprised and confused by his presence.

"Sorry, Detective," stated the senior officer once the silence became a little uncomfortable. "Someone has misled you about this case. It's only a B and E at this point. There was no homicide there."

Detective Drummond put up his hands and waved them dismissively. "No, don't worry. I'm not here in an official capacity," he explained. "Trent and I are old friends, and he called me when this happened. He and I were rookies together back in Jamaica with the Intelligence arm of the Constabulary Forces. He may be an investment banker now, but Trent was quite impressive until he was injured in the line of duty. So, I can assure you that Miss Goodchild will be very safe with him. Now, you should know that Trent lives in Greenwich, so Miss Goodchild will need to leave the state in order to stay with him, but I'm sure that would not be a problem, right? She is clearly the victim in this crime, and Trent will make sure she is available if you gentlemen need to speak with her further."

The three detectives eyed each other before both Brown and his partner conceded that Renee was fine to leave the state.

Renee sensed the awkward tension between the

officers, but her focus was on Trent and what she had heard. He was looking at her intently, as though he knew questions were brewing in her brain, and was braced for the attack.

Eventually, the two detectives investigating her case quickly concluded their interview and left the room.

"Renee, I would like you to meet my good friend, Detective Robbie Drummond with the Homicide Division of the NYPD."

"Hi, Detective Drummond," she stated politely, and extended her hand.

"Please, call me Robbie," he replied with a big smile as they shook hands. "And it's a pleasure to meet you, Renee. Trent here has told me quite a bit about you."

"Really?" Renee asked with genuine surprise. "I would like to say the same, but unfortunately, he's never even mentioned that he used to be a police officer."

She tried to sound flippant, but her tone revealed her annoyance. Trent had the good sense to look embarrassed while Robbie laughed heartily, looking back and forth between them.

"It was a long time ago, Renee," Trent tried to explain, but it sounded flimsy.

"Well, maybe he was just being humble," Robbie replied, still grinning. "He was rising quickly in the ranks until he was shot during an investigation."

Trent seemed content with them talking about him as though he were not there, but his gaze remained fixed on Renee. She had no clue what to think about all this information, much less how to respond to Robbie's teasing. Suddenly, the events of the evening seemed too much to deal with. She just wanted to pretend the whole thing never happened. At least until tomorrow morning.

She nodded politely and gave Robbie a tight smile. He was a very perceptive man. Once he saw the exhaustion on Renee's face, he turned to Trent. "Well, I'm sure you both have had enough excitement for one night. I'll leave you two alone. Trent, walk me out, then take care of your lady. She looks like she is about to collapse," chastised Robbie. "And don't worry, Renee. We'll have you back home safe and sound very soon."

"Thank you, Robbie. It was nice to meet you," she replied.

He nodded, and Renee watched as the two men walked out of the room.

Now alone, she looked around aimlessly and bewildered. When Trent returned, she was sitting in the armchair next to the window, looking out into the night and watching the snow come down fast and furious. Somewhere off in the distance, she heard Trent make a phone call. He approached her softly a few minutes later.

"Thank you for offering to let me stay with you, Trent," she stated, still looking out into the night. "But it's not really necessary. I'll call my friend Jennifer in the morning. Or I can just stay here for a few days. . . ."

"Renee, you're staying with me. We need to get you out of the city," Trent replied in a tone that allowed no argument.

Renee was too exhausted to argue. He might believe she had given in, but she planned to readdress the issue again in the morning.

"I'm sure you're as hungry as I am, so I've ordered dinner for us," he told her. "Why don't you take a bath or something and relax? I'll let you know when the food arrives."

It was a great idea. A long soak was exactly what she needed.

Renee stood up slowly, and as she turned to walk toward the bathroom, Trent stopped her with a gentle brush of his hand.

"I promise you, Renee, everything will be okay. Don't worry about anything. I will keep you safe."

He looked down at her with such sincerity and conviction that Renee took a second to look deeper into his eyes.

"Why do you keep saying that? Why does everyone think I need to be kept safe? Why would anyone want to hurt me?" she asked, her gaze still fixed on his.

"Renee, someone destroyed your apartment. They destroyed everything you own. Clearly, whoever they are, they are very dangerous people."

"But they're not after me. There is no reason why someone would do that to me on purpose. So it was a mistake, right? The wrong apartment or the wrong person. Or maybe just some kids looking for money. Either way, nobody is after me!"

Her voice slowly escalated until it was loud and shrill. Trent tried to pull her close, perhaps to comfort her, but she resisted.

"It's okay," he stated soothingly.

"No, it's not okay. You're looking at me like those detectives did. Like I know something about all this. Do you think I'm lying too?"

Trent let out a deep breath and dropped his hands, looking guiltily to the floor.

"You think I'm lying, don't you?" she demanded again.

"No, I don't, Renee, but . . ."

He trailed off, and Renee watched as he struggled to find the right words.

"But what, Trent?"

"Look, you've been through a lot tonight, and I'm sure you're exhausted. Why don't you take that bath; then we'll eat dinner. We can talk more after that."

"No," she stated simply. "We will talk now, Trent. Explain the *but* in your statement."

He looked down at her with clear frustration, but Renee held her ground. She lifted her chin stubbornly. He took a deep breath and turned away from her before letting it out slowly.

"Someone has been using your identity to extort money from men."

Renee had no clue what she thought he would say, but as his words hung in the air between them, they sounded so ridiculous that she found it hard to take him seriously.

"What? Trent, that's crazy! Where did you come up with something like that?"

He finally turned back around to face her. She was surprised to see that the look of guilt was back on his face, along with what appeared to be regret and dread.

"I know it, Renee, because a woman pretending to be you slept with my cousin, then threatened to tell his wife if he didn't pay her ten thousand dollars," he told her slowly. "Renee, you weren't referred to me by one of your clients. I sought you out to save my cousin's marriage."

Chapter 19

Trent was usually pretty well spoken. He hardly ever struggled with his words, even in the most stressful or unpleasant situation. In his current position as an investment broker, there had been many situations in which he had to inform his clients of their financial misfortune, particularly within the last couple of years. As a police officer in Jamaica, he sometimes had had to tell parents or other family members the worst possible news: that their loved ones had been killed in a gunfight or a car accident. All of those conversations were difficult, but Trent had always been able to find the right words to explain the circumstances and console those affected.

Now, standing in front of Renee, with her piercing eyes looking deep into his soul, his mind was blank. He could not find an appropriate explanation for the circumstances they were both in.

The minute he saw the destruction of Renee's apartment, Trent knew this conversation was inevitable.

And since that moment almost five hours ago, he had been struggling with how to tell her about his participation in the situation.

Two weeks ago, when he and Nathan discovered that Nathan's lover was a fraud and that the real Renee Goodchild was a victim of identity theft, Trent was left with very mixed feelings. On one side, he was concerned about the unscrupulous woman with no identity. She had the ability to destroy his cousin's life if she wanted, and they had no idea who she really was. And to what extent had this woman implicated Renee in her crimes? If she was bold enough to impersonate Renee around New York City in order to commit extortion, it was very possible that she also used Renee's identity for other financial fraud.

Yet, while his police training told him to be wary of the whole state of affairs, Trent could not deny that he was very relieved. *His* Renee was actually the beautiful, smart, and successful woman whose companionship he grudgingly enjoyed.

Up to that point, he had tried to deny feeling anything for her other than contempt and scorn. He dismissed the excitement and attraction he experienced for her as a strictly physical and primal reaction. The alternative—that he had somehow become captivated by a skanky gold digger who was also his cousin's leftovers—was just unacceptable.

Now as Trent looked into Renee's eyes as she waited for an explanation, he wondered what advice his dad would have for this situation. What do you do when the right woman finally comes into your life, but you've done something so horrible that she would likely never forgive you?

He took a deep breath and leaped forward with his best attempt to explain everything to Renee.

"I sought you out on purpose to save my cousin's marriage."

She wrinkled her forehead, then shook her head, clearly struggling to understand his words.

"What? Someone pretending to be me did what?"

"Renee, it's pretty complicated, and I don't think you're in the right frame of mind."

"Trent, there is nothing wrong with my frame of mind, all right? So you better tell me what's going on right now."

Trent let out another big sigh. His shoulders were slumped and his head fell forward in defeat. "I'm not sure where to start, to be honest," he confessed in a soft voice.

"Start from the beginning," she demanded without sympathy.

"Okay. Well, I guess it began a couple of months ago. My cousin, Nathan, met a woman and they had a brief . . . thing. Then she threatened to tell his wife if he didn't give her money. Ten thousand dollars, to be exact."

"So, what does that have to do with me, Trent? What does any of that have to do with the break-in at my apartment?"

"Renee, that woman told him her name was Renee Goodchild and that she was an interior designer with a firm called the Hoffman Group."

"That's ridiculous, Trent. I'm pretty sure I never

met your cousin, and I sure as hell did not sleep with him or try to extort money from him!"

"I know that now, Renee. But when I met you, all I knew was what Nathan told me."

"I'm sorry; I don't understand any of this. So your cousin cheats on his wife and calls you in a panic, right? And your solution is to hire his lover as your interior designer, then sleep with her?"

Her voice was dripping with sarcasm. Trent opened his mouth to respond but couldn't come up with a reply that would help his case.

She continued her analysis. "What you're saying to me is you hit on me, pretended to like me, then slept with me, all the while thinking I was your cousin's lover and an extortionist?"

"Renee, it wasn't like that."

He reached out a hand to touch her arm, but she pulled away and walked over to the bed. Her back was to him, and Trent just wanted to pull her into his arms to force her to see that it didn't matter how they met or why. What mattered was how he felt about her now.

"How was it, Trent?" she demanded.

"I didn't mean for it to happen that way."

She turned around and looked at him with burning eyes. "Really? So, what was your end game, exactly? What did you want from me, the woman who used sex to get money from your cousin?"

Trent looked away.

"Oh, my God! That's it, isn't it? You thought you would flash your fancy waterfront house and your flashy car, and I would sink my greedy little claws into you. And, what? Forget all about your cheating, sleazy cousin so he could continue to cheat on his wife?" Renee let out a sharp, ugly laugh, but she looked like she was about to cry. Her eyes welled up with tears, and her lips began to tremble.

"Renee, please . . ."

"Get out."

"Look, I can explain . . ."

"I said get out! Now!"

She turned away from him again, but not before one of those tears spilled onto her cheek. Trent's heart sank and he felt nauseous. He could barely resist the urge to pull her into his arms and comfort her, but he did. Instead, he walked out of the hotel room.

Trent didn't go far. He found himself in the hotel lobby, nursing a bottle of beer at the bar. Images from various moments over the last six weeks flooded his mind, including the day Nathan called him to confess that his infidelity had gotten him into a boatload of trouble with a woman named Renee Goodchild. What was it about his cousin's pathetic cry for help that had compelled Trent to get involved?

The whole story about a sexual fling gone wrong had seemed silly and exaggerated at the time, and Nathan was clearly in a panic. He had even suggested that Trent use his law enforcement persona to intimidate his ex-lover into backing off. That suggestion was out of the question for Trent. He was not going to pretend he was still an officer for any reason, and he certainly wasn't going to deliberately intimidate a woman. Instead, Trent had concocted the ridiculous plot to distract Renee, the fake Renee, with a more eligible, single victim.

The rest was now history, and nothing had gone as planned. Though Nathan had not heard from the fake Renee in over two weeks, they still didn't know who she was or what she planned to do about her threats. Nathan obviously had not learned any lessons from the whole ordeal, nor did he seem remorseful or regretful about his behavior. Trent had not made any more attempts to discuss his cousin's chronic infidelity, but he just hoped Nathan would eventually came to his senses and realize exactly what he would lose if Ophelia found out about his cheating.

Trent took a long drink from his beer, gulping the last of it before slamming down the bottle. He signaled to the bartender to serve him a second. At that point, he noticed a very attractive young woman a couple of seats over from him giving him the eye. Trent nodded to be polite, then went back to his drink. But he wasn't surprised to find her sitting next to him a few seconds later.

"Hi, there," she stated brightly.

She tossed her blond hair back and forth and smiled broadly. Her sea-blue eyes were sharp and inviting.

"Hello," he replied.

"You look like you can use some company. It's quite the storm we're having, isn't it?"

Trent nodded in agreement.

"I'm Leslie. What's your name?"

"Hi, Leslie, I'm Trent."

"So, Trent, what are you doing all by yourself?

You don't look like the type to hang out at hotel bars on a Saturday night. Are you here from out of town?" she asked.

"Not really. Just here for the night with my girl-friend."

"Really. Things not working out as planned?"

"Things are working out just fine," he stated flatly.

She giggled flirtatiously, leaning closer so her hand brushed the sleeve of his jacket.

"Well, your girlfriend is crazy to let you out of her sight. If it were me, you wouldn't have any energy to leave the room."

Trent shook his head and drank more of his beer. She was pretty hot, and there was a time not too long ago when her invitation might have seemed like a good idea. Now, Trent just found her attention intrusive and cheap. The idea of casual encounters no longer held any interest.

"Thanks, but she is more than enough for me," he replied.

"Then she is a very lucky woman."

"No, I'm the lucky one," Trent stated.

He drained his second drink, then pulled a twenty-dollar bill out of his wallet and tossed it on the bar.

"Have a good night," he told the woman, then walked away.

Trent checked his watch. It was only ten-thirty, and it was likely that Renee was still awake. He didn't want to upset or disturb her again for the rest of the evening, so going back to the room was out of the question for now. Instead, he picked a cozy chair in a secluded part of the hotel lobby and pulled out his phone.

Robert Drummond answered after the first ring. "Hey, Trent," he stated. "I was just going to call you."

"Any luck so far?"

In their conversation earlier in the evening, Trent had told Robbie everything he knew about the real Renee Goodchild and the woman who had been using her name. Robbie agreed that the impersonator was most likely the target of the break-in, and it was possible that Renee was innocent and ignorant to the whole scheme. He promised Trent he would see what he could find out in the police databases.

"Yes and no. I did a basic search using Renee's information and everything looks pretty standard. As far as I can see, her background check is clean. And if anyone is using her identity for financial gain, they're being pretty subtle about it."

Trent thought deep for a few seconds. "So, this really doesn't tell us anything new, Rob."

"It tells us that your instincts are probably right. It's likely that Renee's name was used to extort money from your cousin and most likely at least one other man, that being the person who destroyed her apartment. I don't see any signs that Renee is actually involved."

"Okay. Thanks, Robbie. I really appreciate your help on this."

"No problem, Trent. Let me know if you need anything."

"I will."

"And, Trent, just in case we're both wrong, keep a close eye on her. For her safety as well as yours."

"I hear you," Trent replied tiredly before hanging up.

Chapter 20

Surprisingly, Renee fell into a deep sleep that night and woke up feeling rested and alert.

After Trent left the room, the room service he had ordered arrived while she was getting ready for a shower. At first, Renee was so upset and exhausted that she didn't feel like eating. But once she lifted the dish covers, the food smelled delicious. He had ordered steak dinners for them both, with a baked potato and grilled vegetables. The next thing Renee knew, she had polished off almost everything on her plate.

She finally made it into the shower around 10:00 P.M. and collapsed in the queen-size bed about forty minutes later. When she woke the next morning, it took her a few seconds to remember where she was. Then she remembered all of the bizarre and frightening details of the night before.

Renee sat up and looked around the hotel room, half expecting Trent to be there. But he wasn't, and there were no obvious signs that he had returned to the room. The full weight of her situation suddenly crashed down on her, making her chest feel constricted. It was Sunday morning, almost seven-thirty according to the bedside clock, and her life was completely in ruins. Everything she owned of value was destroyed and she was temporarily homeless. With her laptop damaged, so was a large amount of her work done over the years, except what she had stored on the computer in the office or in project folders.

Now Trent was gone, at her demand, and she was alone.

She thought back to their heated argument last night and wondered if she should have let her astonishment and hurt rule her head. There was no doubt that she was justified in her feelings, but despite his role in all of this, Trent had offered her a safe place to stay and his protection. Now she had nothing. Renee was very tempted to go back to sleep and put off reality for as long as possible.

When she finally climbed out of bed, she turned on the television for some company. With the infomercials playing in the background, Renee headed toward the bathroom to get washed up. That's when she realized that the room service tray from dinner had been removed. Before going into the shower last night, she remembered putting her empty plate on the tray on the console beside the television. Trent's meal was still there. Then she had forgotten about it.

Renee looked around some more and noticed that Trent's overnight bag was next to the bathroom, and his toiletry bag sat on top of it. She let out a deep breath, from a mix of relief and anxiousness. Trent had not left her after all. He had come back to the room at some point either last night or early this morning.

As though hearing her thoughts, he opened the door. Renee was about to walk into the bathroom and jumped with fright at the unexpected sound. He juggled two tall cups of takeout coffee in one hand and had a brown paper bag in the other. She watched, still too surprised to move, as he closed the door with his heel. Trent didn't notice her until he turned toward the sleeping area of the room.

They both stood frozen for several seconds, eyeing each other and trying to decide what to say.

"I picked up some breakfast," Trent finally stated to break the silence. He walked toward her and lifted his peace offering for her to see.

Renee nodded and mumbled brief words of thanks. Unsure of what else to say, she turned and closed herself in the bathroom. She took her time going through the motions of brushing her teeth, washing her face, and changing her clothes, stretching the time out until she found new resolve.

Trent was on the phone when she reentered the bedroom. He glanced over at her but the look on his face was unreadable. The conversation lasted only a few minutes longer, but his voice was too low for her to hear his words. Renee busied herself with repacking her things in her bag, preparing herself for their next conversation. When his muted voice became silent, she turned to face him. He was looking out the window, his brows pinched together pensively.

"Trent," Renee called out.

He looked at her, trying hard to remove the signs of stress from his face. She took a deep breath.

"Considering the circumstances," she continued. "I think it's better that I stay with my friend Jennifer. She lives in a very safe building downtown, and I'm sure—"

"No."

Her mouth hung open with shock at his simple, authoritative statement.

"What? You can't decide—"

"I'm sorry, Renee, but it's just not possible."

"Look, Trent. I appreciate your concern, but it's not your decision."

"You're right, it's not."

Trent had been leaning against the desk, and he now straightened to face her. He sounded weary and drained, and the crease between his brows was back.

"Renee, I just spoke with Detective Brown."

"What did he say? Have they discovered who did this? Can I go back to my apartment?"

"I'm afraid not. I called him to get an update, and he very bluntly told me that they have nothing. No clues and no suspects."

"Oh," she whispered. Her shoulders fell in defeat.

"He also thinks you know something that you're not telling," continued Trent. "And he made it clear that he was only leaving you in my custody against his better judgment. The implication was clear, Renee. He thinks you have something to do with it."

Renee let out a long, frustrated grunt. "But I don't know anything! How many times do I have to repeat myself?"

"Well, that may be so, but they are only allowing you to leave in my custody, Renee, and only because of my friendship with Robbie. So, you have no choice. Your only option is to stay will me until this whole thing gets straightened out."

She didn't know what to say. So many aspects of this entire situation were too crazy to understand. Trent must have sensed how confused she was. He approached her and put a gentle had on her shoulder.

"So, you're right, Renee. It's not up to me where you stay for the next little while, but you don't really have a choice," he explained in a more tender tone. "All I care about is that you stay safe, and I can only guarantee that while you are with me."

He sounded so sincere, and in that moment, Renee wanted to believe him. It would be so easy to buy into his motives and his feelings. But his lies were still too fresh in her mind. If she had to stay with him while the police continued their investigation, that did not mean she had to trust him or allow him close to her heart.

Renee stepped away from him and went back to packing her things.

They left the hotel about fifteen minutes later, taking the coffee and bag of pastries with them to eat in the car. The drive to Connecticut was a little slow. The storm the night before had left the roads icy and dangerous. Renee and Trent passed several car accidents and wipeouts along the way. Yet, the ride was pretty silent with less than a dozen words exchanged between them.

Now that it was clear how limited her options were, Renee spent the time deciding what she was going to do about work. They arrived at Trent's house in Greenwich around ten-thirty. The temperature had dropped since the day before, hovering near the freezing mark. There was a strong breeze coming off the lake, making the air feel even colder.

Trent grabbed their bags from the car and she followed him inside.

"I'll put your bag in the spare bedroom," he told her once they were on the main floor. "Would you like something to drink? Are you hungry?"

"No, I'm fine, thanks."

He nodded and continued upstairs. Renee stood and looked around the space. It was shocking to believe it had been only a few weeks since she had met Trent here for the first time. It was even more unbelievable that the whole thing was a setup from the beginning. This project was just a scheme to expose her as a slut who had bartered her body for the gain of ten thousand dollars.

When Trent returned downstairs, she was finally ready to confront him.

"Was any of it real, Trent?"

He stopped a few steps away from her.

"I've been planning how I can continue to work on my projects remotely, from here," explained Renee in a casual tone. "Then suddenly, it occurred to me that your bedroom redesign project probably isn't even real. It was all part of your plan to save your cousin."

Trent stood straight, his eyes fixed on hers with intense focus. Her sarcasm was thick and biting.

"So, you need to explain to me what was real and what was created just to mislead me."

"Renee, none of this was about you."

She let out a sharp laugh. "I know. That has been made very clear, Trent. And maybe that answers my question. Everything you did and said was because you thought I was someone else."

"That's not what I meant, Renee," he replied, throwing his arms up in frustration. "But you're right. At first, I thought you were someone else. However, once I found out that you weren't that person, it all changed."

"What changed? You stopped sleeping with me because I was easy and cheap, and started respecting me for my mind?"

Trent let out a long breath but had the decency to hang his head in shame. Renee looked at him and all of the fight went out of her. Arguing and attacking him wasn't going to get them anywhere.

"It was a serious question, by the way," she added. "I need to know if you still want your bedroom done."

"Yes, Renee. I really think you are a great designer, and I would like you to finish redoing my room—that is if you still want to."

She didn't really have an answer. But she looked at him again and realized there were a lot of things she still did not understand.

"When did you realize I wasn't your cousin's lover?" Renee asked.

He had a steady gaze on her again. "When you did

that television show. Nathan saw it and assured me you weren't the woman he had met."

That was two weeks ago, Renee calculated quickly. Yet, he continued to see her and pretend nothing had changed. She wanted to know why but wasn't sure she would trust his answer.

"Why would someone pretend to be me?" she asked instead. "It doesn't make sense!"

"Well, it's pretty clear now. This woman used your identity to hide her own, Renee. And judging by the extensive damage to your apartment, she had good reason to not want to be found. She may have scared Nathan with her threats, but she has really pissed off someone else as well."

Renee didn't want to feel scared, but she could not prevent her heart from racing.

"But why me? This is New York, Trent. It's a pretty big city with thousands of very important, impressive people. And I barely know three people since I've moved here. This is crazy!" She threw her arms up in frustration. "Why would she choose me?"

"There's only one logical answer. She looks like you and knows enough about your life to be credible," he stated evenly. "It's someone you know, Renee."

Her eyes widened, and she slowly shook her head back and forth. It was one thing for some greedy stranger to use her good name to commit crimes, but to think it could be someone close to her, or even an acquaintance, defied reason.

"I told you, Trent, I don't have a lot of friends here."

"Okay, so the list of women who look similar to you must be pretty short."

Renee shook her head again, but her mind was starting to work pieces into place. Then Trent pulled a photo out of his back pocket and unfolded it.

"Let's start with the girl in this picture with you," he stated.

Chapter 21

"Who is she?"

Renee heard the question, but she grabbed the picture out of Trent's hand and walked away from him. The image showed her and Angela at a homecoming football game in their sophomore year. They were wearing their cheerleading outfits and looked youthful and happy. Even then, the similarity between them was uncanny.

"Where did you get this?" she demanded, turning back to wave the creased and scratched photo in front of his face.

Until yesterday afternoon, it had been framed and mounted on her living room wall.

Trent ignored her question. "Who is she, Renee? If she was behind all of this, then she's in real danger. You would not be doing her any favors by protecting her."

Suddenly, she could easily see him in his previous profession as a police officer. It was clear that he had already been doing his own investigation and drawn his conclusion.

"She's just a friend from high school. I haven't seen her for years now," she replied with a steady gaze.

"Are you sure? Where is she now?"

"I don't know. Last I heard, she was still in Pittsburgh."

Trent watched her steadily, as though reading her body language for signs of the truth.

"All right," he stated simply. "Then tell me about your roommate."

"What about her?" Renee asked blankly.

"Could she be involved? How well do you know her? Maybe she's the one using your identity. She would have access to your information." Trent persisted.

Renee bit her lip, fighting the urge to be honest and reveal her suspicion of Angela now growing in the pit of her stomach. But she didn't say anything. At the very least, Angela deserved the benefit of the doubt. Renee needed some time to ask her directly about her involvement.

"I don't know, Trent," she finally responded. "I wish I had some information that could help identify who was responsible. But I don't."

Eventually, Renee told him she was tired and needed to make some phone calls. Trent gave in to her and led her up to the spare bedroom, down the hall from his. Once alone in the room with the door closed, she waited a few minutes before taking her mobile phone out of her purse. She then cracked the door open to make sure the hallway was empty and he was out of earshot. When she finally felt comfortable, she began to search her address book to find some way to contact Angela. There was an old cell phone number listed under her name with a Pittsburgh area code. Renee knew it was unlikely to still be working, but she tried it anyway. As suspected, it was disconnected.

She hung up the phone and sat on the bed. Her mind was racing a mile a minute.

What in the hell has Angela gotten herself into?

There was very little doubt in Renee's mind that Angela was behind all this. Angela had always been attracted to the fast life and easy money. But what Renee wanted to know was why. Sure, their friendship had become distant over the last few years, then pretty awkward over the last couple of months as roommates. Yet, Renee found it very hard to believe that Angela would do anything to deliberately hurt her or put her in danger. Until Renee spoke to her and understood exactly what was going on, she wasn't going to put the police or Trent on Angela's tail.

First thing on Monday, Renee planned to purchase a new laptop. At that point, she would be able to access her Internet mail account and send Angela an e-mail. Until then, Renee would do the next best thing; she would leave a message with Angela's mom, Janette Simpson. She didn't have Janette's current number, so Renee called the only person she knew who might.

"Hey, Mom," she stated when the phone was answered.

"Renee? Hi, baby. How are you?" asked Anna. "I left a message for you yesterday; then I started to get worried when I didn't hear back."

"Sorry, Mom. I didn't get your message. How are you doing?"

"Oh, I'm all right I guess. Tired as usual, but I can't complain. How are you, baby? Did you remember to send me the copy of your TV appearance?"

"Yeah, I did. You should get it any day now," Renee told her.

"Oh, good! I'm so excited to see it. You were such a quiet child, Renee. Always so serious and focused. Who would have guessed you would be doing television," her mom stated with a deep chuckle.

"Mom, it's just one show."

"I know, I know. But you have to start somewhere, right?"

"I guess. I just don't want you to get too excited."

"Oh, please, Renee. What's wrong with a little excitement?"

It was Renee's turn to laugh a little. "How is Kenneth doing?" she asked.

"Oh, you know him. He's doing just fine. He's now got it in his head that we should go on a cruise. You know, one of those ones that go through the Caribbean? That's all he's been talking about for weeks now. He's like a dog with a bone, that one."

"Yeah, you told me last week. Are you going to go?"

"Oh, I suppose. He'll wear me down eventually."

"It sounds like lots of fun, Mom. I'm sure you'll have a great time."

"How about you, Renee? When are you going to take some time off and come home for a vacation?"

Renee thought about her current situation and how difficult it was going to be to manage her projects remotely without falling behind schedule. Vacation time was definitely out of the question for the foreseeable future.

"I'll try to make it home soon, Mom. At least for a weekend."

"Good. Now that spring's here, you can help me do some gardening."

"Okay," agreed Renee. "Hey, Mom, do you have Janette Simpson's phone number?"

"Janette Simpson? Oh, I haven't spoken to Janette in a long while. Not since we moved out of the neighborhood almost ten years ago. Why, what's going on?"

"Nothing. I'm trying to reach Angela, and I just realized the phone number I have for her is disconnected."

"Oh. But I thought Angela was staying with you while she's getting settled in New York?"

"Well, she was. But she has a new boyfriend and she's decided to stay with him."

"Oh, that doesn't sound good. It's only been three months and she's moved in with a man already? That girl has not changed, has she?" Anna asked rhetorically, her voice heavy with disapproval.

"Do you have a number for Janette?"

"I'm sure I have something in my phone book, but I don't know if it's current. Let me go get my purse."

"Thanks, Mom."

When she came back to the phone a couple of minutes later, she gave Renee a phone number that seemed familiar. Renee assured her mother again that everything was fine and that she would be home soon for a visit. She told her mom to pass on a kiss to Kenneth before they hung up.

Renee checked the hallway again to make sure that Trent was not in earshot before she made her next phone call. She dialed the number her mom gave her and got an answering machine. It was a cryptic recording that didn't mention any names, but Renee felt her only option was to leave a message and hope it would reach Angela's mom.

"Hi, Miss Simpson, this is Renee Goodchild. I'm tying to get a message to Angela. Can you tell her to give me a call on my cell phone as soon as possible?"

Renee ended the message by leaving her phone number and wishing Miss Simpson all the best. The only thing left to do was wait.

Renee managed to stay away from Trent for the next day or so and avoid having to lie to him any more than she already had. Though they were on polite speaking terms, there remained an awkward strain between them. Renee was still unclear about where things stood with their relationship, but she just didn't have the energy to address it. Her emotions were all over the place, and it just seemed easier not to think about things.

She didn't see Trent again that evening. He had already left for work by the time she got downstairs on Monday morning, but he had left her a spare key and a note with the security pass code on the kitchen table. As planned, Renee took a cab into downtown Greenwich in search of a new laptop. Once she found one she liked, she also picked up a good amount of work supplies, then spent the rest of the day walking around and browsing in the various clothing stores. Around noon, she stopped to have lunch and used the opportunity to make several phone calls, the first of which was to work.

First, Renee checked her messages. Then she asked Marsha to put her through to Amanda's assistant, Claire. Amanda was due to return from Aruba later that week, so Renee gave Claire a brief summary of what happened over the weekend. Claire also booked some time for Renee in Amanda's calendar on Thursday so they could review her projects.

Renee then left a message with her insurance broker to advise them of the break-in and report the damaged items. She also left a message for Detective Brown, requesting an update on the investigation and a copy of the police report.

She returned to Trent's house at midafternoon and got settled in the family room to work. Trent called her on her cell phone around three o'clock to see how she was doing and to let her know he would be home by six with dinner. They were both polite and the conversation was brief. Once they hung up, Renee felt confused and torn all over again. But instead of dwelling on the situation and trying to make any decisions, she took a deep breath and went back to work.

Chapter 22

Trent was finding it very hard to focus. It was Wednesday afternoon, and he had been watching the clock for the last two hours. Somewhere around noon, while he was eating a sandwich at his desk, he wondered what Renee was doing. Had she eaten lunch? Was she getting some work done?

He toyed with the idea of calling her but dismissed it pretty quickly. What would he say? They had barely said more than a few sentences to each other when they were in the same room. Clearly, Renee was still pissed at him, and Trent could hardly blame her. The more he thought about the circumstances in which they had met and become intimate, the more disgusted he was with himself and the whole situation.

The question he'd been struggling with for the last few days was what he was going to do about it now. At first, his only focus was keeping Renee safe until the police discovered who had vandalized her place and why. That was partly because he felt responsible about how far things had gone. If only he had confronted her from the beginning instead of playing head games, or confronted her when he found out she wasn't Nathan's lover, then maybe she wouldn't be in danger now. But instead of thinking through all of the risks to Renee, he had focused on how great it would be to date her for real.

Now, with her under his roof and with him every day, Trent could not stop thinking about a long-term strategy. He had to find a way to get them past how things started and on to what they could have together in the future. Very simply, he had to get her to trust him again.

At twenty minutes after two o'clock, Trent had an idea. He picked up the phone on his desk.

"Nancy, I'm going to leave a little early. Can you schedule the meeting with the analysts for later in the week?"

Nancy said she would, and Trent started to clean up his desk. He fired off a couple of quick e-mails and pulled together a few reports that he could review later that evening. Once in the car and on the road toward the house, he quickly called Ophelia to ask her a favor. By the time he pulled into his driveway, he had all the details of his plan worked out and a smile on his face.

The house was quiet when he got inside, and all the lights were off. Trent didn't think anything of it at first and just assumed that Renee was working in her bedroom. He decided to change out of his suit and into some casual clothes before seeking her out. Wearing jeans and a white cotton button-down shirt,

Trent stood in front of his guest bedroom for several seconds, rehearsing exactly how he would start the conversation. He felt like an inexperienced teenager, and that was comical.

Finally, he knocked on her door. There was no answer after a few seconds, so he knocked again. Still no answer. It was only three-fifteen, so Trent was pretty certain Renee wasn't asleep. He listened intently for a few seconds, and the still quietness told him the room was empty. Trent slowly opened the door to confirm. Everything looked neat and tidy. The only sign of Renee's presence was her knapsack sitting behind the door.

Trent was not sure whether to be relieved or worried. With her bag still here, Renee clearly had not left permanently without telling him. There wasn't a sign of forcible entry into the house or any kind of struggle, so perhaps she had just run to the store or gone out for an errand. He did give her a spare key for just that reason, he reminded himself. The question now was where had she gone and how long had she been gone.

He closed her bedroom door and headed back downstairs. He busied himself checking the kitchen cupboards and creating a mental shopping list, but fifteen minutes later, he was ready to call Renee's cell phone. Trent was dialing the numbers when he heard the door open on the ground floor. Renee came up the stairs a few moments later, then stopped on the landing. She was clearly surprised to see him there in the middle of the afternoon.

"Hi," she stated tentatively.

"Hey," he replied. "Is everything okay?"

"Yeah, everything is fine. I just went out to pick up a few things," Renee replied, and lifted up the two small shopping bags in her hands to show him.

"Good. I'm glad you're getting settled in," he replied. "Actually, that's why I came home early. I need to pick up some groceries, and I was thinking that you probably need some more clothes and stuff. We can go for a ride and do some shopping."

"Oh," replied Renee. "Ah . . . thanks, but I need to get some work done. . . ."

"I promise I won't keep you out too late. We can both catch up later this evening," coaxed Trent. "I'm sure you can do with some sushi, and I know of a great little place."

She smiled a little. "Okay, but I'll have to do some work later, then," she agreed.

"Yes, ma'am. We'll be home no later than eight o'clock."

They left the house a few minutes later.

"How are things going with your insurance company?" he asked while they were driving.

"Okay, I guess. I sent them a copy of the police report, and I should know more by Friday. All of the damage and replacement costs should be covered. But we'll see."

"That's good."

They drove in silence for a few more minutes.

"Listen, I have two tickets to a function coming up in a couple of weeks," Trent stated. "Will you go with me?"

Renee looked over at him with a mix of confusion and surprise.

"It's a charity thing, really. A spring ball that is sponsored by my firm. I bought the tickets a few weeks ago, and I'm sort of obligated to go. I meant to ask you last weekend, but things didn't really go as planned."

She was now looking out the window again.

"Well, thanks for the invite, but I don't really have anything to wear, so—"

"That's not a problem," he quickly interjected. "In fact, I know just the place where you can get what you need."

"No, really, Trent. Thanks, but I'm not in the mood for a big party," Renee insisted.

"Well, let's do some shopping and maybe you'll change your mind."

She didn't respond right away, so Trent took her silence as agreement and continued his drive on the highway toward the downtown area of Stamford, about five miles away from his house. Nathan's wife, Ophelia Frost, owned an exclusive woman's boutique that carried very beautiful formal wear and accessories. When Trent had spoken to Ophelia earlier, they had arranged for Renee to go into the store and pick out the perfect dress for the ball, on his tab.

As planned, Trent parked near Ophelia's store and dropped Renee off with a quick introduction to Nathan's wife. The two women seemed to be friendly from the beginning, and Ophelia kicked him out of the store after a few minutes, assuring him that Renee was in very good hands.

Trent used the next hour or so to do his grocery shopping a couple of blocks away and to stock up on a few household supplies. He also stopped into a men's store nearby to pick up a new shirt and tie for Saturday to go with his basic black tuxedo.

When he returned to the boutique, the two women were sitting in a couple of waiting chairs, chatting away like old friends. Trent was pleased to see a garment bag draped over Renee's legs and another small sack resting by her feet. She looked up at him with a shy smile that also seemed a little guilty. He grinned back.

There was a short but heated debate about the bill. Renee was adamant that she would pay for her own clothes, but Trent and Ophelia just ignored her. They all exchanged warm good-byes, but Renee still looked pretty annoyed as Trent ushered her from the store. She remained sullen as they drove back to Greenwich for their sushi dinner.

Trent, on the other hand, was feeling pretty good. He was practically grinning from ear to ear and made no attempt to hide it. Up until that afternoon, the Children in the Arts Spring Gala was something he had been dreading. Goldwell Group was a major sponsor for the annual event, and Trent was expected to be there. He originally planned to go alone, like he had done for the past two years, but Brianna had invited herself along quite insistently, and there didn't seem to be any reason to object. But now, with Renee at his side, he was certain he would have a good time.

The only thing left to do was break up with Brianna

and uninvite her from the party. It was going to be an unpleasant discussion, but Trent knew he had to do it as soon as possible and would be relieved when it was over.

Brianna had called him from France on Tuesday afternoon to let him know she and her mom were flying back to Connecticut the next morning. Trent anticipated that she would call him from home later in the evening. His plan was to invite her to lunch on Thursday and break the news at that time.

Once in Greenwich, they stopped at a small Japanese restaurant. Their conversation was a little awkward and stilted, filled with small talk about Greenwich and Stamford. Neither mentioned the unresolved issues between them.

As promised, Trent had Renee back at his place well before eight o'clock that evening. She immediately excused herself and went upstairs to get some work done. He stayed in the living room to do the same thing while watching television. As he had expected, the home phone rang about an hour later, and it was Brianna.

"Hey, baby!" she stated brightly. "What are you doing?"

"Hey, Brianna, how was your flight?"

"Oh, just exhausting! It's so good to be home. Daddy picked us up at the airport and took us to dinner at the Hyatt. We just got home a few minutes ago."

"Well, now you can relax and get settled in," he told her sympathetically.

"I was actually thinking you might want some company tonight."

Trent was caught off guard. Her suggestion wasn't surprising since she had come over for late-evening visits several times in the past.

"You should probably stay home and get some rest. I have a lot of work to do anyway. Why don't we meet for lunch tomorrow?" he suggested gently. "I'll call you in the morning."

"All right," replied Brianna with a long sigh. "I can't wait to see you."

Trent closed his eyes and pinched the bridge of his nose. He felt a pang of guilt about the situation.

"We'll talk tomorrow," he told her.

They hung up soon after, and Trent spent a few minutes reflecting on the time he had spent with Brianna. She was a nice girl and he didn't want to hurt her, but he was surer than ever that there wasn't anything there worth pursuing long-term. Now that she was back in town, Trent was anxious to resolve things between them, then move forward from there.

Eventually, he went back to reviewing the financial reports he had brought home. At eleven-thirty, he packed his work away and headed up to bed, intending to watch the rest of the nightly news upstairs. Trent was walking down the hall upstairs, on his way to his room, when Renee stepped out of the main bathroom just as he was passing the door. They both stopped in surprise and to prevent a collision.

She was wearing a white cotton camisole and matching long pajama pants. Her face was freshly scrubbed and her skin smelled like softly scented lotion. Trent could not stop staring down at her.

"Sorry," he finally stated, stepping back to give her space to move.

"No, that's okay," she whispered.

He cleared his throat self-consciously. "I'm, ahh . . . I'm heading to bed now," he stated, sounding lame even to his own ears.

Renee nodded while avoiding his gaze. "Yeah, me too."

"Do you want anything? A glass of water or something?"

"No, I'm good, thanks."

Trent nodded, but his eyes were still fixed steadily on hers. "Okay. Well, good night, then," he stated.

"Good night."

He turned to walk away, but stopped as he felt her touch his arm.

"Wait, Trent," she stated breathlessly.

He swung back toward her, ending up so close that their shoulders were brushing.

"Yeah?"

"I just wanted to thank you for everything. I really appreciate your help and your offer to let me stay here for a little while."

"Renee, you don't have to thank me," he replied solemnly. "I promised you that I would keep you safe, and it's the most important thing to me right now."

"Well, I appreciate it. And I still insist that you allow me to pay you back for the clothes."

Trent took her by the shoulders, pulling her even closer to him. She sucked in a sudden breath in surprise.

"Renee, I don't give a damn about the clothes,

okay? All I wish is that none of this had ever happened and that I had met you under normal circumstances. Then we would be together instead of you hating and distrusting me."

"I don't hate you, Trent."

"I wouldn't blame you if you did," he replied remorsefully. "What I did was horrible, and I regret it with every bone in my body. And I know that it has probably ruined my chances with you, Renee. But I'm asking anyway. I'm asking you to give me a chance, and I'll wait as long as you need to make a decision."

Chapter 23

Renee was completely unprepared for that moment.

Since Saturday night, she had allowed her anger and heartache to take over, creating a wall to protect her from her feelings for Trent. Though she had no choice but to stay at his place, Renee thought that as long as she kept to herself and minimized their contact, she could get through it without too much pain. Once her life went back to normal, she would eventually get over him and be able to move on.

Except now, with Trent's hands holding her tight, she felt the same intense attraction that had been there from the beginning. He looked down at her with such heat and intensity that she felt singed. It was stupid to deny it, and it felt so easy to give in to what she wanted, what her body still craved.

Renee leaned forward and closed her eyes. She felt Trent's brief hesitation, as though he was afraid to believe what his eyes were telling him. Then he groaned and his lips found hers in a deep, soul-searching kiss. After days of tension and awkward silence, neither of them had the ability to hold back or hide their desire.

Within seconds, kissing turned into licking and sucking. Gentle touches turned to teasing and stroking. The passion between them was explosive and got hotter and hotter until soon they were peeling off each other's clothes right there in the hallway. When they were down to their underwear, Trent took Renee's hand and led her into his bedroom. He stopped by the bed and took out protection from the top drawer of his side table. Trent then backed her against the nearest wall before lifting her up and wrapping her legs around his hips.

"Oh, God, Renee. This thing between us is so good," he whispered into the sensitive spot behind her ear. "We're so good."

"Uh-huh," she mumbled in agreement, barely able to string coherent words together.

He gripped her under her bottom to brush his thick arousal against her sweet spot. They both moaned with frustration and heightened stimulation.

"Tell me if I'm going too fast, okay?" he demanded softly.

Renee shook her head while trying to keep breathing. "No, it's fine. . . . It's good . . . perfect."

"Yeah?"

Trent stroked along her mound with the rigid tip of his penis. She was dripping wet. Renee arched her back against the wall, grateful for its support.

"Yes!" she panted.

With a little adjustment, his penis sprung free. He kissed Renee gently on the forehead, then sweetly on the lips as he slipped on protection. With gentle fingers, he brushed aside the thin fabric of her panties and entered her hot passage with one sure stroke. The intensity of their connection left them both still and breathless.

"Hold on to me," he instructed.

She followed his direction and allowed him to take control of the moment. Gently and with complete control, Trent started them on an incredibly passionate ride. Stroke after stroke brought Renee closer to absolute fulfillment until she was hanging off the edge, begging for completion. He was right there with her and pulled her in his full embrace as he finally shuddered in climax. His intense pulsation deep inside her core was the catalyst for her own uncontrollable orgasm.

When it was over, they were both sweating and breathing heavily. Trent still held her tight in his arms, using the wall for support. Renee's legs were still wrapped around him, though they hung limply from the knee with exhaustion.

"Hmm," he mumbled, nuzzling her ear. "Maybe we should head to bed now."

Renee giggled weakly while pressing her face into his neck.

He untangled her legs and swept her up into his arms with one across her back and the other under her knees. When he reached the bed, he lay her down in it, and together they climbed under the sheet. He pulled her close to his chest and they promptly fell asleep.

When Renee woke up alone on Thursday, she had a happy smile on her face and her mood was equally bright. It got even better when she checked her cell phone and found a text message from Trent, stating he was thinking about her and wishing her a good day. The warm-fuzzy feeling lasted all day.

Work was productive. She had temporary solutions for the progress on the Gibson and Armstrong projects, so there might not be any delays to her deadlines. Renee also had a very supportive discussion with Amanda, who was now back from her lengthy vacation. But the best news was a phone call from her insurance appraiser confirming the replacement value of her damaged items.

Renee also told Jennifer about the break-in. Jennifer lived in a small apartment building in the East Village and let Renee know that one of the units was now empty. The landlord was hoping to have a new tenant in there by the first of May, and Jennifer promised to put in a good word for her. Renee hadn't decided what to do with her current apartment. Her lease was month to month but required thirty days notice to leave. She was still quite worried about the idea of moving back in to live there alone, even after the police closed their investigation. And God knew when that would be. It'd been almost a week and there hadn't been much movement yet.

Renee promised Jennifer she would think about moving and let her know soon.

When Trent got home that evening, they shared a nice meal and Renee told him about the insurance claim and the opportunity for a new apartment. He listened but seemed distracted. She asked him if everything was okay, but he brushed aside her concerns with a bright smile, so she let it go. They watched television together, then went upstairs to his room and made love again.

Friday went by pretty much in the same way, and Renee was starting to think that working from Connecticut for a couple of weeks may not be that bad. The Gibson project was still going through the construction phase, and Cree Armstrong's condo redesign might be the only project really impacted. With Cree in California, anyway, many of the decisions were being made by e-mail and phone. Renee also recruited Freddie and Albert to help with sourcing finishes and fabrics, since it was very likely that they would also custom make many of the furniture pieces.

She was still working away when Trent called her from the office at around four-thirty.

"How's your day?" he asked.

"It's going well," she replied. "I'm working on replacing the damaged things in the apartment. The insurance company confirmed they will send the money as soon as I provide the receipts."

"That's great news!" stated Trent.

"I know. I was pretty stressed out about the whole thing."

"Well, I know it doesn't feel this way now, but soon this whole ordeal will be behind you."

Renee wondered exactly how long that would be, but kept the thought to herself.

"How was your day?" she asked instead.

"It was good already. But better now that I'm talking to you."

She smiled shyly.

"I'm almost done here, so I should be home by five o'clock," Trent continued. "I was thinking that I would pick you up and we'd go out for dinner."

"Hmm, that sounds good."

"Great. So I'll see you in a few minutes."

Trent stopped at home for a few minutes to change out of his suit and into jeans and a sweater. He then took her to a casual steak house not far from his office.

"Can I ask you something?" Renee requested seriously.

They were in the middle of eating their meal.

"Sure," he replied with a shrug.

"What's up with your cousin?"

"Nathan? What do you mean?"

"Well, it was a little awkward for me on Wednesday with Ophelia once I realized who she was. She was really nice, Trent. But the only reason you and I even met was because your cousin was cheating on her. I felt guilty just knowing about it."

Trent put down his fork and sat back. She could tell that he was uncomfortable with the topic.

"I can understand that," he stated. "To be honest, it makes me pretty uncomfortable too."

"So, what's going on there? I mean, she's beautiful and seems pretty easy to get along with. Why did he do it?"

"Honestly, I don't understand it, either, Renee. I won't say I was shocked when Nathan told me he had an affair, but I was disappointed. He has a pretty good life with Ophelia from what I can see, and I don't understand why he would put all of it in jeopardy."

"Did you ask him about it? Did he say why he did it? Or is he just one of those guys who cheat because they can?"

Trent was shaking his head. "I've asked him a little, but he's not exactly forthcoming about his motives. Plus, he thinks that since I'm not married, I can't possibly understand what he's going through."

Renee thought about Trent's words for a couple of minutes. "Does he still love her?"

"You mean Ophelia?" he asked, and Renee nodded. "I think so. They've been married for four years, but he probably got married too young. I guess it's not that black and white, right?"

"Was he in love with the other woman? The one who used my name?"

"No, I don't think so. Nathan said they were just casual friends, and he was honest with her about his marriage from the beginning. I have to assume that's true."

Renee felt sad for both the women involved, assuming the other woman was Angela. She wished her friend wanted more out of life than just to have random, fleeting fun.

"Have you ever cheated in a relationship?" she finally asked.

He looked at her steadily, but his face did not show any expression.

"I've tried not to," he told her. "I know I would never even think about it if I was married."

"You've tried not to? What does that mean?" She laughed a little, trying to lighten the mood a bit.

Trent leaned forward and seemed to relax a bit.

"It means that I've never cheated while in a committed relationship. But I have dated more than one woman at a time. It's possible that any one of those women might feel as though I cheated."

"Trent, that sounds a little like a Bill Clinton speech."

He smiled at that one.

"If you were sleeping with both women at the same time without them knowing, I guarantee they would feel cheated on," Renee added. "Wouldn't you? I don't think it's a female feeling."

"You're right, I probably would. And just to be clear, I would never intentionally hurt someone I care about by casually sleeping around. But sometimes it's just bad timing."

"Have you ever been cheated on?" she asked.

"Not that I'm aware of," he replied immediately. "Okay, now it's my turn to ask some questions. Have you ever cheated?"

"Never. But I have been cheated on."

Trent nodded as though hearing more than what she was saying.

"What?" she demanded.

"Nothing."

"You think I'm sensitive to Ophelia's situation because of that? That I'm judging Nathan and every man because of what happened to me?"

"I didn't say anything!" Trent replied defensively.

"Oh, please! It's written all over your face."

He burst out laughing. "Honestly, I wasn't thinking anything, Renee. But now I do think you're a little sensitive."

She rolled her eyes but could not help but see the humor in her reaction.

"Anyway," she continued, dragging out the word with sarcasm. "It was my first real boyfriend and we just grew apart. There were lots of reasons why we weren't going to last. His cheating was just the end result of all those things. It made it easier for me to break up with him. Of course, I didn't know all this at the time, but I see it now."

Trent nodded with understanding. "Well, just so we are clear, Renee, I would never cheat on you. It's not something that you have to worry about."

She smiled shyly, feeling a little overwhelmed by the intensity of his gaze.

"I wasn't worried," she replied.

Chapter 24

The conversation with Renee on Friday evening weighed on Trent's mind over the weekend. His responses to her questions were completely honest and sincere, but he still felt guilty over how things went down with Brianna in the end.

As planned, he had taken Brianna out to lunch on Thursday to officially end their relationship. They met at her favorite French restaurant on Greenwich Avenue. He was already at their table when she arrived, and stood up as the maitre d' escorted her into the room. She looked stunning as usual, wearing tight jeans tucked into knee-high boots with stiletto heels and a rich white leather jacket. Her long jet-black hair was perfectly curled to frame her face.

"Hi, babe," she stated with a warm, coy smile.

They hugged and Brianna brushed her lips against the side of his mouth. Her sweet perfume surrounded him in a familiar cloud.

"Hi, Brianna," he replied with a casual smile.

They sat down and placed their orders.

"I can't believe I've been gone for over a month. It went by so fast, even though I missed you so much. But France was just perfect. Mommy and I are already planning our trip back. And this time, I'm bringing an empty suitcase. I did so much shopping!" she stated with a girlish laugh.

Trent smiled back. Her bright personality was infectious and reminded him of why they had had so much fun together in the beginning. He listened quietly as she continued to tell him about the trip. Eventually, Brianna landed on the topic of the Spring Gala, which was over two weeks away.

"I'll probably just stay over from Friday evening. Hopefully it will be a little warmer by then. I've planned to wear only a light wrap. I guess I could use one of my pashminas if I had to."

He took a deep breath and used the opportunity to get to the point. "Listen, Brianna. I really wanted to meet with you today to talk." His tone, though gentle, had a serious edge.

She paused with her fork in midair. "Why, what's up? You did get the tickets to the ball, right? I asked you weeks ago and you said you would. I—"

"It's not about the ball, Brianna. Well, it is in a way, but not about the tickets. I don't think it's a good idea for us to go together."

"Why? I don't understand."

"I've been doing a lot of thinking over the last few weeks, and it made me realize that we had a good time together, but I don't think we can be anything more than good friends."

He watched her face display an array of emotions

in quick succession, from confusion to disbelief to shock.

"What are you talking about, Trent? We've been a lot more than friends, for God's sake."

"I know. And I have enjoyed getting to know you better in all ways. But I don't see it going beyond where we are now."

"So what are you saying? You don't want to be with me anymore? What happened?" she demanded, blinking rapidly.

Her volume had gone up a couple of levels, and the couple at the table beside them glanced over in curious surprise.

Trent leaned closer to her and replied in a soft voice filled with empathy, "Nothing happened, Brianna. I really like you and care about you. But I just realized that my feelings haven't developed beyond that. I wish they had. You're a beautiful and sexy woman. But that's not enough. I need to feel more than that."

"And you don't feel that for me?"

"I'm sorry, Brianna. I really did not mean to hurt you."

"So you're saying that everything is fine between us now, but it can't grow beyond that?"

"Yes, that's what I'm saying."

"Okay, then. Let's continue the way we are. Why do we have to make a decision now? I mean, maybe you just need more time. . . ."

He was shaking his head.

"But why? What's the rush, Trent? Tell me what I did to make you not want me anymore."

Her voice quivered slightly, and Trent felt like the biggest jerk in the world. She didn't deserve this, but he just could not continue seeing her knowing they had no future. Particularly since he now saw that future with Renee.

"You didn't do anything, Brianna," he repeated. "This is not about you, I promise."

"How can it not be about me?" she asked with a bitter smile. "I'm the one being dumped."

"It's not like that. I'm not dumping you. I'm just saying that I think this thing between us has gone as far as it can, and it would be unfair to you for me to continue our relationship knowing that."

Brianna stared down at her plate for a long pause. Finally, she tossed her head and looked up at him with defiance.

"Are you breaking up with me because of another woman?" she asked quietly.

Trent let out a long breath. He had broken up with enough women to know this question might come up. As he told Renee, the situation he was in now was all about timing. Trent knew without a doubt that he was not breaking up with Brianna because of Renee. He had known almost from the start that Brianna was not the right woman for him long-term. Though their time together was good and enjoyable, he would have broken up with her eventually anyway.

"No," he stated very strongly.

Brianna straightened her spine and put a pleasant smile on her face.

"Well, I can see how going to the ball together doesn't make much sense, right?"

He reached out and covered one of her hands with one of his in comfort.

"I'm sorry, Brianna," he stated solemnly.

She smiled brighter and started to pull on her jacket and gather her things. Their waiter arrived at that point to pick up their dishes, and Brianna was standing by the time their table was clear. Trent also stood and pulled her into a hug.

"Bye, Trent," she whispered.

"Good-bye, Brianna."

For the rest of the day, Trent revisited the conversation several times, wondering if he had approached the situation the right way. While he had a huge sense of relief, he also felt sad that he had caused Brianna pain.

But now, on Sunday morning as walked into his bathroom and took in the image of Renee in his shower with warm water running down her body, it was easy to put Brianna out of his mind.

"Do you mind if I join you?" he stated over the sound of the water spray.

Renee looked over her shoulder with a smile, then nudged open the glass door with her hip. Trent stripped off his boxer shorts and stepped into the spacious shower with her. She had her back against the shower head to get all wet before soaping up, and he immediately started to help by scooping up handfuls of warm water and pouring them over the front of her body.

"I thought you needed some help," he explained with a smile.

"Hmm, thanks," she told him with a giggle.

Trent gently moved Renee so their positions were switched, and he stood with his back under the water spray with her back to him. He then picked up the bottle of her scented bath gel and squeezed a sizable dollop into his palm. They smiled at each other as he began to lather her up in slow circles. He started with her shoulders and worked his way over her arms, then down her back. She closed her eyes and let out a light sigh.

The room soon filled with steam and the soft scent of her soap. Trent's intention had been to help Renee with her shower and allow her to relax. But the sight of her all wet and soapy seemed straight out of Trent's fantasies. Her chocolaty skin was so smooth and slippery that his focus quickly changed from cleaning to caressing. He tried not to give in to his mounting desires, but the dark peaks of her breasts were unavoidable from his view, puckered, quivering, and begging for the heat of his touch.

Still, Trent tried his hardest to stay focused, brushing soap down the sides of her waist, then up her stomach to the top of her rib cage. His touch hovered there as his thumb teased the underside of her breasts. Renee looked over her shoulder, her hot gaze seeking his, telling him of her desires. He filled his hands with her firm, round globes, squeezing them gently to enjoy the fullness.

"You feel so good, Renee," he whispered into her hair.

She reached back and ran one of her hands up the side of his leg until she reached the curve of his glutes. Trent pulled her up against him until their bodies were firmly pressed together. All pretext of showering was gone.

He pressed kisses against her temple and down the side of her neck. His fingers lavished her swollen breasts with attention, tweaking at the sensitive nipples until Renee started to moan softly. She arched her back, teasing the rise of his erection with the valley between her buttocks. Trent sank his teeth into the curve of her shoulder, then circled her tender spot with his tongue.

"Oh. Oh, Trent," she stammered.

One of her hands roamed over his leg and hip feverishly; the other was buried in his hair. She bent her head back and pulled him down so they could kiss. It was open, wet, and sloppy with fervor. Trent slid a hand down her stomach and cupped the mound between her legs. Renee squirmed under his touch. He slipped his middle finger along her hot crevice, now slippery with desire.

"God, I want you, Renee. I need you so much right now," he gasped.

Trent released her long enough to turn off the water and open the shower door. He took her hand and helped her out of the stall, then grabbed one of the towels to dry them off. When they were dry, Trent tossed the towel aside and pulled her back into his arms. The passion and urgency were back within seconds.

Renee took his face into her hands and pressed her lips against his with slow deliberation. She sucked on his lips and ran her tongue along their edges. It was unbearably erotic. Trent felt the beat of his heart through his chest as he waited in anticipation for her next move. While she continued to kiss him with maddening slowness, her hands slid down his chest, down his abdomen, and wrapped around his rigid penis. She stroked her fingers over his full length, teasing the silky tip with the center of her palm.

Trent's moan was deep and vibrating.

With one smooth movement, he picked her up by the waist and carried her to the sink counter, setting her on top with legs parted wide. His mouth fell on hers with hungry intensity, and Trent buried himself into her hot wetness with one deep stroke. They both froze, savoring the feeling of perfect oneness. Their eyes met and neither could look away. Trent withdrew almost completely, then filled her once again, then again and again.

They both came together with their shouts of ecstasy echoing around the tiled walls. Trent held her close in the exhausted aftermath. Everything about Renee was infused in his soul—her smell, her taste, the softness of her skin, and the hot sheath that still cradled him tightly.

There was no doubt in his mind that Renee Goodchild was the woman he had been waiting for, and he had every intention of keeping her.

Chapter 25

By Sunday, Renee still had not received any response to her e-mail or voice mail message to Angela. She was getting worried about her. If Trent was right, someone was very angry with Angela, and God knew what they would do if they found her. She was now seriously questioning if she had made the right decision not to tell Trent and the police everything she knew.

Renee decided to call the police if she didn't hear from Angela by Tuesday. Thankfully, the call came on Monday afternoon.

"Hey, Renee, I got your e-mail. Are you okay?" Angela asked in a voice that was loud and high with concern.

"Oh, Jesus, Angela. I was getting so worried about you. I'm okay, but it's bad. Someone broke into the apartment last Saturday and destroyed everything. My laptop was smashed, and they even tore up my couch."

"Oh, my God!" She gasped. "Thank goodness you weren't home, Renee."

"Angela, what the hell is going on? What are you involved in? And don't even bother to deny it. I know that you've been pretending to be me."

There was silence on the other end of the phone.

"Angela, are you still there?"

"I'm here. Renee, I swear to God it was harmless," she confessed. "When I first got to New York, I met some new people. They all had such glamorous jobs. Next thing I knew, I was using your name and telling everyone I was an interior designer. One thing led to another and . . . Anyway, it doesn't matter. I swear to you, I never meant for anything bad to happen to you. Oh, my God. I'm so sorry."

Angela's voice shook with shame and distress. Renee ran a hand over her forehead. She was overwhelmed with conflicting emotions. On one hand, she was angry and shocked that Angela would violate her trust that way and bring this mess to her door. On the other hand, she could hear the remorse in Angela's voice.

"Angela, I'm really scared for you, for both of us. Who came after you, and what do they want?"

"I can't get into it right now, and we shouldn't talk over the phone. Can you meet me somewhere? I'll explain everything, I promise. Everything is going to work out okay."

"I'm in Connecticut right now, but maybe I can come into the city tomorrow. Where are you?" Renee asked.

"I'm still in Brooklyn."

"Can you meet me in the Bronx? At around noon? I'll take the train in."

"I can't tomorrow, but how about Wednesday?" suggested Angela.

They agreed to meet on Wednesday at a coffee shop a couple of blocks away from the rail station.

Somehow, Renee managed to act completely normal around Trent for the next couple of days. They had developed a domestic routine where they spoke once during the day, then spent the evenings cooking together and relaxing on the couch the remainder of the evening. She now slept in his room every night, wrapped in his arms. Things between them felt perfect, and Renee was not about to jeopardize that as she tried to resolve the drama with Angela.

On Wednesday morning, after Trent left for work, Renee spent a couple of hours working on Cree Armstrong's project before getting ready to meet with Angela. She walked out to the rail station a few blocks from Trent's house and caught the train into New York. When she got to the coffee shop, Angela wasn't there yet. Renee ordered a hot chocolate and a muffin, then sat down to wait. Someone had left a popular tabloid magazine, the *Weekly Voice,* on the table beside her. She picked it up and casually flipped through it.

When Angela arrived, Renee was fully engrossed in a story about one of her favorite young actors back in the day. Chad Taylor had been one of the hottest and most successful teen actors until he went on a huge drug and alcohol binge about eight years ago. According to the *Voice,* Chad was a rising star again. He had just finished a long run on Broadway and was getting ready for the release of his first blockbuster movie later that spring. There were several pictures of him in the story, including one with his new fiancée, a gorgeous and successful supermodel.

"I read that article too," Angela stated as she sat down. "Remember when we used to race home after cheerleading practice to watch his TV show?"

Renee smiled at the memory. "I know," she replied. "It's hard to believe we were ever that young."

Angela let out a deep breath. The two women looked at each other, both trying to think of what to say.

"What's going on, Angela?" Renee finally asked. "Why would you get yourself mixed up with extortion?"

"Extortion?" Angela repeated, feigning surprise and confusion. "What are you talking about?"

"Ang, I agreed to meet with you because you promised to explain everything to me. Don't start with a lie, okay?"

Angela looked at her steadily, and Renee could tell she was still trying to decide how much truth to reveal.

"Does the name Nathan ring a bell?" asked Renee, and Angela's eyes widened. "Well, I had the pleasure of meeting Nathan's cousin, who is a former Jamaican police officer. Imagine my surprise when he revealed that I was demanding thousands of dollars from his cousin and if I didn't get that money, I would tell his wife about our affair."

Angela let out a deep breath but had the decency to look away. "Honestly, Renee, I wasn't serious. I was just toying with the man. I knew he didn't have any real money, but he liked to act so big and rich that I wanted to teach him a lesson. That's all, I swear! I haven't even called him back about the money."

"Well, great! I'm glad it was an empty threat. Except you've still left me with a very nice reputation on the street," Renee replied with heavy sarcasm.

"Look, I'm sorry, okay? I'll do whatever you want. I'll tell Nathan the truth, okay? Then you'll be in the clear."

"Well, that's perfect, except Nathan wasn't the one who destroyed my apartment. So why don't you tell me what I don't know already. And don't lie to me anymore. I haven't told the police anything about you or what I know so far. But I promise you I will if I don't get answers, Angela."

Angela sucked her teeth hard, clearly not happy with being threatened, but Renee maintained a serious, focused stare on her childhood friend.

"All right, all right," Angela finally stated under her breath. "I met a guy a few weeks ago, and now I have something of his. He wants it back, that's all."

Renee continued to look at her hard. "What does that mean, exactly? What do you have? How did you get it? Did you steal something?" she asked pointedly.

"It's not like that, Renee. I'm not a thief! It's just something I stumbled across, okay? Something valuable."

"How valuable?"

"Let's just put it this way: I'm anticipating a decent reward."

Renee could not believe her ears. Angela sounded so cavalier, almost amused, by this whole thing, yet everything that Renee owned had been viciously destroyed, and she was now hiding out in another state.

"Are you crazy? Don't you get it? While you're waiting for your reward, this guy came looking for you to get his property back," she stated forcefully, finding it difficult to keep her voice down. "Did you tell him where you had been staying? You should see what he did to my stuff!"

"I barely know the guy, Renee, I swear. He's just a producer for some play that I met at a party. I really can't believe he would try to track me down like that."

Renee felt the red-hot flare of anger and frustration creeping up her spine and flooding her body.

"You used my name to do this, didn't you? That's why he broke into my apartment. You stupid, selfish bitch," she spit out. "You don't care about anybody but yourself, do you? Of course not. As long as you make some quick money, who cares who you hurt?" Renee stood up. She didn't want to hear anymore and absolutely did not want to be involved in this mess.

Angela stood up, too, and reached out a hand to stop her. "Wait, Renee. Please, it's not like that!" she stammered. "Please. I don't want the money for myself. It's my mom, Renee. Please listen to me."

Renee looked back at her.

"Her lupus has gotten really bad in the last couple of years," whispered Angela. "She can't work anymore, and there's no money for the medication that could help her. I just thought, if I can get a chunk of cash to help her out, she could get some treatment. I . . . It seemed so harmless at first. This guy has money. He will barely miss a few dollars, and I'll give him his stuff."

"Angela, we have to go to the police. He's obviously dangerous."

"No, please. Just give me a couple of days. I have everything worked out. I'm going to meet him this week."

"I don't know. I think that's dangerous, Angela. Just give the cops what you found and let them take care of it from here."

"Please, it's the only chance I have, Renee. Just give me two weeks, okay?"

"What about me, Angela? My name is still going to be linked to this. I'll never feel safe again!"

"I'll tell him the truth, that I stole your identity. He only wants what I have. Then I'll leave New York and the whole thing will be all over. I promise."

"It's too dangerous, Angela."

"Please, Renee. I need this to help my mom."

Renee let out a deep breath. "Fine. You have two weeks. Otherwise, I'm telling the police everything I know."

She left Angela and the coffee shop and headed back to the subway. Instead of taking the train headed toward Connecticut, Renee went farther south into the Bronx. It seemed like the perfect opportunity to stop into Henry Interiors to check on the progress of the custom furniture she had ordered.

She was still completely blown away by everything that Angela had told her. It was hard to believe that two women who had come from the same place could go in such different directions. At nine years old, they were like twins, not only in looks but also in thoughts and ideas. But their personalities had always been polar opposites, with Renee quiet and shy and Angela loud and outgoing, but those differences balanced each other out within their friendship and made them both stronger. But somewhere along the line, it also tore them apart.

Now, Renee could only see a glimpse of that street-wise, independent girl who Angela had once been and who Renee had always secretly envied. The injustices of life had taken her down a path that was bound to lead to disaster, and Renee felt powerless to prevent it.

When she arrived at Henry Interiors about thirty minutes later, Frederic and Albert were standing in the middle of the showroom having a very loud argument.

"Hey, what's going on?" she asked, walking toward them.

They stopped yelling to look over at her, but their eyes still shot fire. Freddie was the first to lower his shoulders and walk toward her. He hugged her with a tight squeeze. Albert finally seemed to calm down a little and welcomed her also.

"What are you doing here?" Albert asked. His disapproval was etched into his face.

"I was meeting a friend in the Bronx, so I figured I might as well stop in while I'm here. I want to see how things are coming along."

The men looked at each other.

"Renee, I thought the police told you to stay out of New York until they solved your break-in?" Albert continued.

"Well, that's not exactly what they said. It's not like there is a Mafia hit on my head," she replied. "They just suggested that I stay with a friend for a few weeks."

"In Connecticut," added Frederic sarcastically.

"Renee, someone may be looking for you. It's not safe until the police figure out who it is."

"Okay, let's not blow this out of proportion, guys. No one is out to get me," Renee told them. "I'm not sure if I'll ever live in my apartment again, but I'm not going to hide out either. No one would look for me in the Bronx anyway. And if they did, I'm sure you both will protect me."

The men looked at each other again, and it was clear they were in agreement for once.

"I'm here already, so there's no point in arguing about it now, right?" she continued. "Come on! Let's go look at how the furniture is coming along. And I need to replace some furniture of my own, so I'm thinking you guys can help me with that."

Renee shot them a bright smile. She looped her arms through both of theirs and started walking toward the warehouse. After a little tugging, they finally started walking.

"So, what was all the arguing about?" she asked.

"My idiot brother wants to bring in a cheap line of fiberboard crap," Albert stated in a disgusted voice. "Can you believe that? I'm trying to explain to him that we have a brand to protect, that our customers expect a certain amount of quality. That's what makes us different from every other retailer."

"Al, why can't you ever listen to someone else's opinion?" protested Frederic.

"I'll listen if it makes sense!"

"You mean you'll listen if you agree with it!" his brother shot back.

"Forget it, Freddie. It's not going to happen. I'm not bringing that cheap crap into my store."

"*Your* store? It's mine too. I have some say in this, and I'm tired of you acting like I'm just one of your employees!"

"Why do you want to bring in this line, Freddie?" Renee asked before Albert could shoot back another hotheaded comment.

Freddie took in a deep breath.

"I'm not saying that I do. I saw a few of the pieces at an industry show last week and they looked very cool. I'm just asking Al to look at them, see their construction. But he's so stubborn, he won't even do that."

"Because it's crap," muttered Albert.

"See?" Freddie said to Renee, gesturing at his brother with a wave of his hand.

"Al, why not just look at it? What's the harm? You two are the best furniture designers I know, and I completely trust your judgment. You know I'm not a big fan of low-quality mass production, but there are some newly engineered products on the market that are pretty impressive. And there's a real market for them."

Albert looked at her with a hard face, but she could tell that he was thinking about it.

"I guess it can't hurt to have a look at them," he finally replied, but his tone said he was still dead set against the idea.

Renee and Freddie exchanged a secret smile of success, and he squeezed her arm to say thanks.

"Now that that's settled, show me how my orders are coming along," she demanded in a bright voice.

Chapter 26

Renee stayed at the store with Frederic and Albert much longer than she expected. They had eleven pieces of furniture in production for her, ranging from sofas and club chairs to various tables and storage units. The most exciting item was the headboard and bed frame for Trent's bedroom. It wasn't completely finished, but it looked exactly as they had designed. Renee could not wait to see it in his finished room.

She also spent some time working with Freddie picking out a new couch for herself, something soft and inviting but also functional and timeless. They selected the perfect design and a beautiful linen fabric in a creamy caramel color for the cover. Renee was so engrossed in the process that she didn't check the time until it was almost five-thirty.

As quickly as possible, Renee wrapped things up with the guys and they made plans to talk again by the end of the week. She did not get on the New Haven train line until after six o'clock. Her plan had been to be back in Greenwich before Trent got home, but that was now highly unlikely. Renee tried not to panic. She knew that he was not going to be happy with her trip into the city and had hoped to avoid the discussion completely. But at least she had the excuse of going to Henry Interiors to do some work and could be partially honest about the purpose of her trip.

As she anticipated, Trent was home before she was. He called her while she was still on the train.

"Will you be home soon?" he asked after his greeting. "I brought home some Chinese food."

Renee checked her watch. "That sounds good. I should be back in about thirty minutes."

"Okay. Did you want me to come pick you up?"

It was clear that Trent assumed she was somewhere in Greenwich, running an errand. She closed her eyes tight, trying to think of the best way to respond.

"No. I'm actually on the train."

There was a brief silence.

"What train? Where are you coming from?"

"I went to the Bronx to visit one of my suppliers."

"What?" Trent demanded in a raised voice. "You went back into New York? Renee, what were you thinking?"

"Trent, I just went into the Bronx to get some work done. I was nowhere near my building or even my office. It's not a big deal."

"Then why didn't you tell me you were going there today?"

"I didn't realize that I had to tell you everything I plan to do," she shot back defensively.

Renee didn't mean for the conversation to go in that direction, but his line of questioning got her back up.

"That's not what I meant, Renee. I'm just saying that if you had told me you needed to go into the city, I would have gone with you, that's all."

"Look, let's just talk about it when I get home."

She heard him let out a deep breath.

"Fine. What time does your train arrive? I'll pick you up."

Renee told him the scheduled arrival and they both hung up.

She was not looking forward to discussing the whole thing with Trent any further. How did she get in this awful situation? When did she become a person who told lies and half-truths to protect illegal behavior? Everything about it made her very uncomfortable and nervous.

As promised, Trent was parked near the front of the station. He stepped out of the car the minute he saw her and opened the passenger door. Neither of them said anything, but he pulled her into a tight hug before she sat down.

"I'm sorry about the way I reacted," he stated once they were driving back to the house. "I overreacted."

Renee looked over at him with wide, blinking eyes. That was not at all what she expected him to say.

"I was just surprised, that's all. The only thing I care about is making sure that you stay safe until this whole thing is resolved. But I didn't mean to make you feel like a prisoner or something."

"I'm sorry too. I shouldn't have gotten so defensive," she finally told him. "You were right. I didn't tell you I was going into the Bronx, because I knew you would try to talk me out of it."

"Well, you're home and you're safe. So let's just forget about it, okay?" suggested Trent. "If you need to go back into New York, just let me know and I'll take you, okay? For my sake?"

"Trent, we can't do this forever," Renee told him in a quiet voice. "I have to go back to my life and my job eventually. I mean, I've been able to get a lot done from your house, but it's just a short-term solution."

"Well, it's only until the police find out who broke into your place or rule it a random incident."

"But what if they don't find out anything? Am I supposed to hide out forever?"

He parked the car inside the garage, then turned to face her. "It's only been a week and a half," he replied in a soothing voice. "I know you're frustrated, but we'll just have to give the police some more time. Is staying with me really so bad?" He brushed the side of her face gently, then placed a soft kiss on her lips.

"No," Renee admitted with a smile. "It's not so bad."

"Because I kind of like your company. Even though you always steal the blanket halfway through the night."

"I do not!" she denied hotly, slapping his arm in protest.

"Yeah, you do," Trent insisted, laughing. "But that's okay. Having you next to me keeps me warm enough."

He kissed her again with sweet, gentle brushes. Renee felt like her heart was going to explode. This thing between them was growing like wildfire, and she wanted to step into the flames without reservation. The only thing keeping her at the edge was the ongoing drama with Angela. Once it was finally over, and Renee no longer needed to lie or hide facts to protect her friend, she could let herself fall in love. She only hoped their relationship would survive in the end.

"I spoke to Ophelia today," Trent told her later while they were cleaning up after dinner. "She's invited us up to her parents' place for the weekend. They live in an estate just outside of Stamford, and she and Nathan are up there a lot."

Renee looked at him with a deep frown.

"What?" he asked.

"Nothing."

"You're thinking about Nathan's cheating, aren't you?"

"I'm sorry, I'm not trying to be judgmental. It just seems wrong for me to take advantage of her family's hospitality knowing what I know."

"Renee, it's not your responsibility to address problems in their marriage. I love my cousin to death, and I want to knock him out for what he's done, but in the end, they are the ones who need to fix their problems."

"I know, you're right. I guess it's a woman thing."

"Well, maybe we'll bring out stuff for the whole weekend, but we can leave Saturday evening if you feel too uncomfortable," he suggested.

She agreed and Trent let her know on Thursday that it was all confirmed. The plan was that Ophelia was going up on Friday evening, and Nathan would ride up with Trent and Renee on Saturday morning.

As she packed her bag on Saturday morning, Renee started to think about Nathan Frost and everything Angela had admitted. After meeting Ophelia, Renee had to admit that she was secretly glad that Angela's threats put the fear of God into him. He deserved everything he got and more. But Renee wondered if it was enough to stop him from doing it again.

On the other hand, Nathan was Trent's first cousin, his family. If she and Trent had a future, Renee was going to have to spend time with him, even if she didn't approve of his behavior. For Trent's sake, it was important that they all got along, and she would do whatever she could to make that happen.

"Are you all set?" asked Trent when she came downstairs.

"Yup. I don't have much to choose from, so it was pretty easy to pack," she joked.

"We can do some shopping tomorrow. You should get some more clothes until you can get back to the apartment."

"Okay," she agreed.

Trent grabbed their bags and they were soon on the road to Stamford to pick up Nathan. When they arrived at the apartment building, Nathan was not ready yet. Trent commented on his cousin's chronic tardiness and decided to go upstairs to urge him along. Renee chose to wait in the car. The two men were back in about fifteen minutes. She stepped outside as they approached.

"Renee, this is my cousin, Nathan Frost," Trent stated.

"Hi, Nathan," Renee said as she extended her hand.

He took it with a soft shake. "Wow," he stated after looking her up and down for several uncomfortable seconds. "I feel like I know you really well already."

Nathan laughed at his own joke, but Renee didn't think it was funny, and from the look on Trent's face, he didn't either. Trent smacked his cousin on the back of the head.

"What? I was just trying to ease the tension," Nathan added, rubbing the bruised spot like a naughty child.

"Get in the car," commanded Trent.

They all took their seats, Renee in the front and Nathan in the back behind her; then Trent started the drive up into the outskirts of the city. The men did most of the talking, and Renee just listened politely. Her mind was preoccupied with her first impressions of Nathan Frost.

There was no denying that he was a very good-looking guy, though in a way that was completely opposite to Trent. Where Trent was tall and solidly built, Nathan was a little shorter than average and slender. Trent had a warm brown complexion a shade or two lighter than her own, and matching cocoa eyes, but Nathan was so light she wondered if he was mixed. His hair was light brown and wavy, and his eyes were somewhere between green and hazel. He would have had no problem catching Angela's eye. And judging from the exclusive building where he and his wife lived, he also had some money.

About twenty minutes later, they were at the northern end of Stamford, and the landscape become more rural. Trent turned off a major street onto a more narrow side road with two lanes. He then turned again a few yards later onto what looked like a winding road but was actually a long driveway. It cut through a dense forest of narrow trees that took them to two large iron gates. Trent entered a code into the keypad, and the gates swung open slowly. A couple of minutes later, the house became visible.

Renee's jaw went slack and she looked over at Trent with disbelief. It was a plantation-style mansion that sat on top of a hill, with a circular driveway in front and elaborate landscaping all around it. It looked like something out of the movies. Renee could not begin to guess at the square footage but imagined something north of ten thousand. She could not wait to see the inside.

"Amazing, isn't it?" Trent said to her once he had parked the car in front of the four-car garage.

Nathan had already gotten out of the car.

"It's unbelievable. Ophelia's parents must be incredibly wealthy," she replied, still looking over the property—what she could see out of the car windows.

"That's an understatement. Her father's family owns several large companies that have been around for over fifty years. This is just one of their houses."

"Wow," was all that she could say in response.

"Ready to go inside?" he asked.

She nodded.

Chapter 27

When Ophelia had extended the invitation to her family home for the weekend, Trent thought it would be a good opportunity for the two couples to spend some quality time together. He knew it was an awkward situation, particularly for Nathan, but having the four of them together in the same room had to happen sooner or later.

Before Trent told Renee about the weekend plans, he called Nathan to give him the heads-up. His cousin was not happy about the suggestion.

"I don't think it's a good idea," he told Trent bluntly. "It's bad enough that you're dating Renee. Now you want us to all hang out? Not cool."

"What's the big deal, Nate? Yeah, it's going to be a little weird for you, but you'll get over it. Renee has nothing to do with you and your crazy lover. She doesn't even know the woman."

"What's weird is that she knows I messed around a bit. Not to mention that she looks like the woman I was with. I don't need it right in my face, that's all."

Trent shook his head. Sometimes Nathan's total fixation on himself was mind-boggling.

"Well, I'm sorry your cheating made things uncomfortable for you. But you're just going to have to deal with it," Trent told him without sympathy. "Renee is not going away, so get used to it."

"Sure, we'll see," he shot back with a snarky laugh. "She'll last about as long as all the others."

"Nathan, you're being an ass," stated Trent bluntly. "You created this whole mess, remember? So I suggest you live with the result and be on your best behavior. I'll see you on the weekend."

Their call ended after that. Trent assumed that Nathan got the message and would behave himself even if he didn't like the situation. It was in his best interest not to make waves. But for some reason, Nate didn't see it that way.

A couple of hours into their weekend, Trent was ready to smack him in the face and knock some sense into him.

He and Renee entered the house a few minutes after Nathan. They took their time walking from the driveway as Trent pointed out the various features on the property, like the stables, tennis court, and infinity swimming pool. Ophelia was waiting in the front foyer when they arrived.

"Hi, Trent, Renee. I'm so glad you guys decided to come up," she stated with a bright smile.

They all hugged warmly. Nathan was nowhere to be seen.

"Ophelia, thank you for inviting us. Your parents' home is just beautiful," Renee told her.

"Thank you, Renee. I guess that's a pretty big compliment coming from you. Trent told me that you're a bit of an interior design celebrity."

"Trent exaggerates," replied Renee with a shy smile.

Ophelia giggled. "Do you guys want to put your stuff away? Trent, I'll put you guys in your regular room," she explained. "When you guys get back, I'll take you on a tour of the house."

"Sounds good," agreed Trent.

He had both their bags over his shoulder and led Renee upstairs to the room they would share. Like the rest of the house, it was decorated in a classic style with heavy, ornately carved wood furniture. The bed was a massive four-poster king with a luxurious duvet and layers of feather pillows. There was an equally lavish bathroom en suite with marble tiles and countertops.

"Wow," Renee said again as she looked around.

Trent laughed at her expression. "Over the top, huh?" he suggested.

"Well, it's a little opulent," she agreed. "But each piece of furniture is like a work of art."

He smiled and shook his head. It all just looked like antique stuff to him.

"Let me guess, Nathan wasn't thrilled with the idea of me hanging out with his wife, right? I guess I'm the next best thing to his lover being here," Renee stated.

"Something like that," Trent admitted. "But I made it clear that he has no choice and that you weren't going anywhere, so he better get used to it."

He could tell the discussion made her a little

upset. Trent pulled her into a hug and let her head rest on his shoulder.

"Remember what I said. If you feel uncomfortable, we don't have to stay long," he reminded her.

"No, I'm okay. I wouldn't want to upset Ophelia. And I'm looking forward to getting to know her a little better."

"Okay. But if you change your mind, just let me know."

Back downstairs, they found Ophelia in the family room just off the kitchen. She was flipping through a magazine with the television on in the background.

"Where are your parents Ophelia? Are they not here this weekend?" Trent asked.

"No. Daddy had to go to Boston for work for a couple of weeks and Mom went with him. They even took Glenna, our housekeeper."

"That's too bad. The weather is so nice, I was looking forward to beating your dad at tennis again," he told her with a grin.

"He's such a sore loser, isn't he?" she said with a laugh. "I'm sure he still plans a rematch."

"Where's Nathan?"

"I'm not sure," she replied. "In the den probably."

While Ophelia took Renee to tour the rest of the house and gardens, Trent went looking for his sulky cousin. He found him in the game room on the lower level. It was a bright space with nine-foot ceilings and several walkouts to the backyard. Nathan was playing pool while watching an NCAA game on the large wall-mounted flat screen. They nodded at each other, and Trent sat back to watch him play for a bit.

Once Nathan had sunk all the balls, Trent chalked a cue and they played a few games against each other.

There wasn't any real conversation other than the occasional comment about a shot, but by the end of their third round, Trent could feel less tension between them.

The women found them playing about an hour later and let them know there was lunch ready upstairs.

"How do you like Greenwich so far, Renee?" asked Ophelia as they ate in the sun-filled breakfast room.

"It's a really pretty town," she replied. "I had never been to Connecticut before, so I didn't know what to expect. But I love the mix of old and new homes."

"I've lived here my whole life," Ophelia told her. "I love visiting big cities, but I'm a small-town girl at heart."

Renee nodded with understanding, then turned to look at Trent. "I was surprised that you chose such a small city when you returned from Jamaica, Trent."

He shrugged. "I didn't really think about it. This was where the job at Goldwell Group was, and it was close enough to both New York and Nate in Stamford, so it made sense," he told her.

"Why not go back to Chicago?" Renee asked.

"I thought about it. I even had a job offer based there, but I couldn't identify with the kid I was when I left. In a way, returning there to live, even in a different neighborhood, felt like going backward. But I definitely miss not being closer to my mom and some of my other family."

"Do you go back often?" asked Renee.

Trent was about to respond when the doorbell rang. Ophelia exchanged a confused look with Nathan, then excused herself to answer the door. It was clear that neither of them was expecting anyone.

"I visit my mom in Chicago a couple of times a month. And she's come to Greenwich a few times."

His voice trailed off as the sound of raised voices emanated from the front of the house. He and Nathan looked at each other and stood up at the same time. Then there was a shout from Ophelia that sent them all running down the hall.

When they reached the foyer, Trent could not believe his eyes. There was a woman lying flat on her back on the floor with Ophelia standing over her repeating the same words over and over again.

"How dare you come to my house? How dare you come to my house?"

The woman crawled backward on her feet and elbows, her eyes filled with terror. Ophelia charged after her and started pulling her up by the arm. They struggled a bit, both shouting obscenities.

"Get off me, you crazy bitch!"

"You want to see crazy?" demanded Ophelia. "Get the hell out of my house!"

Trent was frozen in shock for only a few seconds; then he ran toward Ophelia and pulled her away from the stranger. Ophelia was incredibly strong in her rage and whipped her arms around to avoid being restrained.

"Let go of me! Let go of me!" she shouted.

Somewhere in the background, Trent thought he heard Nathan muttering nonsensical statements.

"Oh, my God! Oh man. Oh, my God!"

Or was that Renee?

The whole scene was completely chaotic.

Finally, Trent managed to get Ophelia to stop fighting him by holding her firmly but gently and telling her to calm down, that he would take care of everything. She eventually went limp in his arms and started crying hysterically.

"She came to my house, Trent. I can't take this anymore. I'm not going to deal with this anymore. She's in my house! Damn him! Damn him to hell."

He brushed her back with long strokes, telling her it was going to be okay. At the same time, his eyes swept the room. He noted the clumsy attempts of the stranger to get on her feet again. He saw Renee clutching the banister, trying to make sense of everything but clearly not knowing what to do. Then he found Nathan pacing back and forth, looking between the women with panic in his eyes. His eyes met Trent's, and he looked like a guilty child caught stealing from the candy store. In that instant, Trent understood exactly what was going on.

Ophelia was still sobbing, but she seemed to have better control, so Trent handed her over to Renee. Renee took the cue and wrapped her arms around Ophelia, then started guiding her toward the back of the house.

"You need to leave," Trent stated to the woman who was now standing at the door, fixing her clothes and regaining her composure.

"Nathan, aren't you going to do something?" the stranger demanded as though Trent had not spoken.

"That bitch is crazy! Did you see what she did to me? She tried to pull out my hair. Who the hell is she, Nathan?"

Trent looked over at his cousin, who was still pacing, his mouth opening and closing soundlessly like a fish.

"Aren't you going to do something?" Trent demanded of him. "What the hell is wrong with you?"

"This is just crazy!" Nathan muttered to himself.

"Do something now, Nathan. If you don't, then I will. Do you understand?" shouted Trent.

Nathan seemed to finally snap out of his trance and walked aggressively to the woman. "What the hell are you doing here, Louise? What's wrong with you, just showing up like this?"

"But, Nathan, you told me that you were coming up here by yourself to do some work. I wanted to surprise you with some company."

Trent could tell that this woman was completely clueless. Whatever story Nathan had weaved had her completely duped.

"You need to leave now," Nathan stated coldly. "If I wanted you here, I would have asked you."

She blinked, completely taken aback by his cruel words.

"But, Nathan—"

"Did you hear me? Get your stuff and go!" he shouted, taking several steps toward her. He picked up her purse off the floor and tossed it in her direction.

It hit her in the chest with a thump, and she stumbled clumsily to catch it.

"I'm sorry, I . . ." She attempted to speak, but

Nathan grabbed her arm roughly and tried to turn her around.

Trent immediately stepped forward to separate them.

"What's wrong with you, man? You're hurting her," he stated to Nathan.

"Fine, then. You deal with her. Just get her out of here."

Nathan threw his hands up and walked over to the staircase and sat down on a step.

Trent turned back to Louise, who was now rubbing her arm.

"Are you okay?"

She nodded but didn't say anything.

"What are you doing here? How did you find the house? How did you get past the gate?" Trent asked her quietly.

"Nathan brought me here a few days ago for the evening," she whispered in a small voice. "I remembered the security code from when he punched it in."

"What?" Trent asked, truly surprised by Nathan's stupidity.

"She's lying!" Nathan stated sharply, jumping to his feet like he was ready to fight.

"Oh, my God!"

These words came from Ophelia, who had returned to the foyer without making a sound. Her hand covered her mouth with horror.

"Nathan? You brought one of your women to my home? My family's home? How dare you? How dare you!"

"What are you talking about? Nathan?" asked Louise as she stepped around Trent and walked up to Nathan. "You told me this was your house. Who is this woman?"

Now Ophelia started to laugh like she had just heard the funniest joke.

Everyone looked at her with a mix of expressions. Trent and Renee were concerned, while Louise still looked confused. Nathan's face showed a mixture of fear and nausea.

"Nathan? Are you going to tell her who I am?" she finally asked once her laughter calmed down a bit.

"Ophelia, baby. She's lying, okay? This woman has been harassing me for weeks. She's crazy."

"I'm his wife," Ophelia finally stated to Louise, punctuating each word sharply. "This house belongs to my parents. And despite what I'm sure Big Man Nathan here has told you, he doesn't own anything but the clothes on his back."

That did it. Louise started shouting questions at Nathan, while he threw back all sorts of accusations and denials to both women.

Trent had heard enough.

"That's enough!" he declared loudly. "Renee, please take Ophelia upstairs."

He waited until the two women reached the upstairs landing, though Ophelia resisted most of the way.

"You need to leave. Now," he told Louise. "I don't care what he told you. Nathan is married. That was his wife. This house belongs to her parents."

Louise screeched in outrage and tried to run past Trent toward Nathan. Her fingers were bent like claws ready to do serious damage. "You bastard! You disgusting pig!" she yelled.

Trent caught her around the waist and physically carried her toward the front entrance. Her limbs were flailing and she was completely out of control. It took him several tries before he was able to open the door and deposit her gently but forcefully outside.

"Go home and forget all about him," Trent advised her. "Otherwise, I will call the police. Do you understand? Just forget about him."

Chapter 28

Renee had been worried about spending the weekend with Nathan and Ophelia while knowing the kind of man he was. Never in her wildest imagination could she have anticipated what had happened. As she stood back and watched the shocking drama unfold, and while her heart was breaking for Ophelia, Renee could not deny feeling a small amount of satisfaction. Men like Nathan needed to see the pain and damage their behavior caused people they claimed to love. And there was no doubt in her mind that Ophelia was better off knowing exactly what kind of man she was married to.

Once Renee managed to get Ophelia upstairs, they went to the bedroom where she and Trent were staying. It was the only place Renee recognized, and Ophelia was in no shape to provide directions. Along the way, they could hear the woman downstairs start to scream and curse at Nathan. The front door opened and closed again; then there was silence.

She and Ophelia sat on the bed for almost an hour.

For most of that time, Ophelia just cried, alternating between deep sobs and quiet sniffles. Renee held her close and provided a constant supply of tissue. Near the end, they talked.

Ophelia confessed that she had had suspicions of Nathan's infidelity for the last year or so. He spent many nights out and blamed them on work. There were various unexplained credit card expenses. Then he started to shred his cell phone bill. When she asked him what was going on, he told Ophelia she was insecure. He said that she used her wealth to try and control him, to make him feel like less of a man. Ophelia then became too proud to ask him any more questions or snoop through his stuff.

Trent came into the room at some point. Ophelia rushed into his arms.

"Why would he do this to me, Trent? What did I do wrong?" she cried.

"You didn't do anything wrong, Ophelia. This has nothing to do with you. Do you understand?" he told her firmly.

"How could he disrespect me like this? To bring a woman here? He knew the house was going to be empty with Mom and Dad gone. I just can't believe he could be so evil. I tried so hard to make him happy, to make sure he had everything he wanted, but it wasn't enough. I'm not enough."

The last words were barely audible as Ophelia bent over in despair.

Trent just held her tighter while his eyes met Renee's. She saw deep anger and frustration. Her heart went out to him, and she wished she knew what to do to console him and his cousin's wife.

Nathan was gone. Apparently, he had taken Trent's strong recommendation that he take a cab back home and allow Ophelia some time to process what had happened. Ophelia was clearly relieved that she did not have to face him again anytime soon. Renee felt the same way. After what Angela said about her affair with Nathan, Renee honestly wasn't sure what she would do if she had to listen to more of his ridiculous denials. She might scratch his eyes out before his wife had a chance.

By early evening, Ophelia was emotionally and physically exhausted. Renee helped her into a hot bath and brought her a couple of aspirin and a glass of water for her headache. Renee then went downstairs, where Trent was in the family room with the television on, but his mind was on other things.

"How is she doing?" he asked.

"Calmer, but still pretty upset. She's still in the bath, but I'll check on her in a few minutes."

Renee sat beside him on the couch. Trent draped an arm over her shoulder and pulled her close to his side. He let out a deep sigh. They sat quietly for several minutes.

"I'm so sorry about all of this, Renee. This is not exactly what I had planned for a weekend in the country," he eventually stated.

Renee smiled at his sarcasm. "It's not your fault. But I still can't believe it went down like that," she told him. "Did you have any idea of how bad his behavior was? Cheating is cheating, but I guess there are varying degrees of foulness."

"Honestly, I'm completely blown away. When Nathan told me about the woman demanding money, I wasn't surprised that he had had an affair. He's always been a little self-indulgent. I guess I would have to blame that on my aunt and uncle. They gave him the impression that he deserves everything he wanted. And being married to Ophelia made it worse, I guess. Her family's money has allowed him to live a pretty extravagant life. Her parents have been really good to him."

"See, that's the part that I just don't understand. Why would he jeopardize his lifestyle by cheating? Did he love Ophelia, or do you think he just married her for her money?" Renee asked.

"I don't know anymore. None of this makes sense to me," he replied sadly.

"What did he say when I took Ophelia upstairs?"

"What could he say? I tried to get an explanation from him, but he's still insisting that the woman was lying. He was panicking about what Ophelia was going to do, whether she would tell her parents. Finally, I just told him it would be better if he left."

They cuddled on the couch for a little bit until Trent took a deep breath and sat up. "Renee, I have to tell you something."

She sat up also. His tone was so ominous, and her heart started beating with anxiety. "What?"

He let out another long sigh. "I was seeing someone when I met you. Her name was Brianna, and

I had been dating her for over three months at the time."

Renee did not know how to respond. His words didn't make sense to her.

"She was in France for about a month with her mom and came back about a week ago. I took her out for lunch and broke up with her."

"I don't understand," she told him. "You cheated on your girlfriend to help your cheating cousin get rid of his lover? Is that what I'm hearing?"

"No! Renee, come on. That's not at all what happened."

"That's what it sounds like to me, Trent. What about your pretty speech about never being unfaithful?"

"Look, Brianna and I weren't in a relationship, not in the way that we are. And I never went out with her again after I met you, Renee."

"Okay. So why are you telling me all this?"

"I don't know. After what happened here tonight, I feel the need to be honest with you about everything, even if it upsets you. I regret some of the things that happened between us, Renee, and I don't want to hide anything anymore."

Renee sat back on the couch and let her head fall back as she looked up at the ceiling. There were so many thoughts and feelings rushing around in her head that she felt a little dizzy. Was Trent being honest? Was this a sign of his character? Will he dump her the minute he meets someone better? What else was going on in his life that he hadn't told her about? She had no clue how to get these answers, so she let the matter drop.

When they checked on Ophelia a little while later, she was sleeping soundly. Renee and Trent went back downstairs and made a dinner out of the lunch leftovers. They then spent the rest of the evening watching movies.

On Sunday, two of Ophelia's girlfriends showed up bright and early to provide their support. Trent suggested it was a good time for him and Renee to head back to Greenwich and give Ophelia some privacy to deal with her situation. They shared an emotional moment with her at the door before getting on the road.

"Thank you both for your help with all this," Ophelia told them with a sad smile. "I know it's a pretty awkward situation."

"Ophelia, you and I are family. I'm glad we were here when it happened so you didn't have to deal with it alone," Trent told her as they hugged. "If you need anything, anything at all, please call me."

"I will, Trent. Thank you."

Renee also gave her a hug before they said goodbye.

That week, Trent and Renee fell back into the routine that had become comfortable for them.

Renee continued to work remotely on Cree Armstrong's condo project. She also managed to do some local shopping to get paint and accessories for Trent's bedroom. Renee estimated that she would be okay staying in Greenwich for another week or so, but anything longer than that would make her job impossible.

The police had no additional leads or information in the investigation of her break-in, and it now seemed unlikely that they ever would. Renee now knew that her only options lay with Angela. Renee had not heard from her since their meeting in the Bronx, and she wondered if Angela was going to be able to resolve things within the two weeks as promised. If not, Renee knew the only option was to tell the police and Trent everything she now knew. There was a knot in her stomach just thinking about that possibility.

Somewhere around six o'clock on Friday evening, Angela called her. Renee was in the living room still surrounded by her work.

"It's done," she told Renee.

"What's done? What are you talking about?"

"You know, what we talked about last week. I met up with my acquaintance and gave him what he wanted. So, it's over, okay? Just like I promised."

Renee sat for a few seconds in stunned silence. She could hardly believe the news.

"Are you sure, Angela?"

"Yup," she replied. "I just left him at the W in Times Square. I'm not paranoid, but if your apartment was as bad as you said, it seemed like a good idea to meet him in a crowded place. Anyway, I told him that now that he had what he wanted, there was no point in trying to bother me anymore, since I had given him a false name anyway."

"And that was it?" Renee asked, still very surprised.

She had always secretly admired Angela's gump-tion and ability to handle anyone and anything.

"That's it. Well, except for the twenty-five Gs he paid me to give him the stuff back and for me to keep my mouth shut about the whole thing."

"What? Whoa!" Renee demanded. "What are you talking about? You said there might be a reward, Angela! Not thousands of dollars. This sounds like extortion! Angela, what have you done?"

"Renee, calm down. It's no big deal. He's a sleazy rich guy. So, I lightened his pocket a bit and he got what he wanted. He can afford it. And after what he did to you, he's lucky I didn't sell those pictures to the highest bidder. I would probably have gotten ten times that amount."

"Oh, my God! Pictures? Okay, that's it. I don't want to hear anymore, okay? I don't want to know any more about this."

"All right, all right. I just wanted to let you know you can go back to your place whenever you're ready," Angela stated.

Renee heard the front door open at the moment.

"I have to go, Angela."

"Okay, I'll talk to you later," she replied cheerily.

"Take care of yourself, okay? And call me when you have a permanent phone number."

Trent stepped onto the landing at that moment, so Renee hung up the phone before she heard Angela's response.

For the rest of the evening and all day Saturday, Renee fought the urge to tell Trent about the call from Angela. But that meant telling him about the meeting with her in New York last week, not to mention lying to Trent about Angela from the minute he had questioned their high school picture. Everything was going so well that it didn't make sense to dredge it all up again and introduce new suspicions. Or at least that was what Renee told herself.

At six o'clock Saturday evening, she headed upstairs to get ready for the party. The annual Children in the Arts Spring Gala was being held at a private golf and country club just north of Greenwich. She and Trent agreed to be ready to leave at seven so they could arrive during the cocktail hour before dinner. When Renee came downstairs again, she was running a few minutes behind schedule. She found Trent leaning against the kitchen counter, drinking a bottle of water. He looked incredibly handsome in his slim-fitting, jet-black tuxedo with satin trim, white, crisp shirt, and silver-gray silk tie.

"Wow," he stated when he saw her.

The water bottle was still tilted but forgotten in his hand.

Renee giggled and did a slow turn for his inspection. Ophelia had helped her pick out a soft satin, full-length dress with a deep plunging neckline and an open, knotted back. It was in a deep aubergine with a band embroidery and sparkling sequins around the abdomen. It flared a bit as she spun and revealed dark purple shoes to complete the outfit.

"Do you like it?" she asked teasingly.

Trent grinned back. "I like!" he stated as he finally walked toward her and pulled her into his arms.

They kissed lightly for a few moments until he pulled back.

"I don't want to ruin your makeup. You look unbelievably gorgeous."

His simple compliment made her blush with pleasure.

"Are you ready?" he asked.

Renee nodded and they headed out to the party.

Chapter 29

On Sunday morning, Trent was in the kitchen whipping up a Jamaican breakfast of salted codfish, dumplings, and fried ripe plantains. While he cooked, Renee was in the shower after a morning episode of quick, hot lovemaking. He was still smiling from the memory of it, and of the evening before at the ball.

It had been a great night. Renee looked so good in that dark purple dress that he had difficulty keeping his hands off her. She was by his side the whole time while they enjoyed the abundance of food, talking with his co-workers, and even doing a little dancing. They also had an opportunity to talk, exchanging more information and stories about their parents and families. Renee finally asked Trent about his life in Jamaica as a police officer. Her eyes shone with tears as he told her about the painful physical and emotional recovery after the shooting.

"Like most young men, I never worried about

my safety or mortality until then. I was careful and always followed protocol, but never felt vulnerable doing my job," he explained as they sat at their table enjoying some wine. "Even when I knew I was shot and lay on the ground feeling the blood pooling around me, it never occurred to me that I could die. It was the look on my dad's face when he arrived at the hospital that made it hit home. He got there just before I was rushed into surgery. I don't remember much about those moments, but I can still see the fear on his face and the tears in his eyes as he looked down at me and gripped my hand. I knew then that he thought I wasn't going to make it."

"Oh, Trent," she gasped.

"It turns out that I had lost a lot of blood and the bullet had fractured into several pieces. The doctors were worried that I wouldn't make it through the operation. Even afterward, they had me listed as critical for a few days."

Trent was relieved to share some of the details about the incident that he'd revealed to only very few people in his life. Renee reached out to grip his hand tightly.

"So, what happened after that?" she asked.

"I took a long look at my life," he stated simply. "My recovery took a while and I had plenty of time to think. Eventually, I realized that I only went into law enforcement to please my father. And after facing death while on the job, it just didn't seem worth it."

"So, you chose a safe, boring career in investment banking instead," teased Renee, lightening the mood.

Trent laughed.

"Yeah, something like that," he replied.

They sat talking for a few more minutes before being joined by Nancy and her date who they had run into earlier in the evening.

The only blemish on the evening was that Brianna had shown up at the gala with a new date of her own.

Trent had not spoken to Brianna since their lunch a couple of weeks earlier. But when Trent saw her walk into the party, he froze, uncertain of how she would react. At first, he tried to avoid her, but it became impossible when she come up to him at the bar.

"Well, I'm surprised to see you here, Trent," she stated with a tight smile. "And with a date no less. I thought you hated these events."

"Hello, Brianna," he replied, leaning forward and giving her a polite peck on the cheek. "You look beautiful tonight. How are you?"

"I'm fabulous, Trent, just fabulous. I see you're doing pretty well too. I also see you have a new girlfriend already. How fast was that? Two weeks? I know you're good, but now I'm really impressed."

Her voice dripped with sugary-sweet sarcasm. To anyone else around them, it seemed like a polite conversation between friendly acquaintances. But Trent could see the venom shining in her eyes. Apparently, the breakup hadn't gone as smoothly as he thought. Trent was very aware of how bad his behavior might look, so he kept his mouth shut.

"Oh, here comes my date. You might know him, I think. Travis Templeton? Former goalie for the Boston Bruins? Daddy has just signed him on as the spokesman for the company's new line. Isn't he hot? Turns out he wanted to ask me out even before I went on my trip. Things just worked out perfectly, didn't they?"

"Well, I'm glad you're doing well, Brianna. I really do wish you all the best," he told her solemnly.

Thankfully, his drinks were ready at that point, so Trent took them and made a quick exit. As he headed back to Renee, he silently prayed that Brianna had vented her resentment enough and didn't have plans to attack him or Renee at some point that night.

Trent was brought back to the present as he heard Renee coming down the stairs.

"Hey, I hope you're hungry," he stated as Renee came downstairs and entered the kitchen.

"I'm starving," she declared. "What do you need me to do?"

Trent asked her to set the table and make some coffee while he brought the food to the table. They were almost finished eating and in the middle of a conversation about their plans for the day when the doorbell rang.

It was Robbie Drummond wearing his homicide detective badge on a chain around his neck.

"Hey, Robbie," Trent stated with surprise as he invited his friend into the downstairs front entrance. "What's going on?"

"Hey, Trent, did you get my message?"

"No, what message?"

"I tried you on your mobile phone earlier. Sorry, man. I couldn't find your home number."

"No problem. I haven't checked my cell yet this morning," Trent replied as he led Robbie toward the stairs up to the main floor. "We're just having breakfast. Do you want some coffee?"

"Wait," Robbie stated, touching Trent's arm to stop him. "Is Renee still here?"

"Yeah, she's upstairs. Why? What's going on?"

"We found a body early this morning, Trent. I think it's the woman who stole Renee's identity."

"What? How do you know? Who is she?"

"We're not sure of her identity yet. We found her and another victim, a guy named Winston Thompson, in his apartment in Brooklyn. A neighbor heard signs of a fight and called the police. The guy is in pretty bad shape at the hospital, so we haven't been able to question him yet. It looks like he'll survive, so we have a detective outside his room in case he comes to."

"Why do you think this has anything to do with Renee?"

"Trent, she looks like Renee's twin sister. I noticed it the minute I saw the body. Then we found these while searching the guy's apartment."

Robbie handed Trent a small stack of business cards. They had Renee's name across them in bold letters and her title as associate interior designer in smaller letters underneath.

"Damn it!" uttered Trent.

"Whoever the victim was, she wasn't living with this Winston permanently. We found a few items of clothing but no personal effects. But there was a cell phone that was completely smashed. It was registered in the guy's name, but we pulled the phone records," Robbie explained in an ominous tone. "Trent, one of the last calls she made was to Renee's cell phone on Friday evening. The call lasted over ten minutes."

Trent looked into the eyes of a cop and a former colleague. Robbie didn't have to say anything else. The implications were clear. They both walked upstairs to the kitchen where Renee was still relaxing at the table and finishing off her coffee.

She stood up when she saw Robbie. "Detective Drummond," she stated with her hand extended. "Nice to see you again."

"Hello, Renee," he replied, shaking her hand.

The tension in the air must have been obvious, because Renee lifted her chin and looked between the two men questioningly. Trent's eyes were fixed on her face, scrutinizing every expression for any signs of guilt.

"Is everything okay?" she asked.

"I'm afraid not, Renee," Robbie stated. "Do you recognize this woman?"

He handed her a small Polaroid picture. Trent could see that it was a head shot of the unknown victim. She was lying on the floor, her arms askew and her dead eyes wide open. He watched Renee's face become frozen with shock as she looked at the image. Her hands started to shake.

"Oh, my God. Oh, my God!" she exclaimed before throwing the picture back at Robbie. "Is she . . . is she dead?"

"Who is she, Renee?" Trent asked pointedly.

She looked back at him, clearly dazed. "Angela Simpson," she whispered.

"And how do you know her?" Robbie asked. He took out his notebook and started to write down the details.

Renee stepped back and fell into the kitchen chair. Her focus had moved off of Trent, and she now stared out across the room into space.

"We grew up together, in Pittsburgh. She was my best friend."

"The girl in the cheerleading picture," Trent affirmed coldly.

She looked at him again, her eyes pleading and pooling with tears.

"She's dead, isn't she? Oh, my God! Angela's dead . . ."

The two men looked at each other while Renee fell apart, sobbing uncontrollably, her shoulders shaking. Trent felt his own eyes tear up. Regardless of what this all meant, he just could not stand to see her in such pain. He lowered himself on bent knees and pulled her into his arms.

It took a while for her to regain her composure. Robbie had grabbed a box of tissue from the kitchen counter, and Renee tried to clean up her face.

"What happened?" she finally asked when she was able to speak.

"Well, that's what we're hoping you can tell us," stated Robbie. He was back to his role as detective with pen and paper ready.

Renee let out a deep breath. "I can't tell you much. She and I haven't been close for several years."

"Did you know she was in New York?" Trent asked.

He could tell by her facial expression that she was dreading having to answer his question. Trent folded his arms across his chest, vowing to himself not to feel sorry for her. She had obviously lied to his face without any hesitation.

"Yes, I did. She stayed with me for a couple months but moved out a few weeks ago."

Trent rocked back on his heels. Dark thoughts began to fill his head as the repercussions of her confession began to reveal themselves.

"And, yes, Trent, I already know she used my name when she met Nathan," Renee continued in a tired voice. "But I didn't find out until last week. After the break-in and everything you told me about the woman who Nathan had been seeing, it only made sense. So I called her and demanded the truth. She finally admitted it."

"You lied to me," Trent stated in an icy voice.

She let out another long sigh. "Yes, I did. But you have to understand, the day you confronted me with Angela's picture, I had just found out that everything I knew about you was a lie, too, so I didn't exactly trust you at that point."

Robbie looked between them, clearly not sure what role their personal conflict played in his investigation.

"Renee," Robbie interjected, pulling her attention away from Trent. "We're pretty certain that the perpetrator of your B and E is also responsible for your friend's murder. Who is it?"

"I have no idea."

"Renee, this is serious now. Stop playing games and tell Robbie what you know. These people are dangerous!" demanded Trent, clearly exasperated.

"You don't think I know that!" she yelled, standing up to face him. "They killed her, Trent! My oldest friend in the world is dead, and I'm going to have to look her mother in the eye. And you think I would hide who did this? I don't know anything!"

She walked away from him with her arms wrapped around herself. Robbie touched his friend's arm, silently asking Trent to let Robbie handle the rest of the questioning.

"Renee, we know that you spoke to Angela on Friday. What did you guys talk about? Did she tell you anything that could help our investigation?"

Renee turned back to them but was silent for several seconds, biting her lip and thinking.

"She had told me several days ago that she knew who broke into my apartment, but she refused to tell me more. Apparently, she had something that belonged to him. I told her that we should go to the police, but she refused. She said that she had already made plans to give him back what he wanted. The call on Friday was to tell me that it was done."

"It was a man?"

"Yes."

"Did she tell you what she gave back?"

"Not at first, but Friday she said something about a picture. That's it."

"Anything else at all?" probed Robbie.

"Angela also mentioned getting some money.

Twenty-five thousand dollars, I think. At first, she made it sound like a reward, but I didn't really believe her."

"She was extorting someone else," Trent stated simply.

"Well, we'll look through the crime scene for any pictures. But we didn't find any money there, so either she hid it or they took it back," explained Robbie.

"Angela said it was for her mother. Miss Simpson has lupus and can't work or afford the proper treatment. Maybe she already sent it to her?" Renee added. "And you should check my apartment again. She had left some stuff there when she moved out."

Robbie nodded and continued writing. "Anything else you can think of?" he asked.

"No," whispered Renee. "Wait, I think she said he was a producer. The guy who wanted the picture back. A Broadway producer. And she met him at the W Hotel in Times Square on Friday. She also said she told him about the stolen identity."

Robbie asked a few more questions about Angela's life and acquaintances over the last two months, but Renee had little information to add.

"How did she die?" Renee finally asked.

"Multiple stab wounds," Robbie told her. "But it looks like she put up a hell of a fight. I don't think you should return to your apartment until we catch this guy. Can you stay away from your office also? We don't know what he thinks your involvement is in this whole thing, and he's obviously willing to shut you up permanently."

Trent watched her nod with understanding but could tell she was still in shock.

Robbie left shortly thereafter, promising to keep them posted on the investigation. Renee sat back down at the kitchen table while Trent made them some more coffee. When he handed her a fresh cup, she accepted it with a grateful nod.

"Why did you lie to me, Renee?" he finally asked.

She buried her head in her hands, clearly emotionally exhausted. Trent wanted to hold her, soothe her, and try to bring her comfort, but he forced himself to remain stoic and clearheaded. There were too many lies and unanswered questions for him to rely on his feelings.

"I told you already, Trent. When you asked me about Angela, I didn't know what to believe. I've known her for almost twenty years, since I was nine years old. I felt like I owed her the benefit of the doubt, or at least the opportunity to explain herself," she stated wearily.

"Fine, I get that. That was three weeks ago, Renee. What about yesterday or the day before? You never even mentioned speaking to her. But now I find out you knew about her plot to extort twenty-five thousand dollars? What am I supposed to think?"

"I don't know, Trent. What do you think?" she shot back. "You think I was in on it from the beginning? That I let her use my name and was going to cash in on the deal?"

Trent didn't respond. He didn't believe that, not in his heart. But the analytical, investigative side of his nature stubbornly refused to dismiss the possibility outright.

Renee nodded her head and clenched her teeth. She walked away from him and went up the stairs without saying another word. A minute later, Trent heard the spare bedroom door close sharply.

Chapter 30

"The rent includes the use of the common areas like the backyard and the laundry facilities in the basement. Utilities are billed and monitored separately in each unit, and you will have to arrange for it to be turned on."

It was Monday afternoon, around the lunch hour, and Renee was walking through the second-floor apartment of Jennifer's building. Jennifer lived on the third floor. It was a renovated mid-nineteenth century four-story firehouse in the East Village. The landlord, a friendly older man named Oscar Fleming, had already given her a detailed tour, and Jennifer was also there to help Renee make a decision.

"Now, Oscar as I told you, Renee can't go back to her old apartment and is staying in a hotel nearby for now. Can she move in right away rather than waiting until the first of the month?"

"Oh, of course," he replied with a big smile. "If you want the place, Renee, it's yours and you can move in as soon as it's convenient. No additional charges, of course."

"That's very generous, Oscar. I appreciate it," Renee told him. "Are you open to a month-to-month lease?"

He folded his arms and looked at her intently. He was a tiny man, at least an inch shorter than Renee and several pounds lighter. His white hair was a little long and windswept, and with his pale, flushed skin, he reminded her of Albert Einstein.

"How about this: We'll do month to month, but with a sixty-day notice to leave. That seems like a good compromise, right?"

Renee smiled, liking his attitude and approach. "That's a very good comprise."

"Well, do we have a deal, then, young lady?"

Renee looked at Jennifer, then back at Oscar. Though she absolutely loved the apartment and the building, she needed some time to make a decision. There had been so many changes and challenges in her life in the last couple of weeks that she felt pretty overwhelmed.

"Can I think about it for an hour or so?" she asked him.

"Absolutely, take your time! You have all the paperwork. If you want it, just give me a call and leave the forms with Jennifer," he told her kindly.

She thanked him, then the two women went up to Jennifer's apartment to talk.

"What do you think? Are you going to take it?" her friend asked as they sat on her couches.

"I love it, Jen. It's a little bit expensive, but with all the renovations and upgrades, I think it's worth it."

"Perfect," Jennifer replied, clapping her hands with excitement. "Then we'll be neighbors."

Renee smiled back, but it was lacking its normal shine. Her heart was aching and it was hard to feel anything good.

"I just have to figure out so many details, that's all," explained Renee. "I'm still catching up at work, and I'll have to pack everything of value at the old apartment once it's safe to go back there. Then there's the funeral. It's this Saturday morning, which means I have to be in Pittsburgh on Friday."

Jennifer moved from the sofa she was on to sit beside Renee and enveloped her into a big embrace.

"Renee, it's okay. We'll figure it out."

They hugged for a few minutes to give Renee some time to collect her composure.

"Now, let's talk this through," suggested Jennifer. "You have to replace all your major furniture, right? But you're a designer, so I know that won't be a problem, especially if your insurance is going to reimburse you. Just have them deliver it here when you buy it. Oscar's great about stuff like that. If you tell him what time you're expecting the stuff, he'll let them into the apartment for you."

Renee nodded, trying hard to focus on the solution.

"And you said the insurance company is reimbursing you for the out-of-pocket expenses for accommodations, right? That should cover the hotel for at least another week. So, don't worry about actually moving in until after the funeral. We'll see if we can book a mover for next weekend, but once you give your thirty-day notice to vacate your current place, you'll have the whole month to do the final move. But I bet you can be moved in here with most of your new stuff by the end of next week. That doesn't sound too bad."

Jennifer made it sound so logical and simple that Renee found herself nodding again in agreement.

"Is there anything we've missed?" asked Jen.

"No, I don't think so," Renee stated.

"Well, then there is nothing stopping you from signing on the dotted line, right?"

"Right," replied Renee with conviction.

In the end, there were very few other options. Angela's murder made it impossible for Renee to ever go back to her Upper East Side apartment and feel safe. And finding a decent apartment at an affordable price in Manhattan was tough, particularly within a few days from the beginning of the month. Jennifer's building was a beautiful, charming old place, and it was safe and well maintained. There were few luxury amenities, so the price wasn't outrageous. Jennifer's calm approach helped her to see that the right solution was obvious.

"You're right, Jen. It looks like we're going to be neighbors," she finally confirmed.

Jennifer squealed and hugged her again. Her joy was so infectious that Renee grinned also.

"Now, we both need to get back to work," Jen instructed.

"Yeah, it's getting late," agreed Renee. "I'll call

Oscar with the news, and I'll fill out the forms and fax them to him."

The women hurried out of Jennifer's apartment and walked together toward the subway station two blocks away. Renee's hotel was only a few streets north of there, off 6th Avenue.

"Have you spoken to Trent since you left his house yesterday?" Jennifer asked.

"No, and I don't plan to."

She could tell that Jennifer wanted to ask more questions, but the look on Renee's face probably told her it wasn't the best idea. All Jennifer knew was that she and Trent had a fight on Sunday and Renee had left his place to return to New York. Renee had told Jennifer about dating Trent almost from the beginning. She also told her about the apartment break-in, but she never told Jennifer about Angela's illegal schemes. Since Angela and Jennifer had never met, and now that Angela was gone, it seemed disrespectful and disloyal for Renee to talk about her old friend's mistakes with someone who didn't know her.

"Well, he sounds like a really good guy. Just give it some time and I'm sure things will work themselves out," her friend predicted optimistically.

Renee mumbled something appropriate in response, then changed the subject.

The women separated at the subway entrance as Jennifer headed back to the department store and Renee returned to her hotel to work. Once she was back in her room, she sat at her desk, turned on her laptop, and started to work through the long list of to-do items in order to get her projects back on track.

Cree Armstrong was in the city for a few days, and they had a meeting on Thursday to decide on some of the features and finishes.

Then there was Margaret Applebaum's room redecoration that was scheduled for completion tomorrow. Everything was ready to go, so she anticipated a smooth finish. Thank God, Margaret had been very understanding and gracious about some of the delays in the last few weeks.

The only project outstanding right now was Trent's bedroom redesign. Renee had no idea what to do about it. The way she felt now, and the way in which she left his place so abruptly yesterday, made it impossible for her to finish the work. The only thing Renee could think to do was pass it on to one of her coworkers.

Once she made the decision, Renee sent out an e-mail to the other associate designers at Hoffman Designs to see who had the time available to pick up something new. It might be a hard sell considering the work was almost an hour away, but to her surprise, she got a response within ten minutes. Nadine Walsh was a couple of years more senior than Renee, but she was in between projects. Renee set up some time to talk with Nadine later that afternoon to exchange the background information and review the design file.

To prepare for the meeting, Renee flipped through her notes from the first meeting with Trent, and her measurements after. She also attached recent pictures of the custom furniture taken at Frederic and Albert's studio. But she did not have a copy of the presentation she had given Trent. The original files were on her old laptop, now destroyed.

Sighing with frustration, Renee started to write up a descriptive e-mail of what Trent wanted from memory, but then stopped after a few sentences. She suddenly remembered the day she met Trent for dinner to present her design ideas. Her printer had been out of ink, so she had saved the presentation on a USB flash drive in order to take it to the print shop down the street. Renee had tossed it into her oversized purse after using it and had not seen it since. It must still be there.

Renee grabbed her bag and shuffled everything around, digging her fingers into the crevices until she found it in one of the inside storage pockets. She plugged it into her new laptop and opened the folder. Her presentation for Trent was there as expected, and she sighed with relief. With no time to waste, Renee attached the presentation and finished typing up the e-mail to Nadine. She sent off the message a few minutes before the women were scheduled to speak by phone.

The meeting with Nadine went quite smoothly, and Renee felt comfortable that Nadine understood her vision for the design and what Trent wanted for his bedroom. The presentation was clear, and Renee provided all the additional details of every aspect of the project. She also gave Nadine the contact information for Henry Interiors, for the stores in Greenwich where she sourced some of the materials, and for Trent.

Nadine was very excited about the project and more than happy to help Renee complete it. According to her, everyone in the office was aware of Renee's situation and was concerned about her safety and well-being. Nadine passed on their well wishes. Without getting into too much detail, Renee let her know that it was likely things would be back to normal within a week or so.

The day went much longer than expected, and Renee was still on the phone negotiating with suppliers and sourcing samples on the Internet well into the evening. Finally, at about eight-fifteen, when her hunger could no longer be ignored, she stood up from the desk and started to clean up her files and shut down the computer. As she closed all of the open program windows, Renee paused at the two items on the flash drive. Besides her presentation, there was a second file, a folder that Renee did not recognize. The title was just a date, February 20 of that year.

She opened the unknown folder and found a series of JPEG files.

Renee sat down again and clicked on the first picture, then sat looking at it for several moments. She leaned closer, her brows scrunched with focus. The image was blurry and grainy, almost impossible to make out, but it looked like two naked people photographed without their knowledge.

She took a deep breath and one by one opened all the pictures, seven in total. Her mouth dropped with shock and disgust at the graphic images.

"Oh, my God!" she whispered, staring closer at the final one.

Somehow, Renee was in possession of very graphic pictures of Chad Taylor, former teenage heartthrob, being pleasured by another man, and with obvious enjoyment.

Chapter 31

Renee walked into the 66th Precinct of the NYPD in Brooklyn on Tuesday morning. She approached the reception desk.

"I'm here to see Detective Drummond in Homicide, please," she informed the man behind the counter.

He instructed her to take a seat in the waiting area. Robbie Drummond arrived about ten minutes later and ushered her into an interview room nearby.

"I was surprised to get your call, Renee. Did you remember something else that Angela told you that would be useful?" he asked when they were both seated.

"No," she replied. "But I did find this."

She placed the flash drive on the desk between them.

"What is it?"

"It's the pictures that Angela tried to sell to the man she met at the hotel on Friday."

Robbie looked between her and the drive several

times before he picked it up. "Where did you find this?" he asked.

"I had it the whole time," Renee told him. "I thought the drive was mine, and I had it in my purse for the past month and a half."

He looked puzzled. "I don't understand."

"I'm not sure I do either," she replied with a sigh. "I bought a flash drive identical to this one a month ago and left it in my office in the spare bedroom. Angela slept in that room while she was staying with me. The only thing that makes any sense is that she and I had bought the same kind of flash drive. I had bought it at the drugstore near my apartment, so it stands to reason that she did too. So, somehow, we mixed up our flash drives without realizing it."

Robbie just nodded.

"Did you find any sign of the money Angela said she received?" Renee asked.

"No, nothing. Her boyfriend is still in the hospital, but we were able to talk to him, and it's pretty obvious he doesn't know anything about what Angela was up to. And there is no evidence that she sent it to her mother in Pittsburgh. Right now, the only conclusion we can make is that her assailant took it."

"Detective Drummond, I think that's why Angela was killed. She told me she was given twenty-five thousand dollars in exchange for these pictures," Renee stated, her finger tapping the small storage device. "If she gave them my flash drive by accident, it would have been blank. Maybe whoever she was dealing with thought she deliberately cheated him?"

Robbie sat back, and Renee could see that he was processing all of the information.

"Who's in the pictures? Do you recognize anyone?" he asked.

"Well, to put it bluntly, it's two men having sex. I would assume that one of them is the producer that Angela knew and met to get the money. His face isn't familiar to me, though."

"So you're thinking the person in these pictures is our perp?"

"I don't know. But based on what Angela told me, it's a good place to start."

"Okay," he announced as he stood up. "I will have one of our analysts run a facial-recognition search. We should have his identity pretty quickly."

Renee stood up also. "That's good, Detective Drummond."

"Robbie, please," he requested. "Thank you for finding this and bringing it in. This is the break we need to catch Angela's killer. And it's probably also the person who vandalized your apartment, so I'm sure you must be relieved."

"Yes, I am. And I hope you can catch whoever did this. But there is something else you should know."

He was about to escort her out of the room but now turned back questioningly. "What's that?"

"I think the other man on the tape is Chad Taylor."

Robbie looked at her hard. "The actor? The one who just got engaged to the supermodel?"

"Yes. And with his blockbuster movie career about to launch, I don't think this would be the right time to announce that he's gay."

It took a moment for the significance of her statement to sink in; then the detective catapulted into action, leaving her in the reception area with the promise that he would call her with an update. As Renee walked out of the police station, there was a flurry of activity behind her as Robbie barked out orders and his team of investigators got to work on the new lead. Her face lit up with the first genuine smile in over two days.

Before Renee went back to her hotel, she had one more important stop to make. The funeral was on Saturday, and she wanted to return to Pittsburgh with a gift for Angela's mom from her tragically deceased daughter.

The rest of the week was incredibly hectic. Renee picked up the keys to her new apartment in the Village and started shopping for the essentials. Frederic and Albert had put her personal furniture pieces at the top of their priority list with the promise that they would be finished within a couple of weeks. She was more than happy to leave it in their hands.

The meeting with Cree Armstrong had gone very well, and the project was finally moving. Renee was relieved that it was back on schedule for completion around mid-June. She also had two meetings set up next week for prospective clients, and she was talking with Margaret Applebaum about her need to decorate yet another room in her house. Renee was finally starting to feel like her life might eventually go back to normal. She just had to get through the weekend and the funeral.

And then there was Trent.

On the day that Angela's body had been found, Renee had been in so much pain. The instant she saw the picture of her friend's assaulted and lifeless body, she felt such a sense of loss that it surprised her. There was also acute shame and regret for how they had wasted the last three months. At that point, Renee had needed the comfort of Trent's strong arms and broad shoulders to help her feel safe. Instead, she got more accusations and insults. It was too much.

After they fought, Renee had immediately packed up her things and called for a taxi back to New York. She then booked a room at a smaller hotel near some of her interior design projects. Finally, she went downstairs with her overstuffed knapsack on her back and her purse in hand. The only thing she left behind was the purple dress and matching shoes she had worn to the gala the night before. She could see the surprise on Trent's face the moment he saw her.

"What are you doing," he asked as she walked past him toward the stairs to the ground floor. "Renee, where are you going?"

She stopped for a moment but could not turn around to look into his eyes.

"I have to go, Trent. I can't stay here anymore."

"Renee, you can't leave. It's not safe," he stated forcefully. "Renee, just wait! We can work this out. Let's talk about it. Renee, please just wait!"

Renee refused to give in to the concern and urgency in his voice. There were too many lies and accusations between them, so much distrust. She just did not have the energy to find the truth anymore.

"Goodbye, Trent," she stated softly before she

walked down the stairs. He didn't follow her, and that was the last time they spoke.

As promised in their meeting at the police station, Robbie kept her posted on the progress of the investigation. By Tuesday night, they had indentified and interrogated Broadway producer Nigel Bloom about his connection to Angela's stabbing. Apparently, he caved pretty quickly. He admitted to meeting with Angela about the pictures and to giving her the twenty-five thousand dollars in exchange for the evidence she had on his scandalous gay affair.

But the money wasn't his, he claimed. He had just been acting as a broker to resolve the situation. He also swore he knew nothing about the murder. All he did was give Chad Taylor's manager, Derek Whitman, the files Angela had given him on a flash drive.

The police caught up with Derek Bloom on Thursday in the Caribbean and had him flown back to New York. The story broke in the news on Friday, and every major station in the United States showed the pictures of Chad Taylor being taken into custody for questioning.

Renee was on the train to Pittsburgh during the evening news, but she got a call from Jennifer with the details and was weak with relief.

Like most funerals for anyone who dies too young and very suddenly, it was bittersweet. Renee was staying with her mom and Kenneth for the weekend, and they all went to the service together. The church was packed with all the young people who considered Angela a friend. Her energy and passion for life were consistently evident in the stories they shared among themselves. Everyone there knew Angela as the vibrant woman who loved to be popular and part of the crowd, but Renee felt proud to have known her deeper. They had been best friends and like twin sisters for many years and had shared all of their girlish secrets. Even though they had taken different paths as adults, Renee would always treasure those memories of their shared childhood.

Shortly before the service was to start, Janette Simpson walked into the church. As she slowly made her way down the aisle with the aid of a cane, it was obvious that she was in pain and struggling to move forward with every step. Renee cried like a baby. Janette's lupus was just as bad as Angela had described, destroying her ability to function until she was just a shell of her former self.

With the stress and chaos of the day, Renee wasn't able to speak with Janette alone until later that evening at the reception, which was held in the home of a family friend. Renee waited until most of the guests had departed, then found Janette sitting in the kitchen.

"Hi, Miss Simpson. How are you holding up?" she asked.

Janette tried to smile, but her lips quivered from the effort. She pulled Renee down into a big hug instead.

"I'm surviving, Renee. Just surviving. How are you doing?"

"I'm okay," she replied. "Miss Simpson, did Angela

tell you that she was staying with me while she was in New York?"

"Yes, she did. It was so nice of you to help her get settled there. She was so proud of you, Renee, and always talked about all the fancy work you were doing. She even called to tell me about the television show you were on," Janette told her with a sad smile. "I was glad Angela was with you, and I hoped some of your seriousness would rub off on her. I told her over and over to be careful. I warned her to just get a good job and forget about all the partying. . . ."

She looked ready to fall apart, so Renee wrapped an arm around her shoulder to provide comfort.

"Well, after Angela . . . passed, I found something at my place that belonged to her," Renee continued after a few moments. "I thought you could use it now."

Renee reached into her purse, pulled out a plain white envelope, and handed it to Janette. The older woman opened the envelope and looked inside at the contents with her face scrunched with confusion and disbelief. It was a money order for one hundred thousand dollars.

"What is this, Renee? I don't understand."

"Miss Simpson, all Angela wanted to do was make enough money to help you get the treatment you need. It was the most important thing to her, the whole reason she went to New York. This money was hers, and I know she would want you to have it."

Janette was too overcome with shock to say anything more. She just hugged Renee over and over while they both let the tears flow. When Renee finally left her, it was with the promise that she would keep in touch and visit Janette often to see how her treatment progressed.

When she returned to her parents' house, they were watching the evening news. Renee joined them, sitting beside her mother, who pulled her into a tender embrace.

"I miss Angela, Mom," Renee stated simply.

Anna stroked her daughter's hair with one hand. "I know, baby. I know."

"I still can't believe she's gone. I was so wrapped up in my life and work that I didn't even try to have a conversation with her. She was going through so much with her mom, and maybe I could have helped, you know? We could have come up with some idea or at least just been there for support. But all I cared about was that she didn't use my stuff or make a mess in my place. I was so selfish!"

Renee buried her face into the crook of her mom's neck and let the tears fall.

On Sunday, Kenneth drove her to the train station. It was very hard for Renee to leave her family, but she promised to return home for a longer visit soon. Before Renee left the house, Anna came downstairs carrying a photo album in her hand and gave it to Renee. It was a collection of pictures from Renee's childhood, and many of them included Angela and Janette. Renee spent the trip back to Manhattan looking over all of the snapshots with a smile on her face, remembering the moment each was taken.

When Renee arrived at Grand Central Station, she walked through the terminal, then stopped at the first magazine stand she passed. The small stand was packed as a steady stream of passengers bought newspapers and magazines for their ride. After a quick search, Renee found what she was looking for: the latest edition of the *Weekly Voice*.

The cover photo was grainy and unprofessional, but clear enough to reveal a shocking image of fallen star Chad Taylor in the throes of passion with his male companion. Renee looked around and saw people buying copies of the publication one after the other, and she grinned to herself with secret amusement about the lucrative tabloid business. She picked up a small stack of them for herself and headed to the cashier.

Chapter 32

The spring weather had been slow to roll in to the northeast that year, but when it did, the world was in spectacular bloom. By early June, the temperature was in the high seventies every day, and everyone was looking forward to an early summer.

Trent Skinner couldn't care less.

He woke up every day, went into the office early, worked late, then headed home to eat dinner in front of the television before heading to bed. The weekends were much the same, with added chores, a call to his mom, and the occasional stop at the gym on the way home. He didn't see the brilliant green leaves on the trees or the vibrant colors in flower beds all over Connecticut. The only thing he noticed was that it was exactly seven weeks and two days since Renee walked out of his life.

But Trent thought he was doing all right. Business was better than ever, and he was tracking toward a record year even in a very tough economy. Sure, there had been a couple of times when he lost his cool a little bit with some of the younger analysts on his team, but it was no big deal. They had to learn that if you do something stupid or make a mistake, you have to man up and be prepared to feel some heat.

"Okay, Trent. That's it!" stated Nancy as she burst through his office door and shut it firmly behind her. "I'm done. Do you understand? I'm tired of your snide, sarcastic comments and your complete lack of tact and patience. I don't want to read one more of your cryptic, one-word e-mails."

Trent put down his sandwich and sat back in his chair. He looked hard at his assistant, then down at the phone that had the speaker button light lit up. She didn't even have the sense to look regretful.

"Hey, guys, I'm going to put you on hold for a second," he told the group of sixteen other funds managers who were on the conference call bridge. "Feel free to continue the meeting without me."

He then hit the MUTE button with exaggerated precision.

"You were saying?" he asked in an icy tone.

"What? Do you really think I said anything that those guys don't already know? News flash, Trent! Everyone is tired of your sour attitude."

"Okay, Nancy, that's enough," he stated, standing up.

"No, it's not," she snapped back, walking up to him until she was right under his nose. "What's going on with you, Trent?"

He opened his mouth to reply with something harsh and biting to put her in her place. Instead, he found it hard to look into her concerned eyes and maintain his shell of cold indifference.

"Look, Nancy," he replied in a softer tone. "I get it. My mood hasn't been the best, and I've been a little short on patience."

"There's an understatement. We've had two of the analysts talk about quitting just this week! And Mandy at reception actually cried after you told her that her blond roots were showing."

"Okay!" Trent snapped.

He fell back into his chair and laid his head against the top. He then covered his face with his hands.

"Okay. Maybe I haven't been at my best," he finally confessed.

"So, what is it?" asked Nancy. "We've worked together for a while now, and this just isn't like you. I mean, I saw you at the spring ball and you looked so relaxed and . . . happy! Now, I find it hard to be in your company without wanting to slit my wrists."

Trent's eyes were closed, but he had to smile at Nancy's comments. *He wasn't that bad, was he?*

"What the hell happened?" she asked again.

He sat up, shoulders slumped, the look of the grim reaper back on his face.

"Ahhhh, I get it," Nancy finally announced.

"What?"

"It's a woman."

He uttered a loud snort, rudely dismissing her statement.

"Who is she, Trent? Please tell me it's not Douglas Chamberlin's daughter. I thought you broke up with her? And thank God for that. I've never met a woman who could talk so much and say absolutely nothing."

Trent didn't bother to reply.

"It's the woman you brought to the party, isn't it? The one wearing that beautiful purple dress? What's going on with her? Aren't you guys seeing each other anymore?"

"Please, Nancy, just give it a rest."

"Okay," she stated with an exaggerated sigh. "What did you do?"

He finally looked back at her.

"What did *I* do?" he demanded, clearly offended. "I didn't do anything! She's the one who lied to my face, then just walked away when I asked for an explanation!"

His voice boomed around the room; then there was dead silence. They looked at each other, both clearly surprised by his outburst.

"Damn it!" he uttered under his breath. "Look, Nancy, it's nothing, okay? I get what you're saying. I'll try to be less of a tyrant. Let's just leave it at that."

"Or," Nancy interjected as she walked toward him, "instead of pretending there's nothing wrong, you can fix the problem."

"I tried, okay?" he burst out. Trent jumped out of his chair and walked over to the office window. The view was uninspiring, but he wasn't looking at anything anyway.

"We had a fight the day after the gala. She got upset, then packed up her stuff and walked out the door. I begged her not to leave; I wanted her to stay and work it out. But she just walked away. I haven't heard from her since. And before you ask, I've tried to call her. I've left at least three messages. She hasn't responded at all."

"God, you men are so stupid."

Trent glanced over at her but didn't bother to respond.

"You have to chase after her, Trent. If you want to be with her, you can't just sit back and allow her to slip away. Get off your sorry, miserable ass and go see her."

"It's been seven weeks. How do I know she hasn't moved on? She's probably dating someone else by now."

"You don't know. But you have to find out."

Nancy made it sound so simple. She was barely out of college and was presumptuous enough to lecture him on love. It was comical.

But Trent could no longer deny that his methods were not working. He had tried calling Renee; then he tried forgetting her. Neither strategy had worked out, as Nancy's tirade had clearly outlined. It was weeks later, and he still felt broken and adrift, as though he had lost something incredibly valuable.

Just like his father had predicted, the right woman had finally appeared. Now that Trent knew who she was, maybe he just had to find a way to get her back.

Eventually, Nancy had enough sympathy to leave him alone. The meeting that he had muted on the conference bridge had long since ended. Trent took a few minutes to reflect on how many people in the office he owed apologies to as soon as possible. It was going to be a lengthy list, so he figured it was better to get started right away, first with the receptionist, Mandy.

His assistant wasn't the only woman to ask about Renee in the last few days. On the weekend, Trent had gone to Stamford to check up on Ophelia and take her out for lunch. It's something he had done a couple times since that weekend at her parents' home.

For most of their meal, Ophelia told Trent about the recent changes in her life. She had been staying with her parents for the past two months.

"I made an offer on a small old cottage home not far from the boutique. It's been completely renovated inside and sits on a really big lot with mature oak and maple trees. I wanted us to buy a house when Nathan and I first got married, but you know him. He complained about all the maintenance it would need," she stated with a hint of bitterness. "So, I'll have what I always wanted, and he can keep the condo."

Trent listened quietly, allowing her to get everything out.

"Daddy doesn't even want him to have that. It's leased by the company, so he's been threatening for weeks to have Nathan thrown out on his ass. But I told Daddy that we should just give it to him. I don't want to fight over money or things. I just want to move on."

"When was the last time you talked to Nathan?" he asked her.

"Last week, but only for a minute. He's still insisting that there was an explanation for everything. I just don't want to hear it anymore," she replied. "How about you? Have you talked to him?"

"Yeah, every once in a while. I think he's finally seeing how bad things are."

Ophelia snorted with disgust. "Forget Nathan. I'm tired of talking about him. How are you doing?" she asked. "You look a little tired, Trent. Is everything okay?"

"Everything is fine. Work is just really busy, that's all."

"I've been meaning to ask you about Renee. How is she doing? I never got a chance to thank her for her support that weekend. I don't know what I would have done if she hadn't been there. God, I barely know her, but I felt like she and I could be good friends. She's really special, Trent. You should hold on to her."

It took Ophelia a few minutes to notice the change in Trent's demeanor.

"What? What's wrong?" she asked.

"Renee and I broke up several weeks ago," stated Trent in a flat voice. His eyes were cast downward.

"What? Why?"

He shrugged.

"Why didn't you tell me, Trent? I've gone on and on about my situation with Nathan, and you've never said a word."

"It's water under the bridge, Ophelia. There's no point in discussing it now."

Trent felt her steady gaze and eventually looked back at her.

"Don't lie to me. It's obvious that things aren't okay. You're in love with her. What happened?"

Trent did not deny her statement. If it was written all over his face, it was pointless to deny it. For obvious reasons, he didn't tell Ophelia all the details, only that they had fought and Renee had broken up with him.

"So, go talk to her and get back together," Ophelia stated.

"It's not that simple."

"Why not? If she is still the woman you want to be with, then it's very simple. Walking away is stupid. Trust me, Trent, if you can find someone worth holding on to, make it work. Otherwise, you will end up alone, or trying to make it work with someone who doesn't deserve you. That was my mistake and look where it got me."

Trent looked away again, her words swirling around in his mind.

"I'm not the best judge of character, Trent, but I do know you are one of the most honest and dependable men I know, and Renee made you happy. Do not let that slip through your fingers. It's really hard to find."

After their lunch, Trent had considered calling Renee again but didn't. Regardless of what Ophelia thought and what he wanted, Renee had clearly made her decision weeks ago. Instead of trying to reach her over and over, Trent decided he would be better off using his energy to forget her.

Now, as he sat in his office on Tuesday afternoon only a few hours since his discussion with Nancy, Trent knew that both women were right. Renee was his future; he knew that with absolute certainty. Now he just had to get her to see it too.

On the Sunday they had broken up, it had not taken Trent long to realize that his brief and momentary doubt of Renee's innocence and motives had just been born from fear and vulnerability. Her lies weren't any more atrocious or insulting than his had been. And when he stepped back to look at the whole picture, it made absolute sense that she would try to protect her childhood friend. But instead of supporting her through one of the most painful moments of her life—the violent murder of her friend—Trent had let his policing instincts take over and forced an interrogation.

Renee may have walked away from him, but he let her down that day. That's what Trent wanted to tell her in person. He just had to create the right opportunity.

That evening, Trent left the office before six o'clock for the first time in weeks. When he got home, he started to plan how exactly he could reconnect with Renee. The last thing he knew for sure was that she had moved out of her apartment on the Upper East Side. Trent had spoken with Robbie a few times during the homicide investigation into Angela Simpson's murder. Robbie had told him about Renee's instrumental role in solving the crime and her continued cooperation throughout the process.

The first thing Trent did the next day was advise everyone he worked with that he was taking Friday off. Next, he booked a room for two nights at a hotel in midtown. Two days later, as he drove into Manhattan during midmorning traffic, he still did not have all of the kinks worked out in his plan, but he was being fueled by adrenaline and determination.

As Nancy had bluntly suggested, by the end of the weekend, Trent would at least be able to walk away with answers.

Chapter 33

Like many days over the last month and a half, Renee and Jennifer rode the subway to work together. Since they had become neighbors, living in the same small building, the two women had become even closer. Renee still worked from home several times a week, but she also enjoyed Jennifer's company when she went into the office. They also occasionally met up in the evenings to have dinner or just do some window-shopping.

On Friday, Renee had planned to spend the whole day on site at Cree Armstrong's apartment coordinating some of the trades. But yesterday, Marsha asked if she could meet with a new client who had approached the firm directly. Renee then adjusted her schedule so she could stop by the office in the morning and be on the project site for the afternoon. She was a little overdressed for construction, in a slender-fitting gray pantsuit and her cobalt-blue pumps, but there was no help for it.

The women parted ways underground after

confirming their plans to meet for dinner and a movie after work. Renee then continued her commute to the office and was there by eight-fifteen. Her client meeting was scheduled for ten-thirty, so she had a couple of hours to get some work done.

"Hey, Marsha, how are you?" she said brightly as she walked into the office.

"Morning, Renee. I'm all right. How are you doing?" Marsha replied.

"I'm good, just glad it's Friday."

"I know. The weather is supposed to be fabulous. I plan to do nothing but garden for the next two days."

"Well, have fun. Don't forget the sunblock," Renee teased.

Marsha laughed. "Oh, no, I won't make that mistake. It wouldn't be very pretty. By the way, there's a delivery on your desk that came in a few minutes ago."

Renee thanked her and was still smiling as she walked toward her desk. Along the way, she chatted with Nadine for a few minutes and said hi to a few other coworkers. When she got to her desk, there was a large rectangular white box wrapped in ribbon. Renee hadn't been expecting any kind of delivery, certainly not a package that looked like flowers. She looked around, confused, then checked the name on the delivery tag in case Marsha had put it on the wrong desk by accident.

Her name was clearly marked as the recipient.

Curious, Renee untied the ribbon, opened the box, and peeled back tissue paper to find a beautiful bouquet of colorful spring flowers. She pulled out the bunch to admire them, and a note card fell out onto her desk. There was only one sentence written in blue ink and bold strokes across the paper, followed by a strong signature.

I would like to introduce myself to you again.
Trent Skinner

Renee sank into her desk chair, her knees suddenly too weak to hold her weight. Her heart started racing with excitement.

It had been so many weeks since the last time she had heard from Trent that she had finally stopped hoping to hear his voice again. Renee was still coming to terms with the consequences of her actions and was still dealing with the loss of both her friend and the man who stole her heart. All she could do was take one day at a time and pray that one day she would feel whole again.

Holding that note and seeing Trent's name boldly printed on it brought back all the raw feelings that she had been trying to overcome.

"Wow, those are beautiful, Renee!"

Renee sat up and turned toward Nadine, who was now standing behind her.

"Thanks," she replied.

"So, who's the lucky man?"

"Oh, ah . . . They're from a client," Renee replied weakly.

"No way. Those are definitely from someone who is trying to impress you. You may want to think about turning that client into something more."

Renee smiled back tightly, then gently put the flowers back in their packaging so she could take them home later. She sat fingering the card for a few more seconds before tucking it in her purse and getting settled in to do some work.

Along with her interior design projects, Renee was scheduled to be on the *Daybreak Show* again in a week's time. In preparation for the show, she got Frederic and Albert to agree to provide samples of their new line of furniture. After weeks of refusing to carry any furniture not made of solid wood, Albert finally agreed to see the high-end fiberboard furniture that Frederic had been so excited about. After inspecting the materials and reviewing the manufacturing process, Albert grudgingly admitted he was impressed and immediately agreed to carry the line. Since then, the manufacturer launched a very successful advertising campaign in all of the major design magazines, and their furniture was being snapped up faster than they could make it. As one of very few wholesalers carrying the line in New York, Henry Interiors was flooded with orders. Renee's feature of the furniture on the morning show was going to send their sales off the charts.

At ten-thirty that morning, Renee was on hold with a flooring supplier when Marsha sent her an e-mail to say her client had arrived and was waiting in one of their meeting rooms. By the time she finished the call, she was almost ten minutes late for the meeting and rushed into the room a little flustered.

"Sorry to keep you waiting . . ." The rest of her words died on her lips, and Renee found herself standing in front of Trent.

"Hi, Renee."

She took a step back, confused and unprepared. "What are you doing here?" she finally asked.

"I'm here to see you."

It suddenly dawned on her that he was her ten-thirty appointment.

"Okay," she replied, unable to think of anything else to say.

"How are you?" he asked politely.

"I'm fine, Trent, thank you. How are you?"

"I'm all right."

There was an awkward pause as they eyed each other hesitantly.

He looks so good! she thought to herself.

"Thank you for the flowers, by the way. They're very beautiful."

"My pleasure."

They fidgeted in silence again.

"How did your bedroom turn out?" Renee eventually asked. "Nadine showed me the pictures. They looked great."

"Yeah, yeah. She did a good job. It turned out really well, exactly like you designed it."

Renee was about to make some other inane comment when Trent let out a deep, frustrated breath.

"I lied, Renee," he stated in a serious tone. "I'm not all right. I'm not even close to being all right. I came here to see you and be completely honest with you. So I might as well start off right and tell you that I'm miserable."

"Oh, Trent," Renee whispered.

She turned and walked away, putting a little distance between them.

"I'm not here to bother you, Renee. I'm not

expecting anything. I just need to tell you that I'm sorry about the way I treated you that day."

"Trent . . ." She turned back to face him.

"I won't take up much of your time, I promise." He rushed forward. "But it's important to me for you to know that I never thought you were involved in any part of that mess with Nathan. You were just an innocent victim in the whole thing, and you had every right to be angry with me for suggesting otherwise."

"Trent, it was a horrible situation for everyone."

His head fell forward and he put his hands deep into his pants pockets.

"Maybe, but you lost someone very close to you that day and deserved some comfort and understanding, not accusations," he rebutted. "I regret my behavior that day more than I can tell you."

Renee nodded. She tried to think of something appropriate to say, but nothing came to mind. After everything that had happened and all the time that had passed, it had never occurred to Renee that he would still have anything to say to her. Not only had her lies and deception helped get Angela killed, they had ruined everything between her and Trent. How would he ever be able to trust her again? It seemed impossible.

Now, as she looked at his face, with caring in his eyes and lines of concern etched into his forehead, Renee felt the stirrings of hope.

"Why are you here, Trent?" she asked.

Renee could tell that her question caught him off

guard. He took a step back and brushed a hand over the back of his head.

"Well, I hoped that I could take you to lunch and maybe catch up. I wanted to find out how you're doing."

"Why?"

Her question came out like a plea and Trent's shoulders stiffened.

"You're right; that's a good question," he muttered. "You made yourself very clear weeks ago. The way I treated you was not right and you've moved on. I came here to apologize and I've done that, so I'll leave you alone now." He started to walk past Renee toward the office door.

"Is that what you think?" she asked. "That I've moved on?"

Trent turned back to face her. "What else should I think, Renee?" he stated in a tortured voice. "I waited for weeks for you to return my calls."

"I couldn't," Renee cried. "I ruined everything, Trent. I just couldn't face you again."

"What are you talking about?"

Renee covered her eyes and tried to regain her composure. Tears threatened to escape from her eyes, but she fought against it.

"I know what I did was unforgivable, Trent. I lied to you, kept information from the police, and Angela was murdered as a result. And I destroyed any trust we had between us. I didn't know how to face you after that."

Trent walked up to her and lifted her face with a gentle nudge under her chin. "Renee, you were trying to help her. You couldn't have known what she was really involved in. How can you blame yourself for any of this?"

She tried to speak, explain the guilt and turmoil that had surrounded her for so long, but the lump in her throat was too big. Trent pulled her into his arms, and silent tears poured down her face.

"How can you ever forgive me?" Renee finally whispered.

"It's easy, Renee. I love you. I don't even have to try," he whispered back.

She lifted her head sharply, shocked by his words.

"It's true," he confirmed with a wry smile. "I wasn't exaggerating earlier, you know. I've been pretty miserable, and there have been several people around me who've pointed it out. So, it looks like I have no choice. I need you back in my life or I probably won't have any friends left."

Renee could not help but laugh as she wiped away the moisture from the corners of her eyes. She was still in his arms, and it felt too good to leave right away.

"I love you too, Trent. I knew that even as I was walking away, and I've missed you every day since," she whispered with her lips next to his ear.

He pulled her close and they kissed deeply and slowly, almost forgetting they were still at her work place.

"So what happens now," she finally asked when they pulled apart.

"That's up to you," he replied, and pressed a kiss on the top of her head.

She thought quietly for a few seconds. "How were you going to introduce yourself to me again?" Renee asked, taking a step back to look into his eyes.

"What do you mean?" Trent asked.

"That's what you said in the card with the flowers. How were you going to do that?" she repeated with a teasing smile.

"Good question, and since I'm completely committed to honesty, I have to confess that I have no idea. I only came with a plan on how to get in the door. The rest was a little sketchy."

"Really? You don't strike me as someone who is usually unprepared, Trent," Renee told him.

He smiled, revealing his strong, white teeth. "Well, I'm a little off my game these days."

Renee smiled back and took another step toward him.

"I missed you, Renee," he stated simply. "Do you think we can try this again?"

She reached up and brushed a finger along his cheek. It was so good to touch him and be near him that she felt a little breathless.

"I don't have to think about it. The Trent Skinner and Renee Goodchild who met the first time weren't real, remember? So maybe everything that happened between them is not relevant or important, and we can now start again as we really are."

"You're wrong, Renee. Some things between them were real and are still very relevant."

Trent leaned forward and brushed his lips gently across hers. A sharp, sizzling string of electricity shot straight down to her knees, just like the first time they kissed. He was right. The attraction had been there from the start and had not faded a bit.

"So, can I take you out on a date for lunch?" he whispered once they finally pulled out of the embrace. "Or maybe you should be the one to pay now that you're a millionaire."

"What?" Renee demanded, stepping back with surprise.

Trent had a mischievous grin on his face. "Come on, Renee. Now it's your turn to be honest. Those exclusive pictures of Chad Taylor in the *Weekly Voice* must have set you up for life. Quite frankly, I was surprised to find you still working as a designer. I thought for sure by now you had bought an island somewhere in the Pacific where you could lie on the beach all day."

Renee smacked him hard on the shoulder in outrage, but he just laughed. She was about to set him straight and explain everything that happened with the pictures, but Trent pulled her into another long kiss, and she completely lost her train of thought.

Want more Sophia Shaw?
Turn the page for a sizzling excerpt from
What Lies Between Lovers

Available now wherever books are sold!

Chapter 1

Did you ever end up in a bad situation, and have no clue how you got there? Did you spend hours wondering how things went so wrong, and why you did not see it coming until it was too late? Monique Evans had been asking herself the same questions for weeks now, and was still waiting for the answers.

She was fully engrossed in a few stolen moments of brooding when she heard her name mentioned somewhere off in the distance. It dragged her attention back to the penthouse-level conference room and to the dozen or so faces staring at her, waiting for her response to a question that she had not heard within a discussion she had not been listening to.

Monique blinked a few times, and then put a thoughtful look on her face. A little flutter of panic rose in her throat as several seconds ticked by and no appropriate answers came to mind. With the calculated practice of a seasoned salesperson, she searched for clues within the whiteboards and open presentations about what her clients wanted to hear. The silence stretched to the point where the coworker sitting beside her started to fidget in his seat.

"I want to make sure I understand your question before I go into detail," Monique finally stated while glancing at the most vocal participants in the meeting. "Can you put it into context for me?"

She was relieved when Robert Tomlin, the head of asset management for the Broadline Logistics, nodded with understanding.

"We would like the new system to have some open source code so that our own developers can customize the software as needed. Then, we need to understand how those customizations will affect your product guarantee."

Everything clicked for Monique at that moment. As the Director of Sales at Sector Asset Solutions, she was responsible for making sure their top clients, like Broadline, were happy with their software. This meeting was to close them on a full system upgrade, a project worth up to ten million dollars. Before her mind had wandered off to reflect on the current chaos of her personal life, Jeff Culvert, her Senior Systems Engineer, had been outlining the various upgraded features in the new version of SPIDER, Sector Asset's core product. Easy and flexible customization was one of the biggest selling features.

"Robert, as you know, our client satisfaction guarantee is the best in the business, and one of our key differentiators," she replied. "SPIDER Release 4 has been designed with that in mind. Because we can't control your customizations, we can only guarantee the functionality of our original code. But, as Jeff explained, the knowledge and document management modules of Release 4 make tracking all modifications very simple. As long as your developers meet the process requirements, we will be able to track any problems."

Without prompting, Jeff took over to delve deeper into the technical details of the issue. Monique listened intently, determined to stay focused, but prayed with every breath that the meeting would end soon. How many more questions could they still have after three solid hours of tech talk?

Her wish came true about ten minutes later. She and Jeff hung around after to chitchat for as long as was appropriate; then they grabbed a cab to go back to Sector Asset. Jeff spent the short ride from San Diego's downtown core out to their office in Mission Hills checking messages on his BlackBerry. Monique had her head turned toward the window, and she wore large, dark sunglasses to cover up her blank stare off into space.

This melancholy had been with Monique all day and really took her by surprise. It had been several weeks since she had finally felt over *him*. *Him* being Donald Sanderson, the boyfriend she had broken up with after almost three years together. It had been really hard at first, but Monique was finally feeling as though the whole messy affair was behind her.

Until today, anyway.

In her calendar, she had bookmarked the coming

Saturday as her ideal wedding day. The reminder notice had popped up when she logged onto her computer that morning. It was a note made impulsively almost nine months earlier, after Donald had assured her they would be married before Thanksgiving. At the time, fully in love and looking for assurances, she had believed him. Several weeks later, Monique had finally accepted that all his promises were lies and he was never going to leave his wife.

"Are you going upstairs?" Jeff asked once they had exited the cab. "It's almost five-thirty."

He was fairly young, probably a couple of years younger than Monique's twenty-eight years, but one of the smartest engineers she had ever worked with. Unlike the other presales technicians in the company, Jeff knew how to explain complicated technology to the most clueless layperson.

"Yeah, I know," she replied. "But, I still have to review some reports for tomorrow morning."

"Well, don't work too late," Jeff advised before he jogged off to the parking lot with youthful energy.

Monique made her way to her office at a much slower pace. It was true that she had a little work to do, but she also had some time to burn before she had to be at her ball game later that evening. On Wednesdays, she played basketball in a recreational league, and tonight the game was scheduled to start at seven o'clock. That gave Monique enough time to wrap up a small project and get to the gym in time to change.

Her league played at the gymnasium at Balboa

Park in downtown San Diego. Monique arrived later than she had expected and rushed to change out of her business suit and into gym shorts, a sports bra, and her team jersey. The last thing she needed was to arrive on the court late and after the starting whistle. She was the only woman playing in an all-men's club, and she'd endured enough aggravation from the guys already.

When she was finally dressed, Monique hung up her work clothes in a locker, laced up her ball shoes, and sprinted out of the changing room. In her distracted haste, she almost ran into her friend and teammate, Gary Cooper, as he stepped out of the men's changing room next door.

"Whoa," he exclaimed, stepping back quickly to avert a collision.

"Hey, Coop," Monique stated, once she realized who it was. She slowed down to walk beside him.

"Everything all right?" Gary asked, looking her up and down.

"Yeah," she replied quickly. "Why?"

"Nothing," he told her. "You just look all made up, that's all. Are you trying to impress someone?"

Monique stopped dead in her tracks and quickly touched her cheeks in surprise.

"Oh, no," she moaned.

She had forgotten to wash the makeup off her face, which meant that her eyes were still lightly rimmed with dark liner and fringed with lashes thickened with mascara. Her lips were probably stained with deep brick-red gloss. Monique immediately rubbed off as much lip color as possible on the back of her hand, then looked back down the hall, clearly contemplating dashing back into the changing rooms.

"Don't worry about it. It's barely noticeable," Gary assured her. "Come on."

Monique allowed him to nudge her into the gym, but she gave her lips another vigorous rub.

The large square room was filled with the sounds of men laughing and balls bouncing on the hardwood floor. It was a full-sized basketball court with several rows of bleachers for spectators. There were about twelve people sitting to watch, most of them the wives or girlfriends of the players. She and Gary joined the six other members of their team, the Ravens, as they did a few minutes of warmup drills.

"Let's pull it in!" demanded Sam, their captain. The six players surrounded him. "Okay, guys, let's go with the regular starters. Gary, I want you to stay on top of number 23. We need to shut down his threepointers before he warms up."

Gary nodded.

"Nigel," Sam continued, firing off the instructions, "you cover number 19. Scott, take 3 and Evans . . ."

When he got to Monique's assignment, their eyes met briefly. Sam paused, and his brows lowered sharply as he scanned her face.

"Evans, you have 35. I'll take 20."

Monique nodded, wondering if she had imagined his momentary reaction. She brushed her hand over her lips again. Unfortunately, Sam was the type of guy who could easily make a woman stare at him so hard and imagine that he was looking back.

Everyone called him Sam or Samuels, but his full name was Tao Samuels. From what she understood, his father was African American and his mother was Chinese, so he had that striking, Tyson Beckford–thing going on, but with skin the color of golden caramel rather than dark chocolate. His face was long and angular, and he had piercing, intense eyes on an exotic slant and generously full lips. And if that weren't enough to remember him forever, Tao was blessed with a tall, lean frame and a natural grace and athleticism.

The ball game started a few minutes later. Though the league was technically for men, there was nothing in the rule books to prevent women from playing. So far, Monique was the only female to take advantage of the opportunity. She had joined the Ravens a few weeks earlier in September, and it did not take long for her ball skills to become obvious. She had played NCAA division basketball in college and was now the team's point guard, playing most of the game.

The opposing team, the Wild Dogs, was pretty good, but by the last couple of minutes in the game, it was clear that the Ravens were much better. This was the second time they had played each other, and the Ravens had won the first matchup by only a few points. Monique had been very new to the league at that time and had only played for a brief period. Tonight, with the flow of the game in her hands, the match was turning into a blowout, and the Wild Dogs were not taking the beating well.

In the last possession, like several times before, Monique dodged the man defending her and made a fast drive to the basket for a clear layup. The spectators on the bench were already snickering in anticipation of an embarrassingly easy play. But just as Monique leaped into the air with her arm extended, intending to roll the ball down the tips of her fingers, she felt a sudden impact against her legs, sending her careening wildly off balance.

It took all her effort and focus to keep her eyes on the basket, and as she headed for the hardwood, she watched the ball bounce around the rim before dropping in. *And one*, she exclaimed in her mind with victory. Then, she landed hard on her side with her left shoulder taking most of the jarring impact. Shouts of surprise and admiration filled the gym as the referee blew his whistle, indicating a foul. There were a few seconds of chaos before everyone realized that Monique was still on the ground and clearly injured.

Tao was the first to reach her, and she could hear the urgency in his voice and feel the warmth of his hand as he searched her legs for any fractures or sprains.

"Monique! Monique, are you okay?"

She squeezed her eyes tight, trying to fight the urge to scream at the pain that ran up from her collarbone to her neck. When she tried to answer him, she could not seem to suck any oxygen into her lungs.

"Monique!" added Gary as he crouched down near her head.

"I'm okay," she finally gasped. "My shoulder . . ."

"Don't move," Tao commanded as he shifted his attention to an area around her upper arm.

"It's okay," Monique told him in a stronger voice. "I just banged it."

"Stay still!" instructed Tao again.

She did as she was told and allowed him to gently inspect the area. He took his time, and Monique eventually opened her eyes to look up at him.

"Does that hurt?" he asked after prodding a tender spot and feeling her flinch.

Their eyes met, and Monique was taken aback by the intense concern reflected in his.

"Just a little," she whispered.

"Is she okay?" asked Gary.

The other guys on the team were surrounding them, all clearly anxious to hear how she was doing.

"I'm fine," Monique replied. "I just got the wind knocked out of me."

To assure them, she sat up slowly. Both Gary and Tao quickly took her arms and helped her to her feet. Monique could not help but wince at the movement in her bruised arm. Once she was seated on the bench, the referee blew his whistle again and the game resumed, with Tao taking her foul shot for her.

There were only six seconds left on the clock, enough time for a final possession by the Wild Dogs. But with the Ravens already winning by twenty-seven points, no one expected much to happen. The few spectators in the stands started to pack up their things, and Monique turned away from the court to grab her towel. By the time she turned back around, a fight had broken out on the court and both teams were yelling and pushing at each other.

Chapter 2

"Let go of me, Gary!" Tao demanded.

Gary had his arms wrapped around Tao's chest, forcibly pulling him away.

"Sam, man, just let it go," said Gary.

"I'm cool, I'm cool. It's over," replied Tao. His fists were clenched tight, ready to respond if provoked.

On the other side of the gym, a Wild Dog player was limping and cursing at Tao with every possible dirty word. The referee was standing between the two teams to ensure the conflict didn't escalate. Everyone else was standing still, wondering exactly what went down and waiting to see what would happen next. It took a few minutes, but the agitated Wild Dogs player was eventually led out of the room by his teammates.

"You tripped him on purpose, didn't you?" Gary asked after things had quieted down.

"Tsk! The idiot tripped over my foot," Tao told him.

"Yeah, sure he did."

"He's lucky I didn't shove my fist down his

throat after what he did to Monique." Tao made this statement in a quiet, emotionless voice, but his face was hard with smothered fury. Gary nodded in agreement.

They both looked over at the bench as Monique touched her bruised shoulder and rolled it to check mobility and pain. Her oval face revealed a little discomfort, with slender, shapely lips pulled back and her even white teeth clenched hard.

Tao found his eyes drawn to her most dominant features: deep, smoky eyes, now surprisingly enhanced with a little makeup. They were one of the first things he had noticed when he had met Monique Evans over a month ago at the start of the basketball season. Even with her hair pulled back and in sweaty gym clothes, those eyes held the promise of sensuality. His first reaction was the natural male instinct to make a move. Then he saw her game skills, and any interest he felt was replaced with respect, almost admiration. Now, Tao tried to think of her as one of the guys.

"How does it feel?" Gary asked when they reached her.

"It's okay, just a little sore."

"You'll have to put some ice on it," Tao told her.

She nodded, and the three of them made their way out of the now empty gym.

"Are we going to get something to eat?" asked Gary once they reached the men's locker room.

It was a routine for the three of them, and anyone else on the team who was free, to clean up, then go to one of the nearby restaurants for dinner after the game.

"I think I'll pass, Coop," Monique told him.

"I'm out too," Tao added. He was about to explain why, when they were interrupted by a woman walking toward them from the front of the building.

"Tao, are you coming?"

The question was more like a command. She stopped behind him, and Tao didn't have to turn around to imagine the annoyed look on her face or the tight fist planted aggressively on her hip. His back straightened with annoyance.

"The game's been over for, like, twenty minutes or something. I've been just standing out here waiting."

"Hey, Tanisia, how are you?" Gary asked after several seconds passed and Tao did not respond to her.

"Okay, well, I'll see you guys later," Monique told them, clearly wanting to avoid the awkward situation. She turned and headed for the changing room. Gary took her cue and did the same.

"What's going on, Tao?"

"I don't know what you're talking about, Tanisia," he replied, finally turning around to face her.

"You don't know what I'm talking about? Do I look like an idiot?"

Tao could not contain the condescending smirk that spread on his lips. But he managed not to say anything.

"What's going on between you and that chick?"

His brows lowered quickly, and his confusion was very obvious.

"What?"

"That chick," she uttered, pointing to the spot that Monique had just vacated. "What's going on? And don't tell me that I imagined the way you looked at her!" demanded Tanisia, her voice getting louder with each sentence. "Then you go and attack the guy because he bumped into her. What the hell!"

Tao closed his eyes and let out a long breath, partly because her screeching was giving him a headache, but also because he didn't really know what to say. He had been really concerned about Monique and had let his anger get the better of him. But it was just because she was his teammate, right?

"Tanisia, I'm not talking to you while you're shouting in my face, all right? So, just calm down and stop being ridiculous. You're embarrassing me."

"Oh, please! I'm embarrassing you? How do you think I feel coming down here to watch your game, and you go to the rescue of some other woman? Then practically ignore me while I wait forever for you? And who do I find you talking to when you finally decide to show yourself?"

"Tanisia . . . !"

"You think you can treat me like this?"

She was a petite girl, maybe five feet, three inches, and no more than 110 pounds. Yet Tanisia had no problem getting up in his face with her finger wiggling under his nose. Her head shook and bobbed to enunciate every statement.

"Like I said," Tao replied, stressing his words and keeping his voice deadly quiet. "I don't know what you're going on about, and I'm not talking to you while you're shouting and getting on."

"Oh, so you're not going to answer me, huh?"

He looked her dead in the eyes to show how serious he was, then turned to walk away. Unfortunately, Monique chose that moment to step out of the changing room and was just in time to hear Tanisia blow her lid.

"Fine then! Walk away like you always do, you bastard! You better lose my number, 'cause there are plenty of men who want some of this! You ain't nothin', do you hear me? LOSE MY NUMBER!"

Tao's back was still turned to Tanisia, but from the corner of his eye, he could see Monique's expression, a mix of guilty curiosity, disgust, and humor as she watched Tanisia storm off, her high-heel boots clicking loudly on the tiled floors. Monique then gave him an assessing glance, as though seeing him for the first time, before also walking away.

Tao could only shake his head, wondering exactly what had happened to send this evening in such a weird direction.

Inside the men's changing room, Gary and a couple of other players were getting dressed after showering. The look on their faces made it obvious that everyone in the room had heard the confrontation.

"So I guess you're free to go get a meal, huh?" Gary asked before bursting into rolling, riotous laughter.

"Tsk! I don't know what's wrong with that girl," Tao said once his friend calmed down a little. "We've only been hanging for a few months. You'd think we were married or something."

"Who told you to invite her to the game? That's always a mistake."

"I didn't invite her! She invited herself, going on about where am I playing and why can't she come? I just got tired of hearing about it."

"Sam, my man, I've got to say, you knew her ass was a little crazy, but you went there anyway," stated Gary, chuckling again at his own words. "She's cute and all, but we're talking 'slash your tires,' 'boil your rabbit' crazy!"

Tao just gave him an annoyed glance, then headed to the shower.

"How about Mexican? I'm craving tacos," Gary continued while still laughing.

Tao could still hear the guys ribbing him until he was standing under the spray of water. Now that the drama had passed, he could see the humor in the bizarre situation. His lips curved into a smile and he started to laugh silently.

Gary was right. Tao should have known that things would not work out between him and Tanisia. He had met her at the grocery store near his old apartment. They had both been picking out bunches of bananas, and their eyes had connected. He could tell right away that she was interested in him, just by the way she flipped her hair and discreetly looked him up and down. Tao had not said anything to her at that moment, but gave in later when they passed each other twice in the frozen food aisle.

There was no doubt that Tanisia was an attractive girl. She had a tight, petite body and a nice, if not exactly pretty, face. But he had hesitated to make a move on her at first. She was a little too made up and obvious for his taste, wearing butt-hugging yoga pants and a tank top that clung to her torso like a second skin. She could have been coming from the gym, except she had on a full face of makeup.

When she finally spoke to him, he was standing near the ice-cream section, looking at the frozen desserts and trying to remember what he still had in his freezer.

"Excuse me? Have you seen any caramel crunch?"

Tao had not been surprised that she approached him. He had been anticipating it, but it still took him a few seconds to figure out what she was talking about. She must have mistaken his confused glance for flirtation, because she gave him a big smile and came several steps closer to him.

"I'm Tanisia," she added.

"Hey," he immediately replied. "I'm Tao."

"Tao?" she repeated, mispronouncing it. "That's interesting. Is it Spanish?"

It was the typical response he got to his foreign name, so it didn't faze him. His face, skin tone, and particularly his eyes often had people confused about his nationality.

"No, it's Chinese," he explained.

"Really? You're Chinese?"

Tao almost smiled as she looked him up and down, her gaze lingering around his crotch as though trying to assess how Asian he really was.

"Half Chinese actually," was his brief response.

Tanisia just nodded, a sparkle in her eyes.

They spoke for a few minutes and eventually

exchanged numbers. Things took a casual course after that, where they spoke a few times on the phone, and then went out to dinner. On the second date, Tanisia invited him back to her apartment and into her bed.

Though Tao wasn't dating anyone else at the moment, he had not considered their relationship to be exclusive or committed. Things between them were fine, and the sex was okay, but nothing more than that. It did not take long for him to realize that they had very little in common.

Clearly, after tonight's outrageous behavior it was over between them, and Tao wasn't at all upset about it. Her loud voice and unnecessary attitude had gotten tiresome really quick. She wasn't *that* cute.

GREAT BOOKS,
GREAT SAVINGS!

When You Visit Our Website:
www.kensingtonbooks.com
You Can Save Money Off The Retail Price
Of Any Book You Purchase!

- **All Your Favorite Kensington Authors**
- **New Releases & Timeless Classics**
- **Overnight Shipping Available**
- **eBooks Available For Many Titles**
- **All Major Credit Cards Accepted**

Visit Us Today To Start Saving!
www.kensingtonbooks.com

All Orders Are Subject To Availability.
Shipping and Handling Charges Apply.
Offers and Prices Subject To Change Without Notice.

Grab These Dafina Thrillers

From

Brandon Massey

__Twisted Tales
0-7582-1353-0 $6.99US/$9.99CAN

__The Other Brother
0-7582-1072-8 $6.99US/$9.99CAN

__Within The Shadows
0-7582-1070-1 $6.99US/$9.99CAN

__Dark Corner
0-7582-0250-4 $6.99US/$9.99CAN

__Thunderland
0-7582-0247-4 $6.99US/$9.99CAN

Available Wherever Books Are Sold!

Visit our website at **www.kensingtonbooks.com.**

Look For These Other
Dafina Novels

If I Could
0-7582-0131-1

by Donna Hill
$6.99US/**$9.99**CAN

Thunderland
0-7582-0247-4

by Brandon Massey
$6.99US/**$9.99**CAN

June In Winter
0-7582-0375-6

by Pat Phillips
$6.99US/**$9.99**CAN

Yo Yo Love
0-7582-0239-3

by Daaimah S. Poole
$6.99US/**$9.99**CAN

When Twilight Comes
0-7582-0033-1

by Gwynne Forster
$6.99US/**$9.99**CAN

It's A Thin Line
0-7582-0354-3

by Kimberla Lawson Roby
$6.99US/**$9.99**CAN

Perfect Timing
0-7582-0029-3

by Brenda Jackson
$6.99US/**$9.99**CAN

Never Again Once More
0-7582-0021-8

by Mary B. Morrison
$6.99US/**$8.99**CAN

Available Wherever Books Are Sold!

Check out our website at www.kensingtonbooks.com.